SURE SHOT

SURE SHOT

SURE SHOT

By Sarina Bowen

Tuxbury Publishing LLC

ONE

Cinderella Gets into a Limousine

BESS

September

WHEN THE BLACK limousine slides to a stop in front of me, I feel a familiar tension right behind my breastbone.

Limos always have this effect on me. The same thing happens in expensive hotels and fine restaurants. For a moment, I feel like there's been some mistake—that this girl from the wrong side of Detroit doesn't belong here.

When the driver's side door opens, I half expect one of Cinderella's footmen to get out. But it's only Duff, my friends' bodyguard. "Hey, Bess! How are you?"

"Great, Duff. I can open doors by myself, though."

"Just doin' my job," he says, halfway around the hood of the car already. He unlocks the door with a key fob and then opens it with a flourish. "Happy Friday."

"You too. Thanks for picking me up," I say as I duck into the back of the sleek car.

"It's our pleasure," my friend Alexandra says, waving to me from one of the two long leather seats. Her ten-month-old daughter is beside her, strapped into a car seat. When Rosie sees me, she babbles a greeting and stretches out her short little arms to me.

1

"Hi, gorgeous!" I coo, seating myself directly in front of her. "How are you both?"

"We're great," Alex says. "Except one of us is teething. Watch that pretty dress if you hold her at the party."

"Oh, what's a little drool between friends?" I glance down at my sundress and wonder if I should have worn jeans. The party is in a backyard. A billionaire's backyard. I never get dolled up, but my sister-in-law talked me into buying this dress, and it would be a crime to just abandon it in my closet.

Alex is wearing a beautiful outfit, too—a flowing skirt and a stylish matching top. She always looks like a billion bucks. That's because she *has* a billion bucks. If we carry this Cinderella metaphor a little further, Alex is the princess who's used to finery, and I'm the villager who spent her childhood in rags before traveling the kingdom to find her own fortune among the knights and thieves.

The baby makes a little noise of complaint, so I take Rosie's small hand in mine, and rub my thumb over her chubby wrist.

Honestly, I'm far more envious of Alex's baby than I am of her Mercedes. I need to snuggle this baby. Although it's rude to unclip a child from her lifesaving car seat just to fulfill one's own hormonally driven baby-snuggling needs. So I have to be content with holding her hand and staring deep into her brown eyes.

"Tell me everything," Alex says. "How was your vacation? How was Vermont? Did you really spend ten days offline?"

"I totally did. It was about as weird as you'd expect."

"Did you experience any withdrawal symptoms?" Alex wrings her hands.

I narrow my eyes at her. "You know I only gave up my *phone*, right? I wasn't secretly at rehab."

She laughs. "I know. But going ten days without my phone would be a real challenge. I don't like what it says about me. As if the world would stop turning if I'm out of reach for a few days."

"Right? I felt ridiculous every time I reached for my phone, and it wasn't there."

Then again, Alex runs a billion-dollar tech corporation with over a thousand employees. People depend on her. I run a company with exactly two employees—myself, plus Alex's boyfriend Eric Bayer—but it feels like more, because my thirty-five clients are accustomed to calling day and night.

That's why Eric challenged me to unplug for a whole week's vacation. "You hired me so that you could get away from your job sometimes," he'd said. "What are you waiting for?"

He was right. So I scheduled my vacation and left my phone behind.

Across from me, the baby babbles loudly, and I don't need a translator to know what she's saying. *Please take me out of this infernal five-point harness.* And when I make no moves to free her, she starts to complain.

"Just a few more blocks," Alex says, stroking the wispy hairs on her daughter's head. "Then we'll see Daddy, and you can crawl around on the grass."

"Speaking of Daddy," I say. "Where the heck are Eric and Dave?"

"Eric and your brother finished up early and headed over to the party. They're meeting us there."

"Okay." I hesitate. "So you don't, um, have my phone, right?"

"Nope!" Alex says cheerfully. "You'll have to wait five more minutes to get your baby back. Eric left this for you, though." She reaches into her laptop bag and pulls out a big manila envelope. *FOR BESS*, it reads. *These are the big emergency items from your week away. Do not open this until after the party! No cheating! We have a deal.*

When I squeeze the envelope, I realize it's awfully thick. I lay it down on the seat beside me while the limo inches forward in traffic.

I last at *least* ten seconds before I grab it off the seat and slip my finger under the flap, tearing it open.

"Uh-oh," Alex says. "I thought you weren't supposed to—"

"Shh!" I hiss. "Don't rat me out, okay? Girl code." I pull the pages out of the envelope. The top one says. *GOT YOU!* And when I flip to the one beneath, it reads, *THERE WEREN'T ANY EMERGENCIES*. And the one beneath that says, *NOW YOU OWE ME A SUSHI LUNCH*.

"Goddamn it!" I squeak. "Your man is such a jerk!"

"What did he… Oh my God." Alex covers her mouth and laughs. "I'm sorry. That is so rude."

"This is *entrapment*," I sputter. "This would never stand up in court."

"Oh, Bess," Alex says. "How did you not see that coming?"

I drop the envelope onto the leather seat in disgust. "That's just mean. I didn't even cheat on this vacation. I didn't look at my email, or even at the hockey news."

For the first time since I'd started my own business six years ago, I'd left it all behind for ten days in Vermont with my brother and sister-in-law. It was time for me to make some changes in my life, and the vacation had been a first symbolic step.

Alex grabs the envelope and shoves it back in her bag. Then she pulls out her phone. "I'm texting him to tell him that we're almost there. And also—as referee—that I consider this an illegal maneuver."

"So illegal." I pout.

She tucks the phone away and smiles at me. "Don't be mad at Eric. He's on your side."

"I know," I admit. "And you can take the boy out of the locker room, but you can't take the locker room out of the boy." Pranking people is a basic life skill in professional sports.

"Eric will have to make it up to you. Ask him for something fancy for your birthday. Are you doing anything special tomorrow?"

My birthday. The big 3-0. Honestly, I'm trying not to dwell on it. "My brother is taking me out for dinner. And then he'll head back to Vermont the following day."

"Make Dave take you to a musical," Alex suggests. "*The Book of Mormon* is funny."

I laugh out loud. "Can you imagine my brother sitting through a musical?"

"Then you definitely should ask. I mean—it's your first birthday in New York!"

Except it isn't. And this is the other reason I've been trying not to think about my birthday. Right after college I'd lived in

Manhattan for three years, before moving back to Detroit to start my own business.

One month into my fledgling New York City career as a sports agent, I'd turned twenty-one. The night of my birthday had been magical and unexpected. It began at a business dinner and ended in the well-muscled arms of a sexy stranger.

Every year on my birthday I remember that night, but this year the memory really haunts me. I'm turning thirty, I'm still single, and I'm starting over in New York. So I'm feeling extra wistful. I'd been such a starry-eyed little optimist at twenty-one. I had thought my life was going to be a long montage of fancy dinners and passionate kisses.

Actually, the fancy dinners still happen. I'm on my way to a billionaire's backyard party right now. My life is amazing.

The passion, though? That turned out to be short-lived.

But I'm working on that, I promise myself. I'm making some changes already. I've moved to Brooklyn and hired Eric, for starters.

The rest of the changes aren't so easy to pull off. My business is flourishing, but my personal life is stunted. That's why I spent part of my vacation drawing up a new five-year plan for my life. It's indexed and color-coded. I'm ready.

"Here we are, ladies!" Duff says from the driver's seat. He glides to a stop in front of Nate Kattenberger's mansion on Pierrepont Place.

Eric Bayer opens the limo's backdoor immediately, leaning in to smile at us. "Hey! All my favorite women in one place."

The baby goes into spasms of joy at the sight of his face.

"Look who's Mr. Popular." Alex snorts. She unclips her daughter from the car seat.

"He's not that popular with me," I complain, even as I take Eric's hand and let him help me onto the sidewalk.

"You fell for it, didn't you?" His chuckle is gleeful.

"It's entrapment," I complain.

He laughs and then takes the baby from Alex and hoists her into the air, where she gives him a big, chubby grin.

"Oh, sure," Alex says. "You're all smiles for him."

And I'm a puddle of goo. Watching Eric play with his baby always knocks me flat. It's the same with my brother and my niece. I've never been a crier, but when Rosie smiles at Eric, or when Nicole smiles at Dave, I just about lose it, every time.

Getting old makes you more emotional, I guess. Yay.

"Let me take her," Alex offers. "You two have some catching up to do. I'll find Nate and say hello."

Eric kisses his girlfriend. Then he kisses the baby. And then he turns to me. "Welcome home, Bessie. You look great by the way. I almost didn't recognize you."

"Why? Because I don't have my phone stuck to my face? Hand it over, by the way."

"No, because you're wearing a *dress*. Wowzers."

"Oh, stop it." I feel heat on my cheeks as I involuntarily glance down at the blue batik sundress. Zara had made me try it on when we'd gone shopping last week in Montreal. "Stop buying dresses for your two-year-old niece and buy one for yourself," she'd said. "My kid has enough clothes to meet the queen. But you wear the same Red Wing's T-shirt everywhere."

She wasn't wrong. But now I feel self-conscious.

"It's a good look," Eric says. "And congratulations on making it ten days away from the office. Are you sure you don't want to go for eleven? Except for that little slip-up just now, you've turned yourself into a woman of leisure."

"There was no slip-up! That was just you being a weenie. Now hurry up and give me my phone back. And fill me in on what I missed. Is it possible that none of my players got traded, injured, or arrested while I was gone?"

He laughs. "You think I'd hide something like that from you?"

"No. But it's kind of wild how quiet everything was." On any given week, someone has a major upset or a nervous breakdown. It's as if I have thirty-five high-strung children in my care. Somebody is always breaking something.

"Nobody got arrested. But Nifty Silva had a tiny run-in with the town of Buckhead, Georgia."

I stop in my tracks. "Omigod. What did he do? Why didn't you call me?"

"Because I handled it." Eric laughs. "And I enjoyed every minute of it. Nifty had outstanding library fines of eighteen hundred bucks. Ask me why."

"Why?" I gasp. "That man makes five million dollars a year."

Eric chuckles. "Five years ago he took a copy of *Field of Dreams* out of the library. Apparently the nice librarians of Buckhead fine you a dollar a day on DVDs."

"And he was too busy setting records to return a fucking movie?" I swear to God this job is like teaching kindergarten but with a better paycheck.

"Not exactly. Right after watching the film, he threw his first no-hitter. So he didn't—"

"—return it. I get it. He's a superstitious crazy man. So how do we smooth this over? Did it hit the press?"

"It was going to. He called the office in a panic. But I handled it, Bess. I had a nice chat with the librarians. I told them that Nifty would donate ten bucks for every dollar he owed, but I suggested she let the fines keep running."

"Oh, Eric!" I burst out laughing. "That's perfect. That's exactly what I would have done."

He hip-checks me on the sidewalk. "I know, boss. And I had a blast talking to that librarian with her adorable southern accent. It's all good."

"Thank you," I say as we walk around to the side of Nate and Becca's mansion. They're the only people I know in New York who can throw a big backyard party. Because they're the only ones with a big backyard. "Thank you for letting me have all that time off."

"It's not a big deal," he says. "People take vacations all the time. Get used to it."

I wonder if I ever will. My childhood was perilous. Dave and I were too busy avoiding my father's fists to notice that nobody ever took us to Disneyland. Or camping. Or any of the things that families do. Summer break had only meant too much time with our angry father.

College was better. But I'd been too busy working my butt off to relax. And after graduation, my dream job kept me busy. And it still does.

"What else?" I demand of Eric. "What other weird calls did you get?"

"There's that rookie who just showed up for training camp in Ottawa. Rollins?"

"Yeah?" My blood pressure jumps. "Is he okay?"

"He's fine," Eric says quickly. "But he panicked his first night there. He locked himself out of his new apartment, and he didn't know what to do."

"Aw." Rollins is only nineteen. He comes from a town in Canada with more cows than people. "Did you help him find a locksmith?"

"Of course I did. I was home with the baby that night, just flipping channels before he called. So I put my earpods in and sat down in the rocking chair with the baby. And I talked to the rookie for ninety minutes while he waited for the locksmith. The kid just needed someone to tell him that it was all going to be okay."

"Wow. Thank you. Bonus points for sure."

"It was great, Bess. It made me understand what this job is for, you know? Negotiating contracts is only half the story. He's just a kid in a strange city. I'd forgotten what that part was like. The only two things he knows how to cook are fried eggs and spaghetti."

"Jeez. Next time I see him, I'll make sure he eats a salad. Anything else? Any gossip? If not, I think I hear a glass of sangria calling my name." Rebecca Rowley-Kattenberger—the new owner of the Brooklyn Bruisers—makes a great pitcher of sangria.

"Oh, there's gossip." Eric chuckles as he finally hands me my phone.

"What kind?" I ask, fondling the phone like a lost lover.

"I think I'll let you see for yourself." He opens Nate and Rebecca's garden gate and then gestures for me to go in first.

TWO

In the Backyard of a Billionaire

The Puckrakers Blog: Preseason Trade Update

"What Brooklyn Needs is a Surly Dallas Player—Said No One Ever"

BRUISERS FANS ARE SCRATCHING their heads this week at the news that Mark "Tank" Tankiewicz was traded from Dallas to DUMBO. While the team could use some more experience on the blue line, Tankiewicz is an expensive choice.

There's some wisdom in poaching a guy who helped cut off Brooklyn's championship dreams a year ago. (And we're told that he brings out the female ticketholders. Tankiewicz is famous for modeling the Jockers line of men's briefs.)

But does Tank have the right temperament for the job? Last season he blew his stack so often on the ice that Dallas fans had a name for his frequent outbursts, dubbing each incident a "Tank Spank."

And if the rumors are true, Tank spanked his own captain late in the season. A scuffle between Tankiewicz and Bart Palacio may have been the impetus for Tank's sudden trade across country.

Time will tell whether this risky trade pays off for Brooklyn. But either way, it's going to be interesting.

Tank

"Welcome to Brooklyn." The team's yoga instructor reaches out a hand for me to shake.

"Thank you so much. It's a pleasure to be here." I've said that ten times in the last ten minutes.

Ariana's grin says she knows I'm a liar. "I'm sure you remember me from this morning's class."

"How could I forget? My hamstrings will never forgive you." I paste a pleasant smile on my face for the pretty lady who's trying so hard to be nice to me. It's not her fault that I'm at a party I never wanted to attend in a city I never asked to return to.

"In addition to making you sweat three mornings a week, I'm also the team massage therapist. We should meet in the next few days to discuss any muscular issues you're experiencing, and to go over any therapies you require."

"Thank you. I'll make an appointment." And now we've run out of things to say to each other. "This is a great party. Do you always kick off the season like this?"

"Every year," Ariana says with a smile. "If I had this lawn, I'd throw a lot of parties, too."

"Right? It's so nice." And it *is* nice, I suppose. It's a perfect September evening, and we're standing in the midst of a sumptuous lawn, surrounded on three sides by high walls. Rose bushes and ivy climb every stone surface. The fourth side of the lawn borders the mansion, where my new team's owner resides with her billionaire husband.

It's beautiful here, but I just want to go home. Except I can't, because I don't have one anymore.

Three months ago I'd been standing in my own damn yard in Texas. The season had just ended after a disappointing loss to L.A. My most pressing engagements were a golf outing with my teammates and a haircut.

Then my wife had said, "I think you should move out."

And the hits just kept coming when my agent called a few weeks later. "Mark, sit down. I have to tell you something. You've been traded to Brooklyn," he'd said. "Now get up again and get your things together."

Worst summer vacation ever.

Patrick O'Doul—the captain of my new team—steps up and slings an arm around Ariana. "Everything okay over here?"

"Of course," she says. "But if you see another tray of those crab fritters go by, feel free to flag them down for me."

"Will do." O'Doul wraps his arm even more tightly around Ariana. It's a gesture that makes a loud statement. *Me Tarzan. You asshole. Get away from Jane.*

I hold back a frustrated groan. *Okay, dude, message received.* I hadn't known that the yoga teacher and the captain were an item, but I'm not the kind of asshole who'd hit on a team employee.

Obviously, O'Doul has already made his assumptions. My shitty reputation precedes me. There've been nasty articles about me. The hockey blogs are spasming with gossip about my life and my sudden trade to Brooklyn.

It doesn't help that I was traded from Dallas—the team Brooklyn hates most. None of it should matter when I'm wearing a Brooklyn jersey. But I haven't proved myself yet. And if tomorrow's practice goes as poorly as today's did, it's hard to say when I'll get the chance.

The last three months have been a nightmare that I'm not allowed to wake up from. I know I'm supposed to keep a smile pasted on my face and just try harder. But I'm really just fucking *tired*. I never wanted to be the new guy in the city. Although this city isn't exactly new to me. I'd been twenty-three the first time I got off a plane at JFK. I'd been a rookie, joining a team just across the river. Another rival of Brooklyn's. I've basically spent my entire career on the two teams they loathe most.

"Have you found an apartment?" Ariana asks pleasantly.

"No, ma'am." I sigh. "I'm in a hotel at the moment. I wanted to focus on training camp before I had to worry about permanent housing. People tell me that Brooklyn real estate is tricky."

"It is. Have you met Heidi Jo?" Ariana beckons to a pretty

blonde woman who's been buzzing around the party. "She works with the GM. But more importantly, she's really good at solving problems. She'll know which real estate agent to use. Heidi! We need you over here."

"You rang?" Heidi says, darting toward us. She's a pretty thing, and young. "Hey! Mark 'the Tank' Tankiewicz! We met a long time ago at some shindig of my father's."

Now that she mentions it, I do have a vague recollection of the league commissioner's daughter. "You were a teenager," I recall. "Mouth full of braces."

"Okay, new rule." Heidi rolls her eyes in a good-natured way. "How about you don't mention my awkward teen years, and I don't bring up your underwear modeling career?"

"It's a deal," I say quickly. I've only been in Brooklyn a couple of days, but I've already heard plenty of snickering about my photo campaigns for Jockers.

Heidi gives me another cheery smile. "Did I overhear that you need to find an apartment?"

"Yeah, just got in on Tuesday. I'm in a hotel. But eventually I'll have to sort that out."

Her eyes light up. "I love apartment hunting! If you're very lucky, something will open up in the Million Dollar Dorm. That's our condo building on Water Street. Some guys rent, but a few guys own their apartments. It's a two-minute walk to the practice rink."

"Sounds amazing." Honestly, that's the only thing that could make me feel better about moving to Brooklyn. A walking commute.

"That building is pretty tight, though. Silas's girlfriend just bought out Dave Beringer. The only other unit I know about is a studio, unfortunately." She puts a hand on O'Doul's shoulder. "Our fearless captain is going to sell because Ariana has a house in Vinegar Hill. There's another nice commute. Five minutes in the other direction."

"I'm *thinking* of selling," the captain rumbles. "Not sure yet. Might keep the place as an investment."

As if it would kill him to sell to me. He thinks my trade was as big a mistake as I think it was. "I won't keep my hopes up, then." I don't bother to keep the snark out of my tone. The dude needs to lighten up.

"Well, anyway," Heidi says, hands on her hips. "The studio probably wouldn't work for you and your wife. How's Jordanna?"

"You have a terrific memory for names," I say. It's easily been five years since we all met. "But Jordanna won't be needing any closet space in my apartment. She's divorcing me."

"Oh!" Heidi gasps. Then she claps a hand over her mouth. "Lord, I am *so* sorry. Holy cow, they're going to take away my license to be a Southern girl after a faux pas like this."

Everyone smiles, including me. "I don't see how you could have known. I didn't even know myself until June."

"Oh, Tank!" She flings her arms around me. "That's terrible."

"Hey, I'll live." I give her an awkward back pat, just as Jason Castro joins our little group, his eyes narrowed and focused on my proximity to Heidi Jo.

"Everything okay here?" he asks.

Oh, for fuck's sake. I step back from Castro's girl and hold in another sigh.

"I am not okay!" Heidi complains. "I put my foot in my mouth. And I am shook."

"Nothing a little cocktail won't fix," he says, handing her a drink. "They're stronger than they look, though. Sip slowly."

She takes the cocktail and takes a nice healthy gulp. "Ooh, tasty."

"Honey…"

"I know." She sighs. "I have the tolerance of a kitten."

"We love you anyway," Ariana says. "Now, who wants to play bocce?"

"Me!" Heidi's hand shoots up.

"Are you as good at this as you are at darts?" Castro asks.

"We'll find out." She hooks one arm in mine and one arm in Castro's. "Let's raise the stakes. A dollar a point. Who wants to bet against me?"

"Why not?" Jason says. "Who needs money?"

Honestly, they make a cute couple. They're both young, and

13

probably in the early stages of their relationship. They don't know yet how fleeting love is—those early years when you haven't let each other down yet.

Jordanna and I had been that way once. We must have been, or I wouldn't have gotten married in the first place.

Jordanna had been the first to admit our marriage was over, but I guess I'd known in my gut that we were doomed. Once the shock wore off, I began to feel some relief. I'm sad, but I no longer have to be that guy who's always failing her.

So here I am in Brooklyn, allowing myself to be led over to the bocce court, which is a strip of sand cut into the manicured grass. The goal of bocce is tossing balls onto the court, trying to land them as close as possible to a target ball. It's as good a way as any for a grump like me to pass a half an hour.

Another game is just finishing up. The winner is Dave Beringer. He's a recently retired Brooklyn player—another guy who's spent the past decade trying to break me in half. We'd gotten into a fight at the beginning of last season, after he'd made a dirty hit on one of my teammates. So I'd punched him in the face.

And if that's not awkward enough, there's this little matter of the fling I had with his sister nine years ago. Not that I'm *ever* telling him about it.

"Hey," he says stiffly.

"Hey," I reply, because nobody ever accused me of being a charmer.

Cue the awkward silence.

"Okay, listen up!" Heidi says with a clap of her hands. "The first round is Tank against Castro. Now I'm going to hand you your balls. Saying that never gets old." Heidi giggles and places a set of heavy wooden balls in my hands. She hands a set to her boyfriend, too.

Castro throws out the pallino—the little target ball. His first toss comes within about a foot and a half of the target.

I know I can do better than that. So I let 'em fly.

Thirty minutes later I've beaten every hockey player I've come up against. I should probably throw the game and let someone else win. But that's lame. And cleaning up at bocce is more fun than making conversation.

Then Heidi steps up to the court. "Okay, big man. It's time someone put you in your place." She throws a ball that lands dead center, rolls two feet forward and stops an inch from the pallino.

"Nice!" I enthuse. "I'm gonna have to bring out the heat."

"Bring it," she growls. "I'm ready."

I lob a ball at hers and push it a few crucial inches off the target.

"Fine, fine," she says with a wave of her perfectly manicured hand. "I'll get you yet." She makes another brilliant toss and pushes my ball out of the way.

"Yeah!" cheers the small crowd around us. "You go girl!"

As if there was any question who'd they'd back. I'd cheer for Heidi, too. She's hilarious. But I can't ease up now. Heidi is watching me with flashing eyes. She doesn't want me to throw the game. So I toss out another winner, crowding her closest ball.

Dave Beringer steps onto the court to squint at our two balls. "Keep throwing, Heidi. He's inside your toss by a half inch."

"No problemo," she says cheerfully. "I'm smooth with my balls." She winks at her boyfriend before her third throw.

"Ooooooh!" The crowd sighs as her roll goes too far to the side.

She's only got one more throw to repair the damage, and it's a beauty. She puts the ball right up against the target again.

"Pressure!" someone yells. Because it won't be easy for me to win now.

My first cautious toss falls short, and all the men snicker. "Yeah, yeah. I got one more." I dust off my hands, and contemplate my strategy. I can only win this if I ease up to Heidi's ball and nudge it aside. Hell.

I line up a careful shot, but just as I'm about to toss, I catch a flash of strawberry curls at my side. I turn for a better look, which is a mistake. As the ball leaves my hand, I'm not even looking at the target. Because Bess Beringer—a woman I haven't seen for nine years—is standing right there, gaping at me.

The ball misses the target. Badly. Heidi lets out a whoop of victory and everyone laughs.

But I can't stop staring at Bess. She's a redhead, like her brother, but her hair color is only one of the striking things about her. She has pink cheeks and flashing bright blue eyes that always tell you just where you stand with her.

And right now they're staring back at me with astonishment. It's been almost a decade since we've come face to face. But, hell, it seems like no time has gone by at all, because it's way too easy to picture her beneath me in bed, straining against me, reaching for what we both wanted and always found together—heady, sweet release.

She's blinking at me, as if she can picture it all, too.

"Hey, Bess!" Heidi says, dusting off her hands. "Welcome back! How was your vacation?"

"Um…" She swallows. "Nice," she says after a beat. "Great vacation."

"Did you win the bet? Ten days without your phone?"

"Yup." Bess's head bobs up and down, but she's still sneaking looks at me.

"Do you know Mark Tankiewicz?" Heidi asks. "Mark, you must know Bess Beringer, agent to the stars?"

I turn to face Bess, and our eyes lock again. Her surprise is so palpable that I have to hold back a chuckle. With the whole world standing here listening, I'm going to have to choose my words carefully.

Bess beats me to it. "Nice to meet you," she says, thrusting out a hand.

Wait, what? That's how she wants to play it?

It takes me a beat to respond. "Likewise," I say, reaching out to shake. When her slender hand lands in mine, I can't help myself. I stroke a finger along the underside of her wrist. "The pleasure is all mine."

Now her cheeks are rapidly staining to a deep pink, and the sight stirs up some long-dormant feelings in my chest. Bess and I had some hot times together. *Really* hot. We'd both been young and new to New York City and so confident that the universe was going to hand us everything we asked of it. And maybe it did for Bess. I sure hope so, anyway.

No wedding ring, though, my asshole brain notices.

Bess pulls her hand out of mine and takes a step backward. "And you're here in Brooklyn because…?"

"Traded," I say gruffly.

"To Brooklyn." Her low voice is so familiar that it gives me chills.

"Right," I say, laughing darkly. "And when I found out, I had the same look of shock on my face that you've got right now."

Everybody else laughs, too, and the sound seems to pull Bess out of her stupor. She straightens her spine, and I'm struck by how familiar her body language is, too. I was always fascinated by Bess. Behind that sweet name and nymph-like body is a tough girl. She's a study in sexy contrasts.

The first time we met, Bess had been a newbie agent, the youngest employee in Henry Kassman's shop. After sharing a business dinner, I'd taken her to my hotel room, where we'd had the kind of up-all-night, energetic, soul-scorching sex that exuberant youngsters sometimes experience but rarely appreciate.

We'd had a friends-with-benefits arrangement that lasted for several months. It had been magic. I'd never hit it off with anyone quite so well as I had with her.

She'd ended it without really saying why, and I hadn't had the good sense to be very upset. I'd missed her, and I'd sure as hell missed the sex, but I'd been riding the high of being a young, successful athlete in the big city. I didn't lack for female attention.

But, man, our chemistry had been on another level. I hadn't appreciated it while it lasted. And now she pretends not to recognize me? *Ouch.*

"Excuse me," Bess says now. She turns her back on me, heading for the house, ducking into the crowd, her hips swaying.

Oh, hell no. She won't get away from me that easily. I eye the boss's mansion and wonder where she'll head next.

"Who needs a drink?" Heidi asks, pulling my attention back to the party. "And who's willing to play the new winner?"

"I'm very afraid," Castro says. "But I'll do it."

"That's my boy." Heidi stands on her tiptoes and kisses him. "I'm going to grab us all a bucket of cold beer."

"I'll help you," I offer. "I need a drink after that whipping you just gave me."

There are a few good-natured chuckles. Losing to the team's favorite assistant was probably a good move, even if I didn't mean to do it.

I head for the bar with Heidi. As I help her tuck bottles of beer into an ice bucket, I feel eyes on me. I finish what I'm doing and glance up.

Busted. There's Bess Beringer, watching me from the food table. She looks away quickly, embarrassed to be caught.

I don't know why she pretended not to remember me, when it's so very obvious she does.

THREE

Creamed Spinach and a Proposition

BESS

IT'S unlike me to panic. I love pressure. I'm an athlete, for goodness' sake. In college, I scored goals seconds before the game-ending buzzer. And in my professional life, I've wrestled fat contracts out of managers who were determined not to pay up. I've removed the hands of grabby, drunk sportscasters from my body without breaking a sweat.

Tonight, though, I'd been unprepared to come face to face with Tank after so many years. I'd seized up completely. Those broody green eyes have always made me stupid.

Thirty-two looks *good* on Tank. His dark, arrogant smirk is the same, but he's aged into a harder, less boyish version of the man I used to know. His body is less bulky, but more cut. The muscles in his forearms are defined, where they used to be just beefy.

I sneak another peek at him. He looks *dangerous*. In a good way. All he's doing is standing in the grass holding a beer, and I still have the urge to scale him like a tree.

The universe is having a laugh at my expense tonight. My birthday looms, which means I've already thought of Tank several times today. *He's* the man who'd made my twenty-first so special. It hadn't been for just the one night, either. Our fling had a shelf life of three or four months. I'd put a halt to it when I realized my relationship with Tank could become a career-ending mistake.

At that point, I'd already landed my dream job as an assistant at the Henry Kassman & Associates. Since I'd skipped a grade in middle school, I'd been a very young college graduate. Young and very naïve. My office nickname had been The Rookie.

By the time my birthday rolled around, all the hockey rookies were turning up for training camp. Since I was based in New York, I'd met a few of the young guys who were playing for New York and New Jersey.

Tank had been one of them.

And the night of my birthday, my boss had plans to entertain a few rookies at Sparks Steak House. "Spend your big night with us!" Henry Kassman had said, inviting me out to the dinner.

"You don't need to buy me a steak for my birthday," I'd insisted.

"Listen, Rookie, it's not like that," he'd said. "After twenty years at this job, I don't really need another steak dinner at Sparks. I'd rather go home and read a Patterson thriller until the book hits me in the face when I nod off. But this is the business. I gotta welcome some young punks to the city and show 'em a good time. If you come out tonight, you'll be doing me a favor."

"Oh," I'd said slowly, trying to decide whether or not to believe him.

"Do you like creamed spinach?"

"I really don't know." Twenty-one-year-old Bess hadn't had much experience with fine dining.

"It's so good. I promise. And the steak is to die for. Come out. Enjoy a glass of expensive birthday wine on me. Chat up some rookies. It'll be great."

So I'd gone, wearing a sleeveless silk top that I'd bought on sale at Bloomingdales on the way there. I'd tried the spinach, and it had been delicious. I'd eaten a filet mignon so tender that it seemed to melt on my tongue like butter. And I drank fine red wine for the first time in my life.

Every time I'd looked across the table, my gaze had locked with a hot twenty-three-year-old rookie from Washington state named Mark Tankiewicz. He'd been handsome and brash, with piercing green-gray eyes. He hadn't been worried about which fork to use or how to pronounce Cabernet Sauvignon.

"My motto is simple," he'd told the table, his wine glass practically disappearing into his big hand. "In any situation I just ask myself, *what can I get away with?* And then I do that."

Everyone had laughed, but the idea had stuck with me. To this very day, I remind myself of his words when I feel intimidated. *What can I get away with?* It had been a powerful dose of wisdom for a young, clueless woman trying to make it in the testosterone-soaked world of professional sports.

Tank had been so comfortable in his own skin. As I'd gazed at him across the table, I'd relaxed for the first time since starting my job six weeks earlier. And when the meal ended, I'd been a little drunk and completely in love with my exciting New York City life.

I was also half in love with Tank, with his wavy brown hair and broody eyes.

Afterward, Henry Kassman had cars waiting outside to take everyone home, but one car had been running late. "You take this one, Mr. Kassman," Tank had offered. "Age before beauty. I don't need a car. Heck, I'll share with Bess. She can drop me at the hotel on her way home."

I'd felt jitters in my tummy at the sound of my name on his lips.

"Sounds like a plan, son, if Bess doesn't object," Henry had said. "Good night, everyone. Go home, get some rest, boys. You're going to need it for the rest of training camp."

I'd gotten into that car with Tank and given the driver the address of the tiny studio apartment I'd rented in a walkup building in the West fifties. "And there will be a first stop, at…" I'd turned to Tank for instructions.

He'd lifted my hand and kissed my palm, sending tingles through my body. "Let's make it one stop, instead. Your birthday isn't quite over yet, right? And I'm really good at celebrating."

After I'd gotten over my shock, I'd stammered out my approval of this plan. Then Tank had placed a hand on my knee, given it a dirty squeeze, and told the driver to take us to the Marriott Marquis.

The man hadn't been lying. He'd been *exceptionally* good at celebrating. Then, and for many nights afterward.

Fast forward nine years, and I'd shaken the man's hand, pretending I didn't remember any of it.

I sneak another look at Tank, wondering how to privately apologize. His gaze jumps right to mine. And then it darkens, sweeping down my body with a bold, possessive slowness.

Holy heck. My neck heats as I turn away. Even after all these years, it's shockingly easy to remember running my hands over his chest, cataloging all the dips and valleys of his muscled torso. It's not an exaggeration to say that everything I know about sex, I learned from him. He hadn't been my first lover, but he'd been my first good one. My *only* good one, if we're being honest.

Not that I should be allowing myself to have these thoughts. I know for a fact that he's married. The day I'd found the wedding pictures on social media was the last day I'd allowed myself to look him up.

I scan the yard, looking for his wife. I've obviously never met her. But maybe I should. It might snap me out of my reverie.

There aren't any unfamiliar women outside, though. She must be in the house. Meanwhile, I'd better get my apology speech ready. It's only a matter of time until I bump into Tank at the team facility. *I'm sorry your hotness temporarily scrambled my brain.*

No, it's bad form to blame the victim. *I'm sorry that old memories briefly interrupted the brain function of this sex-starved woman in the throes of a midlife crisis.*

That's too pathetic to say out loud. Even if it's true.

Avoiding Tank, I eat some excellent barbecue with my brother. When we're finished, I carry our plates into the house. The enormous kitchen is buzzing with caterers, one of whom takes the plates from me. I'm walking toward the door when I spot my new business partner in the dining room, chatting with Rebecca Rowley-Kattenberger.

I duck in to say hello. "Hey guys! What are you plotting?"

"Bessie!" Eric says, waving me over. Rosie is strapped to his chest in a carrier, and when she spots me, she lets out a little squawk of greeting.

"Ooh! How's my girl?" I croon.

"I'm just dandy, thanks for asking," Rebecca jokes. Then she grabs me into a hug. "How are you? Are you settling into your new apartment? Is it great?"

"It's getting there. I barely have any furniture, but I hate shopping." Without asking for an invitation, I unclip the front of Eric's baby carrier so I can hold Rosie.

"Well, *I* don't hate shopping," Becca says, clapping her hands. "Just say the word if you need a little company."

"You don't have time to help me pick out a coffee table." I hug Rosie as she tries to grab fistfuls of my hair.

"Hey, I can make time," Becca says. "Especially if there are rugs involved. And throw pillows. By the way—I love your dress. You must not hate shopping *that* much."

"No, she really does," Eric says. "And I've never seen her in a dress before. I didn't even know she had knees."

"*Eric*," Becca squawks. "That's no way to treat your boss."

"Are you kidding? She teases me all day long," he says. "This is just self-defense."

I give him a poke in the elbow, and he snickers. Eric and I have known each other a long time. I was his agent for eight years, since Clove—Eric's first agent—died in a car crash.

Clove had been a senior agent at Henry Kassman and Associates, and he'd had a lot of clients—both hockey and baseball, which was unusual. Some of Clove's athletes left our firm after he died, and some of them got picked up by more senior agents. But Eric and a handful of others picked me.

"They know they'll get a lot of your attention," Henry Kassman had explained to me. "And they know I've got your back. So put on your game face and fight for your new clients, Bess. You're going to do a great job."

At the time, I'd been both gratified and terrified by the number of clients I'd picked up when Clove passed away. Within the space of a couple weeks, I'd gone from a third-stringer who'd mostly answered phones, to a busy agent in her own right.

I'd never looked back. Two years later I'd left Kassman to start my own business. There weren't many agents in Detroit, and I knew I could pick up a bunch of athletes who wanted local representation.

That feels like a hundred years ago, though. And here I am starting over on the East Coast, because my priorities have shifted once again.

"Hey girls!" We're joined by Georgia, Becca's best friend and the team publicist. "Nice dress, Bess! You look amazing. Wow."

Eric snickers, and I have to give him another poke in the elbow. But the surprise in Georgia's voice is a wakeup call. "I guess I have a reputation for avoiding girly clothes."

"I'm a proud tomboy myself," Georgia insists. "Although Rebecca tries. Did you hear she just bought a Brooklyn nail salon?"

"Oh, neat," I say, feigning enthusiasm.

At that, everyone laughs. Even the baby.

"When I reopen the place, will you let me treat you to a mani pedi?" Becca asks with a smile. "It's fun. I promise."

"It really is," Georgia insists. "I don't care much about nail polish, but I love a nice pedicure. It's all about the foot rub and the gossip."

"Okay, why not?" I say. "I'll try anything once."

"Excellent!" Georgia says, holding out her arms. "Now let me hold the baby. It's my turn."

"I suppose." My reluctance to pass her over is genuine. I love babies in general and Rosie specifically.

"Could I leave her with you two for a minute?" Eric asks. "Gotta hit the little boys' room, and then find her bottle."

"Sure, Big Daddy," Georgia says, taking Rosie from me. "We will do you the favor of snuggling this baby. Where's Alex, anyway?"

Becca points toward the grand staircase. "She and Nate disappeared into his office to talk business."

"On a Friday night?" Georgia scoffs, kissing Rosie's cheek.

"Have you met Nate?" Becca asks. "I'd better greet some more guests. The new guy looks a little lonely out there. Later, peeps." She excuses herself, and I resist the impulse to look out the window to check on Tank.

Lonely? That doesn't sound like him.

Georgia bounces Rosie and gives me a smile. "What's new? And what's your brother doing in town this weekend?"

"Tomorrow night he's taking me out to dinner. This afternoon he sold his condo to Delilah Spark, and tonight he's out drinking with the guys."

"Oh, great. Leo will probably come home bombed."

"Probably," I agree. "Tell me some gossip, girly. You know you want to." And agents live for gossip. It's how we find our clients.

"Let's see. The new guy is Mark Tankiewicz. I'm sure you heard about the trade."

"Right. From Dallas," I say, sidestepping the fact that we know each other. "Your coach is hoping to deepen the experience on the bench after losing a couple of veterans."

"Yep," Georgia says cheerfully. "But the transition is looking rocky. The younger players aren't quite ready to listen to a guy who stole the Cup away from them a year ago. The first two practices were..." She chooses her words carefully. "Not smooth."

"Bummer," I say, allowing myself a glance out the window at the veteran in question. He's standing by a rose bush, looking grumpy. Trades are rough on a guy. They just are. Even if you're a superstar.

Georgia drops her voice. "Leo was pretty testy last night. I guess Tank and Jason Castro had words. The new guy is a little prickly."

I groan inwardly, because Castro is my client. And I really hope the rift is only superficial. "They'll sort it out," I say. *They'd better*.

"Oh, of course they will. Tank seems pretty angry about the trade, though. I don't think he saw it coming."

"It's a big deal to have your life uprooted," I say. "New teammates, new home. His wife probably had to quit her job, or at least say goodbye to her friends."

Slowly, Georgia shakes her head. "The wife isn't coming."

"What?" The question flies out of my mouth. I forget to cushion it with indifference.

"It's true. I always sit down with the new players to get a feel for their publicity needs. And the first thing I asked him was about his wife. He flat out told me that she filed for divorce a few weeks ago."

I gasp. Because that's just harsh.

"Isn't it awful?" Georgia winces. "I guess she really didn't want to move to New York."

"That can't really by why," I whisper. "Can it?"

Georgia shakes her head. "Of course not. But it's bad form to speculate. The blogs are inventing all kinds of reasons already. I heard he fought a teammate. You and I both know not to trust that stuff, but..." She breaks off, looking uncomfortable.

"That bad, huh?" My traitorous gaze goes right to the windows again. "That's so sad," I whisper. I'd just assumed he was happily married. Honestly, I *always* assume that anyone who's married is happy about it.

Georgia kisses baby Rosie on the head. "Trades are hard enough when you have a partner by your side. I can't imagine getting traded and divorced at the same time."

"Georgia!" someone calls from another room. "Are you in here?"

"Coming!" she calls. "Sorry, if you'll excuse me?"

"Go!" I insist, taking the baby back from her. Rosie smells like baby powder, and the scent is like a drug to me. I want to stick my nose on her little fuzzy head and inhale.

So I do. Because we're alone in the dining room now, and nobody is around to see me. Rosie makes a soft coo, and then sticks her fist in her mouth, and I wonder if Eric has found that bottle yet. I walk closer to the leaded-glass windows, so we can both look outside.

My eyes find Tank immediately. Of course they do. He's deep in conversation with Silas, the backup goalie. My brother sold his condo to Silas's girlfriend this afternoon.

I wonder where Tank has been staying. At a hotel, probably.

Trades are brutal. You get no warning. One phone call will uproot an entire family.

Or a marriage.

And I just shook his hand and pretended I didn't even recognize him.

Nice work, Bess. Real smooth.

Baby Rosie squints at me, as if trying to decide whether or not to yell at me. And I can't say I blame her.

FOUR

People Will Write Anything on the Internet

TANK

I'M DONE with this party. As soon as I can shake our hostess's hand, I'm out of here. There's only one person in the yard who's smiling at me. It's Ivo, the other new trade. He's a young Finnish kid who arrived only yesterday.

"Nice party, right?" I ask him.

He smiles.

"Did you try the brisket? It was almost as good as Texas barbecue. Almost."

He smiles again.

"You have no idea what I'm saying right now, do you?"

He smiles one more time. "No English."

"Poor kid." I give him a friendly tap on the elbow. "Actually, they like you better than me already. Doesn't matter if you speak the language. Hell, it's probably easier that way."

He smiles.

At last, Rebecca Rowley-Kattenberger finishes her conversation and turns to me. "Mark Tankiewicz! Do you have everything you need for the golf tournament this weekend?"

"I do, ma'am. And thank you for the party. Your home is amazing." I hold out my hand to say goodbye.

"Isn't it?" She hugs me instead of shaking my hand. "I didn't have a thing to do with this place. And you don't have to call me ma'am. Everyone else calls me Becca."

"It's just Texas manners," I promise her. "I spent eight years there."

"That's a long time," she says kindly. "But you grew up in Washington state?"

"That's right. Good memory."

She waves a hand around the yard. "It's my job to know everyone's business. Let me know if you have any trouble settling in," she says. "If you don't like the real estate broker we recommended, there are others."

"I haven't even called them yet," I admit. "I need to focus on hockey first and the chaos of my life later."

"I can't even imagine how you're holding it together." She squeezes my arm, her face full of sympathy. "I'm sure you've had easier months. Just let me know if there's anything you need. And thanks for coming today."

"My pleasure." She gives me another warm smile, and I return it even though my neck feels hot.

Everyone knows about my divorce, giving me either dirty or pitying looks. They're both a drag. I've already cycled through a wide range of feelings—shock, numbness, sadness—but I seem to have landed on embarrassment, instead of utter heartbreak.

If that's not a sign, then I don't know what is.

"Hey, Rebecca!" another player says, grabbing the owner's attention. He's not just any player. Eric Bayer is one of the veterans I was meant to replace. Bayer is only a year or two older than I am, but he retired last season after one too many knee surgeries. "Did you happen to see... Oh, there it is!" Bayer reaches under the caterer's table and emerges with a tote bag. It's covered in bright pink bunny rabbits. He pulls a baby's bottle out of the sack and begins to shake it. "Just in time," he says.

I search my brain, trying to remember if I ever met his wife. But I come up blank. I thought he was single.

"Do you need to heat that up?" Becca offers.

"Nope. The little miss likes it cool or warm or any temperature at all." He pops the protective top off. "Here she comes now."

I glance toward the half flight of stairs to the house, and my heart fails. Because it's Bess who's carrying a chubby little baby girl out into the yard. The baby is propped snugly on her hip and clutches a lock of Bess's striking red hair in her tiny hand.

Bess is too distracted by the baby to look at me, which is a good thing because I know there's shock written all over my face.

"Wow, Rookie," she says to Eric. "That's a very manly diaper bag you have there."

"You shut up," he says with a smile. "Thanks for the free babysitting."

"Who says it was free?" Bess asks, handing the baby over.

That's when I remember to breathe. Because Bess isn't Eric's wife, and that's not her baby. Not that I should care. It doesn't have a thing to do with me.

What the heck is wrong with me? Back in the day, Bess and I weren't even serious. We had a wonderful, physical fling.

Before she broke it off, without telling me why.

Eric pries his daughter's fingers off Bess's hair and casually tips the baby back into his embrace, the bottle sliding into her mouth like he's done this a thousand times before. All the women in a twenty-foot radius are watching him with hearts in their eyes.

Even Bess. "Need anything else?" she asks, taking the baby's chubby little bare foot in her hand and giving it a gentle squeeze.

"No boss, I got this."

Her brother Dave calls over to them. "Don't call her *boss*, it will go right to her head."

"That's the idea," Eric insists. "It helps to gloss over my general incompetence." Then he turns his head and spots me listening in on this friendly drama. "Hey, man. It's been a while since I faced off against you."

"It has, right?" I say stiffly. "Last fall, maybe?"

"Yeah," Bayer agrees. "I only got six weeks of the regular season. Welcome to Brooklyn. I'm sure you're questioning all your life choices right now, but this is a good group."

"I can tell," I lie.

"Uh-huh." He gives me a grin, like he can see right through me. "What are you up to these days?" I ask.

"Working for this tough lady here." He jerks his chin toward Bess, who rolls her eyes at him. "Trying my hand as an agent."

"Oh, cool." I'd heard that Bess was doing well with her business in Detroit. She's rumored to be a tough negotiator. And it makes sense that she'd want someone on the East Coast to help her grow the business.

"I'm still learning the ropes," Eric says. "You're Henry Kassman's client, right?"

"True story."

"Well done, Rookie!" Bess says to Eric. She's still avoiding my eyes. "Look at the memory on you."

"Hey, I pay attention. You two must have met Kassman at about the same time?" he asks her. "You must have overlapped by a year or so."

"*Overlapped*," I say slowly. "Yeah, I guess you could say that."

"Briefly," Bess stammers, lifting her chin to show me a pair of startled, guilty eyes. She takes a deep breath. "Kassman runs a great shop" she says coolly. "I loved working with Henry."

I hold her gaze. Now we're having a staring contest. I win it. Bess's eyes drop first.

The victory doesn't sit right with me, though. To this day I don't know why she cut me loose. We had a really good thing going there for a little while.

But then she cut me off with no explanation. She only said she was too busy to spend time with me. But it was probably the other way around. Her next boyfriend was probably a guy who didn't spend sixty nights a year on the road.

"Bessie, I'm heading out," her brother says, interrupting our second awkward moment of the evening. "You sure you won't come out drinking?"

Bess shakes her head. "You go ahead. I don't feel like getting as drunk as you're about to get."

"How do you know?" he asks.

"Oh, please. One last night in the city with the team?" She waves a hand, like the math is too easy. "Just don't get arrested. No two a.m. calls from the city jail, please."

"Like that's ever happening," he scoffs. "Bayer, you in?"

Eric looks toward the house. "Probably. But first I'll make sure Alex and Rosie get home. Text me when you land at a bar."

"Will do." Dave crosses a few feet of lawn to kiss his sister on the top of her head. "Don't wait up. And I promise not to be too hung over to hang out on your birthday."

Your birthday. Whoa! I'd forgotten the date. But I haven't forgotten any of the details.

Neither has Bess. Her blue eyes cut right to mine. She quickly looks away again, and I see it—the telltale blush leaking across her cheeks and up her forehead. Nobody blushes like Bess.

And there's plenty to blush about. I remember everything about our first night together. The hesitation on her face when I'd invited her to my hotel room. The shock and lust in her eyes as I'd kissed my way down her body. The sounds she'd made...

Fuck. That was a long time ago. But it made a powerful impression on me.

"Hey, Tank." The backup goalie—Silas—arrives beside me. "Coming out with us tonight?"

Beside him, his buddy Castro scowls, as if he can't stand the idea.

That's okay, because I've had enough togetherness already. "You kids have fun," I say. "I'll see you tomorrow morning."

When I turn around, Bess has disappeared.

Before leaving the party, I make a pitstop in the mansion's sumptuous guest bathroom. Then, since I still need to shake Nate Kattenberger's hand, I go looking for the billionaire. Every ground-floor room is more impressive than the last.

I'm just passing the kitchen when I catch a few words the chattering caterers are saying.

"She left him! Can you believe it?"

"He must have a flaming hemorrhoid for a personality, because I wouldn't kick him out of bed. Did you see those arms?"

Feeling paranoid, I stand there, listening.

"She must love Texas more than she loves his dick," someone says with a snicker.

"I read that he cheated."

"Right? All that temptation from puck bunnies."

"They say he cheated with a teammate's *wife*. That's why he got traded."

Oh my fucking God. People will write anything on the internet.

This is why I'd spent the summer hiding from everyone, living in my Russian teammate's house, taking care of his dogs, trying to decide which Dallas neighborhood would be my home next year.

And then the hockey gods made a completely different choice for me.

I force myself to walk away from the kitchen. I finally locate Nate Kattenberger in his front parlor and thank him for his hospitality.

"Great to have you here," he says with a firm handshake.

"Great to be here." Another lie.

After a few more platitudes, I'm free of the party. As I duck out of the garden gate and walk down the sidewalk, I realize I don't know where the hell I am. I pick a direction and walk a block, but my path dead-ends into a park-like walking path along the river. There's a terrific view of lower Manhattan, but nowhere to meet a taxi.

So I reverse course, pulling my new phone out of my pocket. Everyone on the Bruisers team carries the same phone. It's manufactured by the billionaire whose barbecue I just enjoyed. It feels foreign in my hand, and when I open up the Lyft app, I realize I haven't linked my account to the new device yet. It doesn't know me, along with everything and everyone else around here.

I walk toward the traffic on what might or might not be Hicks Street. I need a yellow cab, hopefully with a driver who knows where the Marriott is. As I approach the corner, I see a taxi slowing down.

I'm just about to raise my hand when I notice it's stopping for someone else—a beautiful woman with lush red hair. As I walk toward her, she gives me the death glare that one New Yorker gives another when staking a claim on a taxi.

Then Bess realizes who she's glaring at, and her eyes widen.

I can't help but chuckle. Rattling Bess Beringer is the only fun thing that happened to me today. Although the day's not over yet.

FIVE

Cinderella Makes a Bad Decision

BESS

TANK STALKS TOWARD ME, and my heart begins to pound. When it comes to this guy, I have no chill. I never did.

But I finally understand my twenty-one-year-old self a little better. She'd made a terrible mistake—an agent should *never* sleep with a client—but now it's suddenly so easy to remember why it happened.

All it takes is one look from Tank, and I remember everything. The way his eyes used to darken while he undressed me. The way he used to pin my wrists together in his hand. The way he ordered me to unzip his pants, and how I obeyed, using my teeth.

He made me feel like a real woman. When he pinned me with that green-eyed stare, I wasn't the neglected little girl I'd been at fourteen. Nor the college jock with frizzy red hair. That look in his eyes made me into someone else entirely. I've never been as brazenly sexual as I was with him.

Twenty-one-year-old Bess hadn't known what hit her.

"Bess," he says in a low voice. "Want to share a cab?"

"What?" My throat goes dry. "Did you really just ask me that? We aren't headed in the same direction."

"We could be."

"*Tank,*" I gasp.

"What? Tell me one good reason we can't. Is there a guy waiting at home for you?"

It takes me several seconds to respond, because I'm so startled. "No. That's not the problem."

"Then what is? Maybe you forgot my name for a minute at the party. But we both know you didn't forget the rest of me."

"I didn't forget your name," I argue. But I can't have this conversation right here in the middle of Hicks Street.

And now the taxi, tired of waiting for us to argue, abruptly pulls away from the curb and abandons me.

"Hell," I curse, watching him go. Now it's just me and Tank. And he's propositioning me. I think. Maybe he's just trying to rile me up as payback for acting like an awkward idiot at the party. "You know what? I'm not twenty-one anymore."

"But wouldn't you like to be?" he asks in a low voice. "Happy Birthday, by the way. I'm still really good at celebrating."

I open my mouth to argue when he raises two fingers to his lips and lets fly with a sharp whistle. Another yellow cab pulls an illegal U-turn and stops at the curb. Tank opens the door and steps back, waiting for me.

I'm stuck to the sidewalk, staring at him. Because parts of me really want to be twenty-one again, damn it. My pulse is racing and my skin feels hot. Nobody has made me feel like this in a really long time. Nine years, actually.

"Get in, Bess," he says quietly. "It doesn't have to be a big decision."

Says you. But standing here on the sidewalk gaping at him isn't a really smart move, either. Anyone leaving Nate's party might spot us.

So that's my justification for getting into the cab—it's better to have this conversation privately. I slide across the seat to make room for Tank. My dress rides up, so I smooth it down primly.

Tank lowers his muscular body onto the seat beside me. "The Marriott at the Brooklyn Bridge, please," he says to the driver.

And then? He puts a possessive hand on my knee, and gives it a dirty squeeze.

It should feel wrong. But instead it just feels familiar. My breath hitches. Nine years later, and I'm still anticipating his firm grasp and the heat of his skin.

This is a terrible idea, I remind myself. *Get out of this cab at the next traffic light.* The Marriott is barely a mile away. I probably have less than five minutes to prevent myself from making another big mistake.

My stomach dips as I imagine what might happen when we arrive. It's been a while since I've been with any man. Maybe it would be awkward and terrible between us.

But maybe not.

Spoiler alert: I don't jump out of the cab.

The driver looks over his shoulder, and then unleashes a torrent of fan-boy ramblings. "Holy fuck! I got Mark Tankiewicz in my cab! You play for Dallas, *da?*"

"Yessir. Recently."

"You know my countrymen, Sergei and Igor Petrov?"

"Of course," Tank says. "Good guys. I was taking care of Sergei's dogs this summer. He keeps vodka in the freezer that will scramble your brain."

The cab driver laughs uproariously and demands an autograph.

Tank agrees. He isn't even looking at me, but his naughty hand slides slowly up my thigh and under my skirt. I hold my breath.

The cab pulls up to the hotel, and Tank's hand vanishes as the bellhop opens the cab door. Tank pays the cabbie and autographs his newspaper. I've almost recovered my wits when Tank hops onto the curb beside me and tucks an arm around my waist.

"Spasiba!" the cabbie calls. "Thank you!"

Tank doesn't bother responding. He's following the bellhop into the hotel lobby, tugging me along. He marches me toward the elevator, and the doors part as if he's commanded them to.

"Well, you have one fan in Brooklyn," I say, trying for nonchalance.

"Only one?" he asks. Then he takes my face in his hands and gives me a smoldering look.

I gaze back at him in wonder. I'd forgotten how it feels to have Tank's undivided attention. The heat in his eyes gives me a high like no drink or drug ever will. I stare at him until he says, "The elevator is here, Bess. Get in."

Jesus. My heart is racing. I have to get a grip. "Look…" I clear my throat as we step inside. The doors slide shut as he punches one of the buttons. "I'm sorry about the party. I'm sorry I implied that I didn't remember you."

"Oh I *know* you remember me." He smirks. "That was never in doubt."

Right. "Here's something you don't know, though. I remember something you said to me the first night I met you. And I never forgot it."

"Was it, 'Oh baby, don't stop'?"

I'm trying to make a point. So I step forward, squaring my shoulders to his, and look directly into his eyes. "Shut up a second, would you? I'm trying to pay you a compliment."

His eyes widen.

"That night we met at Sparks, I was new to the city and new at the agency. I read your file before dinner so I could memorize facts, but I didn't know what the heck I was doing. I was terrified of screwing up. But you sat across the table from me with that fifty-dollar glass of wine in your hand, looking as comfortable as a king…" I can still picture the whole scene like it was yesterday. "And even though I knew you were just a rookie in a strange city, you didn't show any fear. In fact, you told the whole table that your motto was: 'What can I get away with?'"

His smile turns wicked. "That sounds like something I would say. Not that I remember saying it."

"Well, I never forgot. And I've been saying it to myself on and off for the last nine years. When I don't know what to do, or I don't understand the rules, sometimes it just comes to me. 'What can we get away with?' So…" I clear my throat. "Thank you for that."

His expression softens. "That's the nicest thing anyone has said to me in a long time."

"You're welcome," I say, feeling a little more rational. A little more like myself.

But when the elevator doors open on the twentieth floor, and Tank waits for me to step out, I'm back to goosebumps and a fluttery tummy. At the end of the hallway, he pulls out a key card and swipes us into his room. Against my better judgment, I follow him inside.

The suite is spacious, with a kitchenette and a dining table. Soft lighting shows off the sleek lines of the low, leather sofas. I skirt the edge of the room, trying to keep my distance. It's surreal to be alone with him after so many years. It's even more surreal that I woke up this morning thinking about him.

The coincidence is easily explained by the date of my birth, and the start of hockey season, but I still feel like I've somehow conjured him with my thoughts.

With forced nonchalance, I stand in front of a set of floor-to-ceiling windows that look out over Brooklyn at twilight. The bridge is lit up in the distance, with the skyscrapers of Manhattan just beyond. The Empire State building is illuminated in green and blue. And a million other lights twinkle in the span between.

It's a view that can make any girl feel small and lonely. In New York, everyone is Cinderella. There's always a party going on somewhere that you weren't invited to.

"Would you like a glass of red?" Tank asks me. "Isn't that how it all began?" He stands at the kitchen counter, uncorking a bottle of wine with a confident twist of his muscled wrist.

"Sure," I say as he pours two glasses.

I watch the burgundy liquid mold to the goblets' shape. Then my dark prince lifts both glasses and stalks toward me at the windows. "Happy Birthday, Bess" he says, his eyes roving my face.

"Thank you." I take a glass, and my hand only shakes a little. Our glasses touch in a silent toast, and goosebumps rise on my arms as I hold his gaze and take a sip.

"How does it feel to turn twenty-one?" he whispers.

Since I'm taking a sip, the joke catches me off guard, and I swallow too fast. "Who's a funny guy?" I say, trying not to cough.

He gives me a smile that belongs in the bedroom scene of a Hollywood movie. In fact, everything Tank does has a sexual awareness to it. The way he walks across a room? Pure sex. The way he holds his wine glass? He might as well be cupping a breast.

I'd blame my dry spell, but I've always looked at him with my tongue practically hanging out. Always. I'm ashamed to say that I tore one of his underwear ads out of a magazine and pinned it to the refrigerator in my first Detroit apartment.

He ruined me for other men, I think. Maybe that's why I'm still single.

"Serious question," he says. "If you could snap your fingers and rewind nine years, would you like to be twenty-one again?"

"I don't know." Not that I'm thinking clearly right now. "There are things I'd like to change about my life. But I've been lucky, you know? It would be a crime to complain."

"Would it?" he asks softly.

"Absolutely." I take another sip of wine and then set the glass down on a nearby table, so that I don't guzzle it.

Tank sets his glass beside mine, and the moment crackles with tension.

When I gather my courage and raise my eyes, he's studying me. Slowly, he lifts a hand, threading it into my hair, catching the back of my head, and angling my face to look up at his handsome one.

Another man might say something self-deprecating to break the tension. But not Tank. He regards me with a gaze that's full of expectation. It doesn't ask permission. He simply dips his head, until his mouth finds the juncture of my neck and shoulder. Then he tastes my skin with firm lips and a sultry tongue.

At the contact, my body flashes first with chills, and then with heat. This ought to seem incredibly weird. We've had two minutes of conversation and barely a sip of wine, and now he's sucking on my neck. But Tank has always occupied an alternative reality—a foreign place where intimate touch is the native language of the land.

I'd forgotten this place existed, but it's good to be back. As he draws me closer, kissing his way up my neck, the scent of his shaving soap washes over me. And my body remembers what to do. Leaning closer, I grip his polo shirt so that he can't get away before I can take another whiff.

"Take it off," he says between worshipful kisses.

"What?" I gasp, because my executive function is starting to evaporate under the heat of his mouth.

"My shirt," he grunts. "Take it off. I need your hands on my body."

In the ordinary world, nobody gives me orders. I've arranged my entire life around my independence. But here in Tank's world, up is down and down is up. Before he even finishes speaking, I'm unbuttoning his polo shirt and lifting it off.

"That's a girl," he whispers, and the praise makes my heart beat faster. And now Tank's chest and I are reacquainted. My hands slide over the ridges of his abs, and I'm just settling in to explore further when he cups my chin and takes my mouth in a kiss.

I go still with surprise. After all, it's been nine years since anyone kissed me with such easy arrogance. It was just the same on that fateful night when I turned twenty-one. His first kiss stunned me with its boldness.

But then his firm lips soften against my mouth, and I'm already pressing back, looking for more. *Oh, right. This man has a black belt in kissing.* He tilts his head to draw me closer, and I open for him like I always did before. His tongue sweeps against mine as he tastes me.

Suddenly I'm twenty-one again, and totally bowled over by Tank's tongue in my mouth. It happened just like this. Red wine, followed by sudden kisses in a hotel room. Strong arms wrapping around my waist, pulling me in. A wide palm on my ass, nudging me nearer to the column of his erection.

I'm all in. I don't try to resist him. I can't think of a reason why I should. I can't think at all.

His kiss grows deeper and more demanding. My poor little body puts up no defenses. I melt against him. My head is full of peaceful static. I'm perfectly content to stay here in this quiet place, lip-locked and breathing in sync with the best lover I've ever known.

But eventually he breaks off our kiss and lifts me.

"Tank," I whisper as my feet leave the ground. This is my last chance to be rational.

"Yeah," he grunts, carrying me toward what I can only assume is the bedroom.

"What are we doing?"

He doesn't answer for a moment, possibly because I weigh a few more pounds than I did at twenty-one and he needs to concentrate. He drops me on the bed and answers the question. "What I always do, Bess. Just seeing what I can get away with."

He settles beside me on the mattress, scrutinizing my heaving chest and the way my dress rides up on my thighs. His body flexes as he leans over me—sculpted by intense physical conditioning, plus a generous helping of genetic good fortune.

And I forget why I asked the question at all.

SIX

The Cave Man in Action

TANK

BESS STARES up at me with wide-eyed wonder. But a second ago, she'd tried to call me on my bullshit. *What are we doing?*

Like I even know. Like I *ever* know. She might've thought I'd seemed wise at twenty-three, but I'd been a stupid kid with three skills—hockey, smack talk, and sex.

Now we're having another go at that last thing. I feel wild tonight, and I know Bess feels it, too. I've spent the last couple of weeks trapped deep inside my head. I want out, and I know just how to get there.

"Kick off your shoes," I growl. "Let's go."

For a split second, I think she's going to roll her eyes and tell me to fuck off. She pushes me out of the way and stands.

My heart drops.

But instead of leaving this madman's hotel room, she takes my face in two hands and kisses me sweetly. And then? She toes out of her shoes.

Hallelujah. I lay another scorching kiss on her. We were always so good together. And maybe it's like riding a bike, because the kiss goes from zero to sixty in under six seconds. I push my tongue into her mouth to show her just what I need. And her hands skate across my chest as she lets me know that she needs it, too.

I lift the little dress she's wearing and shove her panties down. Bess moans, and unbuttons my khaki shorts with quick fingers.

I'd weep with joy if it wouldn't slow down the action. Instead, I yank down her zipper, remove her dress, and toss it aside. And— holy hell—I've got a hot, naked woman in my arms. Her face is flushed, her lips bitten by my kisses. And the expression in her eyes is one I haven't seen from anyone in years. Pure lust.

"Goddamn, honey," I babble, my gaze sweeping down her lovely body. "Thirty looks hot on you." I skim a grateful hand down her milky skin, my fingertips just brushing the trimmed red hair at the top of her sex.

"*Fuck*," she gasps.

The shocked, dirty word makes me absolutely throb. I yank my shorts down, finishing the job she'd started, kicking off my briefs after that. "Lie down," I practically snarl, my self-control paper thin.

Bess steps back to do exactly as I say, and I feel another rush of gratitude, followed immediately by a wave of white-hot desire as she lays herself out for me on the white duvet.

It's like being handed a full platter of food after a year of near starvation. I don't even know where to begin. I prowl the bed, lean down, and take one of her pert nipples into my mouth.

"Oh, Tank," she moans, arching off the bed, threading her fingers into my hair.

The sound makes me *ache*. I can't even remember the last time I heard my name as a moan. I'm trembling now as I kiss my way across her chest, swirling my tongue around her other perfect breast, taking the pebbled tip against my tongue.

My cock is as stiff as a pipe, bobbing heavily against the bed as I lick and kiss and nibble my way down her body. I part her legs with shaking hands and then drop my mouth unceremoniously onto her pussy. She sobs my name again, and I'm drunk with the taste of her on my tongue, and the tug of her hands in my hair.

This is everything I forgot I needed. I bury my face between her thighs, losing myself in the clutch of her legs and the slide of my tongue against her slick heat until she's shaking and sobbing my name.

She has no idea at all what this means to me. I haven't felt desire like this in years. Haven't been *desired* in years.

When I can't stand it any longer, I hoist my hungry, desperate body over hers. I grip her hips, knowing that if I hesitate, we'll both just think too much. I slide inside her tight heat, my jaw clenching against the sudden, unbearable heaven. We inhale sharply and in unison.

Propping myself on my elbows, I look down at Bess. She's staring right back up at me as if she's just woken from a dream, her breath fast and warm against my face. We both blink at each other as if we can't quite believe our luck.

Being here again with Bess? Miraculous. I'm overwhelmed by all the intimate, familiar details of this moment. The texture of her hair against my skin is just the same. She still has freckles on her chest, and I want to kiss each one of them. She still has a strange, round scar on the inside of her arm.

That look on her face is the biggest miracle of all, though. She's just as stunned as I am. We're the two craziest, luckiest people in the world right now. And it makes me feel wild.

"Hold on tight," I grunt like the caveman I've become. "Gonna be a rough ride."

Breathing hard, eyes still locked on mine, Bess reaches up and grips my shoulders. And I finally let myself go. My hips draw back on their own volition, and I begin to move.

This is a moment that deserves to be savored. But there's no way either one of us could manage to go slow. Within seconds I'm picking up the pace, until I'm thrusting like a stud horse—more power than finesse. Our mouths join and our teeth click and our tongues tangle. It's rough and graceless, but I've never been more alive than I am right now.

The last nine years never happened. There's only heat and Bess's knees clamping around my eager hips. She tastes like red wine and sex and everything I ever wanted in my whole goddamn life.

She's on the same page, straining against me, boobs bouncing, hips lifting to meet mine stroke for stroke. She takes a deep, hungry breath and then gives me exactly what I need—a high, keening moan, followed by the telltale clench of her pussy around my rock-hard cock.

That's what finishes me—the utter joy of making Bess come. My balls tighten, and I experience a bright, energetic wave of jubilation as I pour myself into her quaking body. Once. Twice. Hell, I need one last hard thrust to wring myself out. And then I collapse like a sweaty dead man, sliding halfway off her body and onto the bed.

"Holy shit," I gasp. I let out an exhausted chuckle.

"Holy shit," she echoes, her chest rising and falling like she's just run the hundred-meter dash.

My brain is full of static. I smile as I close my eyes and stroke Bess's skin, enjoying the rhythm of her heart beneath my palm.

"Tank," Bess whispers before I'm ready to talk.

"Hmm?"

"Is this a terrible time to say that I was sorry to hear about your divorce?"

A bark of laughter escapes me. "It's as good a time as any." I try to slow down my breathing. I roll my head and glance at her pink-cheeked face. "You're not feeling guilty right now, right? If you are, don't."

"Okay," she says, sounding unsure.

"Really, don't," I repeat. "You have no idea how badly I needed that just now." I raise my head to look at her. The room is lit only by the city lights outside, but it's enough to see the uncertainty in her eyes.

"I would never want to make your life more complicated," she says softly.

"You couldn't possibly," I insist. She doesn't know the magnitude of the gift she just gave me. I haven't been to bed with a woman who didn't resent me in *years*. I'd forgotten how it even felt to use my body for pleasure and nothing more. But I can't explain all that to her. I won't ruin the bright, shiny moment we just had. "Please don't make me talk about my divorce right now."

"Okay," she says, smiling. "Sorry."

I shake my head before settling it on the pillow again, willing to forgive her anything. "Can I ask you a question?"

"Sure. Anything."

"Why did you ghost me before? When I played for New York. You just dropped me, and I never knew why."

She's silent for a moment. And then she asks, "Nine years later, does it even matter?"

"I guess not." I give her half a shrug, like I don't care. "I've always been curious. But you don't owe me an explanation."

She sighs. "I was twenty-one, Tank. I was young and green and afraid to screw up my life."

"I get it," I say quickly. "I wasn't much of a catch back then." I'd put hockey first.

"No—you don't understand," she argues. "Don't ask a girl for an explanation and then interrupt her."

"Okay. Sorry. Carry on."

"This is actually embarrassing," she whispers. "Nine years later, I still don't like thinking about it. But something happened at work."

"Hey." I put a hand in the center of her smooth tummy. "You don't have to tell me."

"No, it's okay." She tucks her head against my shoulder. "Do you remember Jane Pines? She covers golfers and tennis players."

"Sure." She'd been Kassman's partner at the time. "She left the firm, right? But I think she's still in the business."

"Yeah. Well, she called me into her office nine years ago." Bess takes a deep breath. "She told me that there was gossip about you and me."

I yank my head off the pillow again. "No shit? I never talked about you at all. You asked me not to."

Now it's her turn to shrug as if it didn't matter. But I'm getting the feeling that it did. "I don't know who talked. But we weren't that careful. You rented an apartment with other players, right? They picked up the landline sometimes when I'd call."

Oh hell. It had never occurred to me that Bess might get in trouble at work. "What did Pines tell you? Did she say you had to drop me like a hot potato?"

"She told me that if I slept with the athletes, my reputation would be ruined. That nobody would take me seriously. It's not the

47

same for women in this business. Her exact words were—'What do you call a woman who takes money from the man she's banging? You call her a whore.'"

"Jesus Christ," I hiss. "That's harsh. It's not like you were *my* agent."

"Oh, please. My boss was your agent. I knew Pines was right."

It's dark in the room, and I can almost feel her blushing from embarrassment. And it pisses me off on her behalf.

"She *wasn't* right," I scoff. "It wasn't her place to lecture you like that."

"Wasn't it?" she argues. "I didn't enjoy hearing it, but she did me a favor. I didn't want that reputation, Tank. I needed to be taken seriously. And that's why I told you that I was too busy to see you anymore. If that seemed like a brushoff, I apologize."

"You could have explained. I would have understood." Even as I say the words, I wonder if they're true. I was an arrogant little fuck at twenty-three.

"I was *so* embarrassed," she whispers. "And so young. And more naïve than you can imagine. It was my first real job, and I needed to do well. I just…"

"All right. Don't sweat it now. Not after that spectacular encore performance." I lean over and kiss her quickly.

She laughs, and her tummy quakes against my hip.

"Should I find our wine glasses?"

"I need a shower so badly right now."

"That's a fine idea," I say, swinging my legs off the bed. "Step right this way."

SEVEN

Employee of the Month

BESS

I'D BEEN EXPECTING to shower alone, since that's how I usually do it. I need a minute to process what's happened and to put my game face back on.

But Tank follows me into the walk-in shower, whistling and gloriously naked. He turns a dial, and water begins to rain down from a luxury showerhead the size of a large pizza. Then Tank pulls me under the warm spray with him and kisses me again.

My game face is probably destroyed forever. Who could spend an evening under this man's hard body, drinking down his kisses, and then manage to look rational afterward? Not me, that's for sure.

I've been very reckless tonight. I've violated my cardinal rule — no sleeping with players. And the man is still *married* — at least on paper. Nobody can ever know about this.

His hands are tender as he slides the soap up my back and kisses my neck. I know I'm just his rebound girl. Tonight is a fluke — a fantastical moment brought to us by luck and memories. We're both feeling a little wistful and lost, right?

He pushes me up against the tile wall and sighs into my mouth. "You're just what I needed tonight," he whispers, as if reading my thoughts. "Happy Birthday."

My heart swells. I kiss him back, because it would be a crime

49

not to enjoy this while it lasts. This will be my last, brief trip into the strange world that Tank and I used to occasionally inhabit. Where bodies are made for pleasure, and no rules apply.

Two hours later I wake up with a start, my damp hair snarled against the pillow. Tank snores softly beside me. Outside, the sky is as dark as Brooklyn ever gets. The clock on the bedside table reads 1:18. Although hotel clocks are often wrong.

Panicked, I slide off the bed. Tank doesn't stir from the place where he collapsed after doing me again in the shower. He's thirty-two years old and has the sexual stamina of a college boy. How is that even fair?

I find my crumpled panties on the floor and pull them on. Then I shake out my dress and step into it, reaching around to zip it up as best I can. My body feels well used, in the best possible way, but I probably look like a disaster. Even worse—my brother is probably letting himself into my apartment right this second, wondering where I am.

I pick up my sandals and tiptoe into the living room, where I recover my clutch purse. My phone confirms that it's twenty past one in the morning.

I'd received a text from Eric Bayer at 12:01. *Happy Birthday! Am I the first to say it? What do I win?*

He's not the first, but I'm never admitting it. *Thank you. You're the employee of the month. Your wall plaque is forthcoming. Are you still at the bar?*

The moment after I hit Send, I slip into my sandals and head out the door, closing it behind me as softly as possible. *Goodnight, Tank.* I feel a bit ridiculous doing the walk of shame in the wee hours of my thirtieth birthday. But here we are.

Eric replies while I'm in the elevator. *Still here at the tavern! Winning at darts, because Heidi already went home.*

Congrats, I reply. *Is there any chance my brother is still with you?*

Yeah. Dave said he was leaving, but he's still talking to Beacon by the door. Want me to grab him?

No, I text back in a hurry. *I was just checking on him. Night!*

When the elevator doors part, I dart through the lobby, fly out the revolving doors, and stick my hand in the air. A taxi swerves and halts at the curb. *Thank you, taxi gods.*

I open the door and jump inside. "Two-twenty-seven Water Street," I say to the driver. "There's a ten buck tip in it for you if we get there inside of ten minutes."

The tavern on Hicks Street—where the hockey players hang out—is between here and my apartment. But if Dave yammers with Beacon a few extra minutes, I can still beat him home. And it's such nice weather that he may decide to walk.

My phone vibrates with a new text from Eric. *Where are you, anyway?*

Why? I reply, paranoid.

Just curious, he replies. *It's almost like you're trying to beat your brother home.*

Oh dear. I hired Eric because he has a sharp mind and great intuition. That feels like a mistake now. *You can be Employee of the Month for the rest of the year if you just forget we had this conversation.*

Awesome. Can't wait to see this plaque.

I snort as the driver flies up Jay Street. Traffic is so light at this hour that I think I'm going to make it.

He just walked out, comes a new text a minute later.

"Damn it!" I squeak, and the driver turns his head in confusion. "It's fine!" I tell him. "Just late for my curfew."

He guns it.

I have never run up three flights of stairs so fast. There's no strip of light coming from under my door as I turn the key. *Yes*.

I step inside, happily noting that the place is empty. I turn on a lamp and rocket into my bedroom, where I hop around like a monkey as I try to unzip my dress. I throw on an old Detroit Tigers

T-shirt and some sleep shorts. Then I try to get a few tangles out of my hair.

The apartment door opens and shuts not more than three minutes after I've returned. He must have taken a cab.

Gently, I open my bedroom door. "Dave?" I call, trying to sound sleepy.

"S'me," my brother slurs. "Did I slam the door? Shorry."

I emerge from the bedroom, ditching all pretense. Maybe I don't need to be subtle, because Dave is *blitzed*. "Did you make it up the stairs okay?"

"I'm very coordinated," he says. And then he burps.

"Right. Well, let's get your coordinated self into bed. Did you have a good time?"

"The best time. Except I lost at darts."

"Can't imagine why." I remove the couch's cushions and extract the pull-out bed. "How about some aspirin?"

"Yes, please. Hey — Happy Birthday! I'm the first to tell you, right?"

"Right," I lie cheerfully. *Take a number.* "Thank you."

I spend the next few minutes shaking out the sheets and helping him make the bed. When I look up, he's watching me. "Isn't it kinda late?" he asks suddenly. "Weren't you asleep?"

"Not at all," I say breezily. "I just got home from a wild night of naked debauchery with a random guy I picked up after the party."

Dave lets out a belly laugh. "You're hilarious. G'night, Bessie."

"Night!" I toss him a pillow and go back to my bedroom.

Ten minutes later the apartment is quiet, and I'm lying in my bed in the dark. *What. A. Night.* I'd worn a dress, for starters. And things had only become weirder from there. *I had birthday sex with Mark Tankiewicz again. Twice.* Unbelievable.

I wonder if he'll wake up and think — *what the hell did I do?* He hadn't used condoms — a fact that might hit him in the morning. I'm a faithful user of birth-control pills, but Tank doesn't know that. At some point tomorrow he'll remember that a single guy is supposed to be vigilant about such things, and he'll panic. I can picture him grabbing his face in two hands and letting out a scream worthy of *Home Alone*.

He has nothing to fear on that front. Just because I have baby fever doesn't mean I'm dumb enough to have a child with a man who doesn't love me.

You're just what I needed tonight, he'd said.

Note the temporary nature of that statement.

Still, it lit me up to hear it. But I won't delude myself. Sleeping with players is still not something I do, and a guy who's just been dumped by his wife is not looking for a long-term girlfriend. So there's no point in dreaming about more.

I roll onto my side, let out a satisfied sigh, and make a pact with myself not to regret tonight. Not too much, anyway. I'll look at it as the last, pointless hurrah of my twenties. I'm entering a new decade. I need different things now.

That's why I'd spent time last week making a personal life plan with color-coded sections and a detailed outline. The first section is titled: "Dating." There are action steps for apps to try, and a list of friends who could possibly introduce me to thirty-year-old men who might also be ready to get serious about the future.

I have other goals, too. More time with friends. More time with family.

I'd moved to Brooklyn to change my life, and tonight's adventure didn't really advance my goals. Still, Tank is special. And now I know I hadn't just been building him up in my memories, because *wow*, the man is seriously talented. Talented, and yet unavailable.

It sure was fun, though. There's no denying that.

EIGHT

Remember Me?

Tank: Hey Bess! I hope this is still the right number. Remember me? I'm the guy whose hotel room you snuck out of the other night. Hope your thirty-first year is off to a good start. —T

Bess: Who is this? You must have me confused with someone else. I don't sneak out of hotel rooms. I walk gracefully, head held high, in my rumpled dress and wet sex hair.

Tank: My mistake. But I would have liked to say a proper good-bye. It's not often that we're in the same state.

Bess: You might be surprised. But I couldn't take the risk of waking you up. After all, you got me naked about four minutes after arriving in your room. So I have no idea what "a proper good-bye" might mean to you. Restraints, probably. And a safe word.

Tank: That sounds about right. Next time, then.

Bess: There won't be a next time. You know it's not because I don't want to. But I don't do players.

Tank: Evidence suggests that sometimes you do. Especially this one.

Bess: No, really. Not for nine years. I took Pine's advice and I never, ever have. You're my one slip-up. Ever.

Tank: Damn, honey. I'm flattered.

Bess: You should be. You're my kryptonite.

Tank: Hey, I am FAR more talented than a hunk of alien minerals. Did Superman scream my name in the shower? So there's no

54

reason not to do it again. Your number won't even go up. You'll still have only one career screwup. If you find yourself back in Brooklyn, I'm happy to be the mistake you can keep on making.

Bess: You really know how to sell a girl.

Tank: Where are you, anyway?

Bess: Detroit. I had to talk to a badly concussed rookie.

Tank: Ouch. Is he gonna be okay?

Bess: Yes, after a minor surgical procedure whereby I remove his head from his ass. This genius was not following treatment procedure because he wanted to play.

Tank: Aw. Poor kid. He wants to prove his worth.

Bess: He can't prove his worth with brain damage. Enough about him. How are you? Settling in?

Tank: Just dandy. My new team hates me. So I just made it worse by beating them all at the golf tournament on Saturday. Now they want to drown me in a bucket. Someday this will all seem funny, right?

Bess: I'm sorry. Trades are so hard.

Tank: Don't agent me, Bess. I'm a big boy. You don't have to give me a pep talk. I'll take a blowjob, though.

Bess: No can do. We've been over this. And all boys need agents. Even the biggest ones.

Tank. That's what she said…

Bess: [Eyeroll.] You sound like a guy who needs a pep talk, though. Where's Kassman? He should be delivering it himself. In person.

Tank: He emails every morning. He's only working part time right now.

Bess: ????? Part time? Henry doesn't even know those words. And WTF? Email? He should be finding you an apartment. That hotel where you're staying is too far from the practice facility. You're never going to bond with the guys if they're keeping you downtown.

Tank: Sure I am. We're having a sleepover later. And a pillow fight. Castro is going to braid my hair and Trevi is going to paint my toenails.

Bess: [Eyeroll emoji.]

<u>Tank</u>: But we could have a sleepover. You and me. We play Detroit next month. You and I could have a secret rendezvous.
<u>Bess</u>: Dream on, Tank.
<u>Tank</u>: Oh I will. Goodnight, sexy.
<u>Bess</u>: Goodnight

But You're a Woman

BESS

October

"ALL THE MANICURE stations are up front," Rebecca says, sweeping her arm toward the shop's windows. "This part is basically finished."

"It's gorgeous," I say, taking in the long, L-shaped sofa with bright pillows. "That's a cool painting, too." Adjacent to the windows is a brick wall with colorful wings painted onto it.

"That's for Instagram pics. The wine bar is going in over there." Rebecca points to the opposite wall. "And the pedicure area is in back. We'll have eight stations—four on each side. And a sliding divider, for private parties."

"Private parties," I echo. It would never occur to me to party at a nail salon.

Although maybe it should. Chapter Two of my five-year plan is titled "Nurturing Female Friendships." It's not just my love life that's suffered as I poured all my energy into my business for the past years. There aren't many women in sports management. I have friends, but they're all dudes.

So when Rebecca and Georgia asked me to meet them for a cocktail and a peek at the half-finished nail salon, I agreed in a hot second.

"Who wants a margarita?" Georgia asks. She's got tequila, lime juice, and sugar out on the salon's new gleaming stone countertop, and she's filling a shaker with ice from a bag.

"I do!" Becca's hand shoots into the air.

"I'd love one," I add. "A small one, though. I have a date at seven thirty, and I probably shouldn't show up sloshed."

Georgia sets the shaker down with a thump and lets out a little squeal. "A date with *whom*? This is so exciting."

"It's not all the way to *exciting*," I hedge. "I don't even know if he's *promising*. Internet dating freaks me out a little. So I chose the most harmless guy from the pack."

"What's his name?" Becca demands. "You can learn a lot with a name."

"Brian."

"And what does he do for a living?"

"Something complicated and financial."

"Ah," they say at the same time. "Yeah, a finance guy will never murder you," Georgia agrees. "So he's got that going for him."

"You say that," Becca says, flopping down on the sofa. "But what if he is just *posing* as a banker on Tinder? What if he's secretly an MMA fighter or the leader of a motorcycle gang?"

"Wow, I'm surrounded by conspiracy theorists." I laugh. "Eric said the same thing." I don't mention that I'd actually be excited about meeting a fighter. I'd pick his brain about tactics inside the ring.

"Eric knows about your date?" Georgia asks. "That's cute."

"Yeah, I needed someone to know where I was going and with whom. But if I'd known I was seeing you two tonight, I could have spared him the involvement."

Note to self: it's less embarrassing to tell your girl posse your dating foibles than your business partner.

"Two dates in a row!" he'd hooted.

"We're not speaking about that other incident," I'd reminded him. "Don't make me take away your plaque," I'd said, pointing at the photo I'd hung on the wall with the caption *Employee of the Month, Every Month.*

He'd given me a cheeky salute. My dude friends are really top notch.

"Are you vetting this Brian over coffee?" Becca asks. "Or did you go straight to dinner?"

"Dinner," I admit. "Everyone is more pleasant with food, right? As long as I'm eating a nice plate of pasta, I can be excited about anything." That's what I'm telling myself, anyway.

"We'd better get started on your nails," Becca says, patting the seat beside her. "Get over here."

"What?" I glance around at the half-finished shop. "Won't it be another month until you're open?"

"That has never stopped her before," Georgia says, closing the cocktail shaker tightly and then giving it a shake.

Becca lifts a large tackle box onto the sofa and opens the top. "How about a sheer wine-tinted polish to go with that pretty top?"

"But I don't know how to paint my nails." And—fine—I have a bit of a complex about it. It's one of those girly things that makes me feel like a freak. "When you grow up without a mother, there are certain skills you never learn. I never tried to wear heels until college. My makeup game is also weak. And I can't cook. At all."

Georgia looks up from pouring three drinks, and there's understanding in her expression. "I'm a member of that same club. Sometimes it really messes with my head."

"Really?" I squeak. And now I feel a little foolish, because I forget that there are lots of other women walking around who didn't have moms.

"Yeah. Leo wants to have kids soon," she says, topping up one of the glasses. "And I do, too. But part of me wonders if I'll know what to do."

"Nobody knows what to do," Becca argues. "That's half the fun. I mean—my sister and her man-child boyfriend are the most clueless people alive. And their kid is doing well." She waves me over to sit beside her. "Put your hands on this towel. You're not a nail biter, are you?"

"No way." I show her my hands, and she grabs one to inspect it.

Georgia puts a drink into my other hand. "I know there's no

prerequisite for having babies. And Leo will be the best daddy *ever*." She smiles at the thought of it. And I totally understand why —her husband is a sweetheart. "But I still worry. I lost my mom when I was six. How old were you?" she asks me.

"Almost two. My mom died of a drug overdose before it was cool." I've said this many times before, in the same flip tone of voice. But I can tell from Georgia's soft expression that she sees right through me. "Are you really going to paint my nails?" I ask Rebecca. "I hope you know that I can't return the favor. Not unless you want it to look like a toddler did it."

"Don't you worry," Becca says, shaking a bottle of something clear. "I am too bossy to let anyone else do mine."

"This is true," Georgia says with a shrug. "Cheers, ladies!" She holds up her glass. "To manicures and margaritas."

We touch glasses, and I take a sip of limey goodness.

"I hope this date rocks your world," Becca says as she strokes the polish on one of my fingernails.

"I'm not expecting magic," I insist. "But I need to start somewhere. I need to meet men who are interested in a relationship."

"But only if they're sexy," Rebecca adds. "I mean—I'm living proof that single, hot nerds exist. I married one."

"Yeah," I say with a sigh. "You might have gotten the last one, though. I feel there's a mismatch between hotties and guys who want relationships."

"Hey," Becca says as she strokes the brush over my pinky fingernail. "What's with the sigh? Is there some hottie you're trying to forget?"

"There was someone. A long time ago," I hedge. I can't tell them about Tank, because both these women work with him now. I'm not a gossip.

Although everyone else seems to be. After our interlude last month, I couldn't resist stalking the internet for news about his trade. I'd found a lot more than I bargained for. Tank punched his co-captain? Talk about a career-killer. If one of my athletes had done that, I would've flown down there and kicked his ass myself.

I know better than to believe the gossip rags. So it's impossible to guess what really happened. And speculating about it makes me feel guilty. Tank has only been good to me.

The only way to stop thinking about him is to find a man who makes me feel as sexy as Tank does, but who's also ready to settle down. Is that really too much to ask?

"Ooh, this color goes great with your skin tone!" Georgia says, looking down at my rosy fingertips. "How come you'll give Bess a pink polish, but you make me wear bright colors?"

"This isn't pink. It's rosé. And it matches her blouse," Becca says, capping the bottle. "You're getting orange tonight."

"Why?"

"Because I have a new orange polish, and you're my favorite guinea pig. Sit down already and just take your beating."

"What are you calling this place, anyway?" Georgia grumbles. "The Nail Nazi?"

"The Colorbox Bar, I think," Becca says, ignoring the slight. "Or Sips and Tips. I haven't decided. Input is welcome."

"You can have both," I point out. "Colorbox can be your title, and Sips and Tips is your descriptive subtitle."

Becca looks up quickly. "You're good at this."

"That's my college degree talking. I did a double major in management and marketing."

"Handy." Becca peeks at the clock on the wall. "Go stick your hands under the dryer, okay? It's going to be time to meet your finance guy soon." She waves Georgia into my vacant seat. "Now let's see what I can do with you."

Fifteen minutes later, they send me on my way. "Don't be late. But let us know if you need a rescue!"

"Thank you both," I say, waving my fingers like a maniac, trying to make sure the polish is sufficiently dry. "This was the pregame party that I never knew I needed. Do I look okay? Does this outfit say, 'Fun, but not a pushover? Serious, but not too serious?'"

"That outfit says 'You're lucky to date me.'" Georgia gives me a bright smile. "Now go have fun."

"I'll try."

And I do try. Our date is at Cecconi's, an upscale restaurant in a beautiful room with a view of the Manhattan Bridge out the window. I laugh at Brian's jokes. And I ask him about himself, which turns out to be a good choice because Brian's favorite topic is Brian.

"I've been a derivatives trader for twelve years. Actually, my true function is originating debenture debt from triple-A rated GSEs."

"GSEs?" I ask, as if I understood any of the other words in that sentence.

"Government Sponsored Entities. Like FreddieMac. I under-write their debt, swapping their floating-rate borrowing needs into the fixed-rate callable debt which is more palatable to retail investors. We're selling implied volatility and arbing the flat-yield curve."

I take a hearty gulp of my wine and try to admire the five o-clock shadow that defines Brian's jaw. He's a decently handsome man, as long as you can overlook the unibrow. "And what do you do for fun?" I'm hoping it's something I'll understand.

"Go."

I blink. "Go where?"

"Go is an ancient Chinese strategy game. It makes chess look as simple as tic-tac-toe. The number of legal possible board configura-tions has been estimated to be greater than the number of atoms in the universe."

"That sounds exciting. I mean, it's no hockey game, but..." I wait for a laugh, but it doesn't arrive.

"Hockey?" He frowns. "Now there's a gruesome sport. I don't get the appeal at all."

Wait, what? "Did you happen to notice what I do for a living?"

"Something to do with management?"

"*Sports* management," I clarify. "I'm an agent. For hockey players."

He cocks his head to the side, as if I've begun speaking Yiddish. "But you're a woman."

I'm replaying his asinine statement in my head when two things happen in rapid succession. The first is that our food arrives. A plate of chicken marsala with cremini mushrooms and fettuccini lands on the table in front of me, and I'm really fucking happy to see it.

The second thing is something I'm less happy about. When I look up again, Mark Tankiewicz is seated at a nearby table, handing off a menu to a waiter, and watching me.

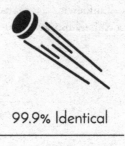

TEN

99.9% Identical

BESS

SERIOUSLY? I don't run into the guy for almost nine years, and now it's twice in the space of two weeks?

I look away, hoping that he'll just disappear. But I'm not that lucky. The next time I happen to glance his way, a waitress is dropping off a glass of wine. I catch myself watching for his sexy smirk when he thanks her.

Goddamn Tank and his goddamn smirk. I'm on this date specifically to forget about him. And now who's drinking a glass of red wine and undressing me with his eyes?

I'm so irritated I could spit.

"How's your food?" Brian asks.

I look down and realize I've eaten several bites without even tasting it. "Wonderful. How is yours?"

"Great," he says, stabbing a piece of macaroni.

I squint at it, because I can't see any sauce or seasonings on it. "You ordered the…?"

"Noodles with butter," he says. "That's my favorite. I'm a purist, I guess." He chuckles.

Yup. My date is officially the least interesting man in Brooklyn. Ten feet away sits a man wearing a tight T-shirt that shows off the hollow between his pecs, where my tongue recently traveled.

I glance at Brian and try to imagine doing the same to him.

Nope. Not happening.

My phone buzzes with a text. Out of the corner of my eye, I see Tank place his phone on the table.

I'm not going to be that rude person who checks her phone. Not during dinner. I stay in the moment and make small talk with the dedication of a medal contender in the Small Talk Olympics. I even laugh at Brian's jokes.

I stay strong for a good fifteen minutes. But then Brian begins an extended conversation with the waiter about the qualities of the house-made vanilla ice cream, and I let myself sneak a peek at my phone.

You look hot in that blouse. Unbutton one more button.

I set the phone in my lap and quickly tap out a reply. *What, are you my pimp now?*

Not for him, he replies immediately. *This is for me*.

I glance up to find Tank's gaze taking a slow, dirty stroll down my body. It's the opposite of subtle. I pick up my wine glass and take a sip while casually giving him the finger.

Brian is still deep in conversation about the vanilla ice cream. He doesn't even notice.

Tank laughs, his green eyes flashing. Then he starts tapping on his phone again. *In Brooklyn again? And I don't get a phone call?*

I guess he's going to figure out my situation sooner or later. So I confess. *Actually, I live here now. Sorry if I didn't mention that before. And you KNOW why you're not getting a phone call.*

First he responds with the eyes-wide emoji. And then he writes: *You sneaky Pete! My change-of-address card must be lost in the mail. How odd that you didn't mention it before. Oh well, I guess you were too busy moaning my name. So how's your date going? Fun guy?*

Totally, I lie.

Did he really order plain macaroni?

My ego demands that I ignore his last text. And anyway, Brian has decided that the ice cream passes muster and orders it.

"Nothing for me, thank you," I tell the waiter, even though ice cream sounds good. I just really need to get out of here.

Of course, Brian eats his ice cream very slowly. He offers me a bite, but I decline out of spite. I polish off my wine and wish I were drunker than I am right now. Maybe this will all seem funnier on Monday morning when Eric asks how the date went.

I sure hope so.

Meanwhile, two tables away, Tank is putting away the New York strip steak, rare, with arugula and Parmigiano mashed potatoes. The muscles in his forearms flex whenever he cuts his meat. And every minute or two he looks up to give me a look so searing and sexual that it's probably punishable by death in several distant nations.

And I'm just so confused. How is it possible that I'm slobberingly attracted to one man, when the other one does nothing for me? Science insists that their DNA is 99.9 percent identical. But, man, that 0.1 percent is like the difference between a rare steak and plain macaroni. One makes my mouth water, while the other is just…

I hold back a sigh and pray for my date to finish his ice cream.

Finally, Brian calls for the check. When the waitress brings it over, I plop my credit card on top of the wallet right as Brian does the same.

He lifts his bland eyes to me. "What's this? I'm treating."

"Well, thank you very much," I say, removing my card. Because I don't want to fight about it.

"I'm an old-fashioned man," he says, passing the wallet and card to the waitress.

"I noticed that when you expressed surprise at my career." *Oops.* It just slipped out.

He chuckles, as if I've said something cute. "I work in a man's world. Sometimes I forget."

"You forget that women exist? Are there no women who…" I try to remember a single word he said about his job. "…do what you do?"

"There's one," he says. "We used to have two, but she went off and had babies." He shrugs, as if this was inevitable.

He's lucky the waitress has already removed my silverware, because I would have stabbed him with it. "You know, this has been fun, but I've got to go," I say, pushing back my chair. "Thank you for the lovely evening."

"Will I see you again?" Brian asks, pushing back his chair to stand up, too.

"Oh, I hope so," I lie, offering my hand for a shake. "It was so nice to meet you." I give him a big smile and then practically run out of the restaurant. When I hit the sidewalk, I take a deep, cleansing breath. *Chin up*, I coach myself. *You can't expect to meet Mr. Right on the first try.*

Except this wasn't really the first try. Every few months I summon the courage to get out there and date, but I always get discouraged. The older I get, the thinner the talent pool.

I'm starting to view single men like the NHL draft. All the best players get snapped up when they're really young.

New York was supposed to help me shake things up. There have to be more single men here than there were in my corner of Michigan. But what if they're all like Brian?

I take another breath and stroll up Water Street, grateful to put distance between me and that disaster of a date. My date might not have been romantic, but Brooklyn's scenery is. The streets are cobblestone, and I'm walking past a Civil War-era warehouse with curved windows and giant shutters. It's half a mile—a ten-minute walk—back to my apartment. I'd planned my getaway when I'd chosen the restaurant. This isn't my first rodeo.

"Bess," Tank's voice calls from behind me. "Wait up."

Except I didn't count on *him*. I don't slow my roll, but I'm not going to be able to outrun an athlete, especially while wearing strappy little sandals. "I can't believe I dressed up for Brian," I grumble to myself. It's just a denim skirt and a silk top. But still.

Tank falls in step with me. "Who was that guy?" he asks. As if it's any of his business.

"Just a guy. I'd tell you what he does for a living, but I didn't understand a word of it."

"Bummer. Where'd you meet him?"

"Tinder," I grunt. Using the dating apps embarrasses me. But when you're in a new city and you've sworn off dating the men you meet at work, there's really no other way. "When I told him my job, he said, 'But you're a woman.'"

Tank stops suddenly. "No he fucking did not." He turns right around and heads back toward the restaurant.

"Tank!" I chase after him. "What are you doing?"

He stops again. "I need to teach him a lesson."

"No, dumbass!" I squeak. "Your agent would kill you."

"Easy, Bess." He reaches out, giving my forearm a squeeze. I'm instantly annoyed by how nice his touch feels. "I didn't mean I was going to punch the man. I need to tell him he's an idiot, because he pissed off a woman with access to the best seats in hockey."

"He doesn't like hockey."

"Oh. Shit." Tank shakes his head. "There's no use spending any time on a guy who hates hockey. Shouldn't you ask that question first? It's a good way to weed out the losers."

"This knife cuts both ways," I point out. "I can't advertise my access to the best seats in hockey."

"Why not?"

"Because then I'll just attract guys who aren't looking to date me. It's bad enough that half the men on Tinder are just after sex."

"Is that really so wrong?"

I make the mistake of glancing at Tank. He gives me a heated smile. And my ovaries stand up in their stadium seats and cheer.

Oh boy. Nothing good can come of this.

Wait. That's not true. Nothing *lasting* can come of this. But that doesn't mean it wouldn't be good.

"I have a five-year plan." I say it aloud more for my benefit than his. It's me who needs the reminder.

"Sorry?"

"There's no page for you in my five-year plan, Tank. I'm trying to meet someone who wants a relationship. And we both know you're not that guy."

"Yeah, well." We stop at the curb, because the light turns red. "You're right. I'm not that guy. I'm never getting married again. But I'm still a good time."

"Is that why you're following me home?"

"A nice guy always walks the single girl home."

"Are you a nice guy?"

"Once in a while."

I snort. The light changes again, and we cross the street, drawing closer to my front door. The point of no return is near. And it's just so easy to rationalize this. *He's lonely. I'm lonely. Who does it hurt?*

Me, that's who. I shouldn't do this. And yet every step brings us closer to my apartment building. "Did you really punch your co-captain in Dallas?" I ask suddenly.

"Been reading the hockey blogs, huh?" He sounds angry.

"It's literally my job, Tank."

"Yeah, I punched him. But don't ask me why, because I'm not going to tell you."

"Okay." Now I feel like a heel for asking. It's none of my business. I'd picked a fight with him, maybe because I was hoping he'd give up on walking me home.

I've failed to scare him off. He's still here, matching my stride. We cross under the bridge, and now we're in the home stretch. "Just in case you're lost," I tell him, pointing back the way we came, "your hotel is in the opposite direction."

"I'm not lost. I'm following you home."

"Why?"

"Why," he scoffs. "Because neither one of us can stop thinking about it." He stops, and when I stop, too, his piercing eyes take in my low-cut top and the flush on my neck. "You know you've been thinking about me. And I sure as hell can't stop thinking about you."

Oh. Wow. Those are the magic words. *Can't stop thinking about you.* My little Cinderella heart swoons against the soot-covered hearthstones, even though Tank is no Prince Charming. He isn't even trying to be. He's raw and hungry. He takes what he wants. He makes no promises, and he tells me no lies.

It doesn't matter. I march up to the front door of my building and pull out my key. "In you go," I grumble, pulling the door open.

"Heck, I didn't know it would be this easy. You're inviting me up?"

"We can't very well stand here and discuss it." I put my keys away. "Half the team lives in that building across the street." I hook a thumb toward the Million Dollar Dorm, as we like to call it. Or, in my brother's case, the three million dollar dorm. He'd owned one of the bigger apartments in the building.

Tank glances across the street, and the look on his face is almost wistful. But then he follows me into my building, pausing in front of the door to my office. "Bess Beringer and Associates. *Nice.*"

"It's small. But I have the best commute in New York." I start up the stairs.

"Yeah, you do." Tank laughs, and then follows me.

When we reach my fourth-floor abode, I'm cursing my little strappy sandals. Tank could do four more flights without breathing hard. I'm not surprised. If I didn't have first-hand experience with his stamina, I probably wouldn't be breaking all my rules again right now.

He follows me into the apartment, and I flip on a lamp and glance around. It's tidy, but small. The only living room furniture is a very plain khaki sofa, because I haven't taken Becca up on her shopping offer yet.

Tank does a quick circuit of the living room. "It's quiet," he says. "Nice."

I burst out laughing. "That's all you could think of to say, isn't it?"

"Maybe." He gives me a smirk. "I'm just not sure why you chose this place, when your brother was selling a sweet pad across the street."

"This is a rental," I point out. "It's cheap, and I didn't have to commit to more than a year. And then there's the commute."

He nods, then sits down on my sofa.

I offer him a beer, but before I can fetch it, my phone chimes. I pull it out of my pocket and find that my dinner date has messaged me, proposing a second evening together. "Oh lord. Let me unmatch this guy or he's going to keep texting me."

I plop down next to Tank and open the app. *Thank you for a lovely meal, but I'm not sure we're a great match. Be well. —Bess.* Then I unmatch him.

"You're awfully polite," Tank says, reading shamelessly over my shoulder.

"Usually," I hedge. "Want to see something funny? I'm still not sure how to respond to this guy. He just sent me his picture today and asked for a dinner date." I tap on the message and show the photo to Tank.

His eyes bulge. "That's Blake Riley."

"I realize," I say with a sigh.

"But...Blake Riley plays for Toronto."

"Yes, genius. That's *Fake* Riley. Some dude *stole* his photo and is trying to pass it off as his own."

"Holy shit." Tank covers his mouth and laughs like a gossipy high school girl. And he looks unfairly handsome doing it. "People are insane. What does he think will happen when you turn up and find some ugly schmo?"

"I honestly have no idea. Maybe he looks a little bit like Riley? Or maybe he's banking on me being too polite to call him out on it."

He takes the phone out of my hand and starts tapping a reply. *I'm really not sure how you're going to fit in a New York dinner between practices in Toronto.* "Can I send it?"

"Sure," I grumble. I take the phone back after he sends it and then unmatch from Fake Riley, too. "You know he'll just try it on someone else, though."

Internet dating is the worst. Tank hasn't figured it out yet, and he probably won't have to. A single hockey player does not require technology to find companionship.

Popping off the couch, I head into the kitchen where I crack open two bottles of Brooklyn Lager. While I'm standing at the counter, it occurs to me that Dallas is playing its season opener against Boston tonight. So I open the league app to check the score. It's 1-0 for Boston heading into the third period.

I tuck my phone away, grab the beers and go back into the living room.

Where I catch Tank checking the score on *his* phone. He glances up at me with a guilty face as I hand him the beer. "Sorry," he says, shoving the phone in his back pocket.

"Don't be. It's one-zip at the start of the third." I take a swig of my beer. "I checked, too. But I didn't see who scored."

We each take a sip of beer. And then we glance at each other. "You think…" He doesn't finish the sentence.

"Should we just check in?" My gaze jumps to the remote control sitting on the TV.

Tank stands up and grabs it. He tosses it to me, and I have the game pulled up on ESPN before you can say *rabid hockey fans.*

"Damn. Palacio is skating with Trane," Tank says.

"Where'd they put Huizing?"

"I don't know. Hang on."

We're both leaning forward in our seats at the shift change. Huizing goes over the wall with a rookie and a recent trade from Tampa. "Whoa!" I gasp as the rookie tries and fails to get the puck back.

Everyone on the ice is skating like his life depends on it. They've got that new-season energy. Bart Palacio comes back out and steals the puck on a lucky poke check, runs it down the ice without Trane's help, and shoots it through the five-hole for a goal.

"Fuck!" Tank shouts.

"Jesus Christ!" I notice we're both standing. "Wait, who are you rooting for?"

"Not Dallas," he snarls. Then he picks up his beer and drains it.

As the commentators cluck over Palacio's goal, I walk like a zombie into my tiny kitchen and get Tank another beer. And while I'm doing some mental math on Boston's chances, I also grab a pint of ice cream out of the freezer and two spoons.

"Do you think Boston is gonna give their backup goalie a few more starts this season?" I ask, handing him a beer and a spoon and sitting down on the sofa.

"They better," he says, waiting while I dig in first. "The Atlantic division is rugged this year. They'll need some relief as the season goes on." He pops a bite of Ben & Jerry's into his mouth and passes me the carton just as the next faceoff begins.

It's a tense period. I'm not sure I even blink as the two teams battle it out. Somehow our ice cream is kicked, and we're both polishing off our drinks when Boston finally puts another one in the net with ninety seconds on the clock.

"YAAAAAAS!" we both scream at the TV.

I flop back against the sofa as they cut to a media break. I look at Tank, whose face is as flushed as mine probably is. There are beer bottles on the floor, and there's a chocolate smudge on my wrist.

"Wow," he says. "We just…"

"Yeah." I start to laugh, because I'd completely forgotten the reason he'd come upstairs in the first place. "No wonder I don't go out on more dates. What is wrong with us?"

"*Nothing.*" He shakes his head. "We're pretty much perfect. The real question is—what the fuck is wrong with everyone else?"

"Seriously. What the fuck, people?"

"What the ever-loving fuck?" he repeats. Our eyes lock, and something in his gaze startles me. It's a mix of humor and warmth. But there's also heat and hunger. That's a potent cocktail, and so much more than I expected to find tonight.

Uh-oh. My inner Cinderella twirls around, giddy. She's got it bad for the grumpy hockey player with the shapely, scruffy jaw and the bad reputation.

And then Tank pounces, pushing me down on the sofa. It's bossy and a little bit rude, and I don't understand why I like it so much. Tension coils inside me as I'm manhandled into place.

But he makes me wait for his kiss. First he rakes me with a hungry gaze, taking in the cleavage revealed by the silly blouse I'd worn for a date I'd forgotten the moment it was over. He makes a sexy, hungry noise, before finally dipping down to take my mouth in a demanding kiss.

I'm putty in his hands. I made this bad decision over an hour ago when I let him follow me home. *One more time*, I tell myself as I drink in his kiss, coasting my palms up the hard planes of his back. *One more reminder of how good it can be*. Then I'll go back to dating available men.

ELEVEN

That Really is the TV

TANK

BESS IS SMART. That's why she's looking at me with a mixture of heat and trepidation. And I know exactly why she forgot to tell me that she's living in Brooklyn now.

She knows I'm a hot mess. And getting involved so soon after my divorce is a dumbass thing to do.

But I'm doing it anyway. I push Bess down on the couch and kiss the confusion right off of her sweet face. Her mouth is cool against my greedy one, but it's not unwelcoming. When I trace the seam of her lips with my tongue, she opens for me.

I up the ante and run a shameless hand up her bare leg. And I'm a little rough when I invade her panties and give her ass a dirty squeeze.

Bess makes a shocked sound against my tongue, but then her arms snake around my neck and she pulls me in closer. Nine years might as well be nine minutes. My body remembers how it is between us. I'm the one who's supposed to push her boundaries. And she's the one who takes it all and asks for more.

I sink into another slow, twisting kiss, rocking my erection against the cradle of her hips. There's no mistaking my intentions. There's no point in hiding how I feel about her.

Maybe I wasn't looking for this. I thought I was too raw and angry to be anyone's good time. But here's Bess with her big blue eyes and her questing hands sliding under my shirt, asking for more skin. More heat.

For the first time in days, I know I'm exactly where I'm supposed to be. The ugly noise of my life quiets as I sit back and yank my shirt over my head. "Need you, Bess," I rasp.

And then I spend the next hour showing her just how much.

When I begin to wake the next morning, I find that I'm buck-ass naked and wrapped around her. She feels perfect against my bare skin. I push my nose into her wavy hair and doze a little longer.

It doesn't take, because images of last night begin to play through my sleepy mind. Carrying Bess into the bedroom and then yanking down her skirt. Laying her out on the quilt and kissing and licking and teasing until she was begging for me. And then turning her around and bending her over the bed...

Ungh. It's been a long time since I woke up feeling happy and aroused.

"Tank," Bess whispers.

"Mmm?"

"Are you awake?"

"You can't tell?" I push my cock against her ass in a blatant display of just how awake I am.

"What time is it?"

"Who cares?"

She does, apparently, because she rolls, pushing me onto my back. I open my eyes. A puffy white cloud is the first thing I see. And when I sit up, the Manhattan Bridge appears against the blue sky. "Nice view. Kind of makes up for the tiny rooms."

She runs a hand down my abs. "I do like the view. And I don't need a big apartment."

"Fair enough. But I want lots of things that I don't really need."

"Like me, for instance?"

"Oh, please." I lie down again and kiss her bare shoulder. "Who says we didn't need that? Both of us." I roll over and trap her under my naked body. "I might need it again right now."

Bess looks up at me with humor in her eyes. She reaches toward the bedside table and picks up her phone to check the time. "Says the man who has practice in thirty-five minutes."

"Aw hell." That's unfortunate. The rink is right up the block, but my gym bag is at the Marriott. She's right, I don't have time. I run the pad of my thumb over her nipple, anyway. God, she's sexy.

This summer I'd thought my dick was broken. I'd been single again after many years of marriage, but I hadn't even glanced at a woman. I'd thought my marriage had permanently killed my libido.

But, nope. Bess makes me feel like a hormonal teenager. I'll probably spend the quiet moments of my day remembering how I laid her out and had my filthy way with her.

Groaning, I lean down to flick my tongue over her nipple.

"Tank." Bess puts her palm on my face and pushes me off her boob, the same way you'd discourage a dog who put his face somewhere he wasn't invited. "Get up, stud. The new guy can't be late."

"I know," I grumble. Thirty-year-old Bess isn't intimidated by me at all, not like she'd been when she was twenty-one. I'm so screwed, because her confidence just makes me want her even more. When she'd flipped me off at the restaurant last night, I'd wanted to kiss her senseless.

It made me crazy to see her dining with another guy. And I've never felt more relief than when she left the restaurant alone. In my haste to follow her out of there, I'd left a hundred dollar tip because it was faster than calculating a reasonable number.

Bess makes me hungry again. Not for steak and ice cream, but for life. I'd spent the summer throwing a tennis ball for my teammate's labradoodles and feeling sorry for myself. But I don't feel that way any longer. "When can I see you again?"

She flinches. "You and I aren't a good idea."

Now there's a blow to my ego. "Not true," I argue. "I'm gonna have good ideas all day long, and you'll be the star of all of them. Besides, you're the only one in Brooklyn who likes me."

"Not true," she echoes, her expression softening. "At least it won't be true for long. You're a good guy, Tank. And a *great* player. They just need a little time to adjust to your way of doing things. Maybe you should spend some bonding time with the team."

"I'm not here to make friends. And you didn't answer the question. When am I seeing you again?"

"I don't know," Bess says softly. "We can't have a fling, Tank. Not like we did before."

"Why the hell not?" And is it just me, or aren't we having one already? "You're not the new girl at the agency anymore, trying to make a good impression."

"You're right. The stakes are even higher now." She trails a hand down my ribcage even as she gives me the brushoff. "I have a reputation to uphold. I can't date players. And it's not like you really need any gossip swirling around you, either."

"I don't care what strangers say about me. They can fuck right off."

This conversation is interrupted by her phone ringing. Or maybe it's mine. I'm still not used to my new phone. "Is that me or you?"

"It's mine. Get off me so I can see who's having today's first emergency."

But I don't. I grab her phone off the bedside table and hand it to her.

"Eric?" she says, answering. "Is something wrong?"

"Yeah," he says, and since I'm six inches from the phone I can hear him. "What's wrong is that you didn't answer any of my texts during the game last night. And then this morning I remembered that you went on a Tinder date with a stranger. So then I worried you were dead."

I chuckle before I realize that I shouldn't.

Bess gives me a very stern look just as Eric's voice says, "Who's that with you?"

"The TV," she says. "I'm not dead." *But you might be*, her eyes threaten.

She gives me a little shove, and I allow myself to be pushed off her body. I grab my briefs off the floor and head for the bathroom so she can talk to her business partner in peace.

"That really *was* the TV," I hear her say. "Believe whatever you want. I appreciate your concern, though."

I can no longer hear the phone, but I'm certain Eric Bayer is laughing.

When I leave five minutes later, I make sure to steal a kiss. I make it a good one, because I need her to realize that she and I aren't over.

Unfortunately, my new teammates aren't as happy to see me as Bess was.

In the heat of a drill, I swing around to catch a pass, but there is no puck flying toward me. Instead, Jason Castro is on his ass on the ice, looking pissed-off, while Ivo skates away with the puck looking pleased with himself.

The whistle is loud and shrill. "Again!" yells the assistant coach.

"What the fuck was that?" Castro spits, getting up.

"You tell me," I grumble. "If you got the pass off, I would have scored."

"Really, *Sure Shot*?" he scoffs, using my old nickname. "You can't get the pass if you're outta position! The blue line is that way." He jerks a thumb toward a spot behind him.

"I was open and ready. It's not my fault you can't find my stick with a compass and a map."

"Because you're in the wrong fucking place!"

"Not hardly," I snap. "Get a clue. I'm not here to do things the same way you've always done them. And I wouldn't be standing here if Coach didn't think your playbook needed a few fresh pages."

Speak of the devil. Coach taps a stick against the boards to get our attention, and I skate off toward the blue line to restart the drill.

"Arrogant fuck," Castro says under his breath as he skates by.

"Dumbass," I hiss.

Castro has skills, though. He's young and fast, but he's been on this same team for all three of his years in the Show. My unusual style of play has broken his little puppy brain, and he isn't taking it well.

There's a long list of good reasons why Brooklyn wanted me

here. I have a lot of experience. Coach Worthington needed some of that. He also needed a D-man who played a different game than O'Doul and young Anton Bayer. It all makes sense on paper.

Although Coach was also hoping to get a share of the calm demeanor and leadership that I brought to the team in Dallas. But that guy? He's left the building. Somewhere between the Dallas/Fort Worth airport and the Brooklyn Navy Yards, I forgot how to be Uncle Tank. My reservoir of patience and advice is dried out completely. I can barely keep my own shit together, let alone handle someone else's drama.

So here we are, sweating like pigs, running the same play for the ten-thousandth time. We're supposed to be fine-tuning our game against Philadelphia, but you can't fine-tune a car that's lying in wreckage all over the front yard. For two hours it's been just like this—total chaos.

At this point I'm praying Philadelphia gets lost on the way to the stadium. It's the only chance we have of maintaining our dignity on Tuesday.

We run the drill again, and this time Castro takes no chances, passing to Drake instead of me. But Drake is blocked by Anton, and the puck is stripped, anyway.

"Fuck a duck," Castro grumbles.

I skate back to the blue line and pray for an end to this torture.

When the end of practice finally arrives, I make a beeline for the rubber matting beyond the practice rink. Unfortunately, several reporters do the same thing, and I find myself face to face with the difficult Miranda Wager and her infernal microphone.

They don't pay her to be nice, I remind myself as I paste on a smile. "Hey there, Ms. Wager. How are you?"

"Excellent. Can we say the same for you? Looked a little hairy out there today."

"Settling in takes time," I say mildly.

"How's Brooklyn so far?" she asks. "Have you found an apartment? The Brooklyn guys are known to take in strays. They're a friendly bunch, aren't they?"

That question is pure Miranda. She's digging for a story about former rivals struggling to become teammates. Nobody has offered me a bedroom, but that doesn't mean anything. "So friendly. But I'm headed home to such a beautiful hotel that I may never leave."

This morning I was surprised to receive a series of messages from my agent's assistant. She'd found me a better hotel room a lot closer to the practice facility. She's sending a car to help me move from one hotel to another, and she's booked me a massage, too.

Honestly, it's all a little odd. I wonder if Bess yelled at Kassman for ignoring me.

"How are your old friends in Dallas faring without you?" Miranda asks. She's still smiling, of course, while she twists the knife.

"I'm sure they're getting their skates under them as well. Shame about that loss to Boston."

As soon as I say it, I realize my mistake. I can't mention Dallas's struggles. If I'm a boring interview, Miranda won't use the footage. I really don't need any publicity right now. Not until I can prove myself.

The team publicist obviously agrees with me. She's wringing her hands behind Miranda Wager, begging me with her eyes to cut things short.

But Miranda isn't done with me. "Your ex-captain says he's looking forward to your January matchup, and that there's no way Brooklyn can win. He's calling for a three-point differential on the scoreboard. What do you say to that?"

I tip my head back and laugh out loud. *Fucking Palacio.* "Here's what I think, Miranda—hockey is fifty percent skill and fifty percent smack talk. Personally, I don't see the point of predicting a point spread on a game that's still months away. But maybe that's just a little quirk of mine."

She gives me another smile, so I brace myself. "Bart Palacio also predicted the matchup to be rougher than usual. He said lingering tensions will probably flare up on the ice. Do you know which tensions he's referring to?"

A flush creeps up my neck as I force myself to hold her gaze. "I wouldn't have a clue, sorry," I say in the calmest voice I can muster.

"Didn't the two of you fight?" she asks, holding her phone up to record whatever I say.

"Well, this might be tough to believe, but my teammate and I did not see eye to eye during every minute of the last seven years. Like all people who work closely together, we fought occasionally. You can write whatever you want, though. I know it's tough to get a good story out of one lousy practice. But if you want to see Brooklyn evolve into a new kind of fighting machine, you stick around."

I'm feeling damn proud of this answer when Miranda levels me with one last question. "Do you have any insight into Juliet Palacio's reasons for hiring a divorce attorney yesterday?"

All my blood stops circulating. "Come again?"

"Yesterday, Bart Palacio's wife retained legal counsel at Darby, Connors and Morgan, the same firm that represented your wife for her divorce—"

Georgia steps between us suddenly, like a skilled referee heading off a fight. "Questions at open practice can only be *game-related*. And Tankiewicz is needed in the dressing room."

Miranda switches off her microphone. "Then I guess I'm done here."

Georgia actually has to give me a hard nudge to get me moving toward the locker room, because I'm trying to wrap my head around this new layer of bullshit.

"Tank," Georgia says the minute we're past the double doors that lead to the locker rooms. "What the hell just happened?"

"Nothing," I say quickly.

She studies me with a frown. "I hate to ask, but…" She clears her throat.

"No," I say, preempting the question. "I never spent any time with Juliet Palacio. I had no idea they were getting divorced. And I do not know why."

"Sorry," Georgia says quickly. "I'm just trying to stay ahead of the news cycle."

"You and me, both."

"Okay." She pats me on the arm. "Good practice."

I just laugh, because it was not a good practice. Not even a little.

TWELVE

Big Hunk of Kryptonite

Daily News and Sports

"Dallas's Palacio Throws Down a Challenge. Tankiewicz Won't Answer It."

BY MIRANDA WAGER

Brooklyn's morning practice was just as squirrelly as last night's game. The team has some work to do, as Tankiewicz fails to settle in.

They used to call him "Sure Shot." But that nickname will have to die if he doesn't get his stick on the puck more often.

Meanwhile, his old team has finally found its footing without him, beating Arizona last night, redeeming their Boston loss.

When asked about the upcoming Dallas / Brooklyn matchup, team captain Palacio was confident. "We'll take them by at least 3 goals," he said. "It's gonna be a gong show, too. There are tensions that need airing out."

Palacio didn't say what those tensions were. However, this week his wife retained counsel with divorce attorneys.

At any rate, Brooklyn fans will be glued to their TVs in early January to find out if their team can take down its nemesis with one of its former players.

When asked for his own prediction for that game, Tankiewicz refused to provide one.

Tank

I read the so-called article in the back of a taxi the next day. It's not Miranda Wager's best work. But hey—she has to file a story whether she finds one or not, or lose her job to someone else. I get it.

The comments, though. They're worse than usual. Miranda opened the door for another round of armchair hockey fans to smear my name.

Tankiewicz gets into a fight with Palacio, then they both get divorced. Coincidence?

I groan out loud. Unfortunately, I'm not the only one to read this article. By the time I step out of the cab in front of my new boutique hotel, my phone is blowing up with texts from my ex-wife. Ignoring Jordanna for the moment, I pay the driver and then enter the spacious and plant-filled hotel lobby.

"Mr. Tankiewicz, welcome back," the concierge says from behind his desk. "Can I offer you a croissant and some fresh-squeezed orange juice?"

"Well, sure," I say as my stomach rumbles. "Thanks."

He hands me a small bakery bag with a smile. "Let me know if you need anything else."

When I let myself into my room a minute later, I'm nearly blinded by the glimmer of sun on the surface of the river right outside. The room is serene and comfortably appointed.

The only unsightly thing in my new space is a bouquet of balloons. They're silver, and each one has an uplifting saying on it. "You've Got This!" "We're Your Number One Fans!" "Go Get 'Em!"

Interesting choice. Kassman doesn't usually send me balloons. I think his assistant might have been trying too hard.

On the bar, I find a plate for my croissant and I bite into it as I glance at my ex-wife's texts.

Mark, you have to make it stop. I'm getting calls. A reporter asked me why we got divorced. Not like it's any of their business. But just tell them, okay? I'm tired of seeing my name on Twitter.

So don't look at Twitter. I actually type that out and then delete it. I refuse to argue with Jordanna, even when she's being ridiculous.

There is nothing to be done, I reply instead. *There is literally no way to kill off gossip other than to ignore it.*

The second I hit Send, those little dots show up, telling me that she's typing a reply.

I open the orange juice and wait, wishing I'd never responded in the first place. The juice tastes like sunshine and heaven. It's funny, but Brooklyn is doing its best to impress me. The Bruisers facility is glorious. This new hotel is lovely. The publicist is nice. The staff is sharp, and living without a car is pretty fab.

If only my teammates weren't trying to drive me insane, I'd have a chance at liking this place.

You could deny it! Jordanna writes. *I look like an idiot. My own friends believe the things they read about you on the internet.*

That's on them, I fire back. *I guess you need better friends. And I'm not giving any interviews about my personal life.*

Somehow I manage not to add: *And if I did, you wouldn't even like what I have to say about the end of our marriage.* I will not pick a fight with the woman who divorced me. No good can come of that.

At least keep your head down, she says. *Don't talk to reporters. Stay out of the gossip pages.*

I'll get right on that, I shoot back.

My phone rings about ten seconds later. Instantly, my famous temper spikes. I'd rather throw my phone across the room than talk to her right now. But when I glance at the screen, I see it isn't Jordanna who's calling me. It's my agent.

"Hey," I say into the phone the second I manage to answer. "Henry! How are you? Long time no see."

"Nobody is sorrier about that than me," the older man rumbles. "How's the new room?"

"Nice," I say, trying to sound upbeat. "Thanks for finding me better digs."

"That was all Kelly's doing."

"Still, I appreciate it," I say, moving over to the king-sized bed, where I flop down with a weary sigh. "Did you call to yell at me for talking to Miranda Wager?"

"Not a chance. I called to remind you—" He stops to take a wheezy breath. "—not to let the assholes get you down."

"Hey, are you okay?" He doesn't sound right.

"Don't you worry about me. Got plans for your afternoon off?"

"None," I say. "Just a few prayers and incantations, and maybe a goat sacrifice or two. It's the only way I can imagine beating Philadelphia tonight."

Henry laughs. "That bad, huh?"

"Practice was just as bad as you read in the newspaper. Luckily, my personal life isn't quite as complicated as you might think from the comments."

My agent snorts. *"Never* read the comments, kid. That's the first rule of life."

"I thought the first rule of life was never order a red wine that's not old enough to go to kindergarten."

He laughs again, and I feel more relaxed than I have in days. Bullshitting with Henry Kassman is one of my favorite things to do on game day. I didn't realize until right now how much I missed this guy.

Bess was right, damn it. A guy just needs his agent sometimes. "Thanks for the presents," I say. "The balloons are a little silly. But I think there's a fruit basket, too."

"That's all Kelly's work. But silly is good. Promise me you won't spend the day brooding. If you can't sleep, go out and do something fun."

"Fun? Like what?"

"Doesn't matter. Pinball. Biking on the river. I know the game is important, but so is your life. You only get one."

His oddly introspective comment has the strangest effect on me. I get goosebumps. Henry likes to win almost as much as I do. His pregame pep talk is usually more along the lines of *knock 'em over and make 'em cry.* "I'll keep that in mind," I say slowly.

"You do that. Now go out and do something fun, and don't waste another second on the haters. Got any new friends yet?"

"No." I chuckle. "That might be a while. They all think I'm a manwhore and a loose cannon."

"They'll come around. You need friends, Tank. No man is an island."

"Yeah, but some men are traded to them."

He laughs, but then he ends up coughing. "I better go," he says, wheezing. "But I'll be watching tonight."

"Thanks, Henry," I say. "Talk to you later." He agrees, and I hang up the phone.

I spend the next few minutes watching the reflection of river light sparkle on the ceiling. I'm probably too stirred up for a pregame nap.

I pick up my phone again and scroll backward through my texts, hoping to see something from Bess, who I can't stop thinking about.

Nothing. Damn it. I guess I have to take things into my own hands. *Hey Bessie. Where are you today? I was just thinking about you.*

She could be anywhere right now. She covers hockey and base-ball players on thirty teams in twenty-one states. I know this because I cyber-stalked her after our first hookup.

Is it egotistical of me to wonder if she's staring out a window somewhere thinking about me? We had a hell of a time together the other night. Bess is terrific. She knocked me out of my funk. Part way, anyhow. I still have issues. But not with the sexiest person I know in New York.

The reply comes one minute later.

Bess: Were you, now?

Tank: Absolutely. Kassman told me to go out and do something fun. And naturally I thought of you.

Bess: Go Fish, Tank.

Tank: I'm not in the mood for cards, thanks. You didn't answer the question. Where are you?

Bess: I'm in Boston at the moment.

Tank: Fuck.

Bess: Are you ready for tonight?

Tank: Of course. The younger guys are still treating me like a turd someone left on their doorstep. And I have no rhythm with the forwards. But no problemo!

Bess: You got this! Yay hockey! <- World's shortest pep talk, because I don't want to be accused of agenting you.

Tank: Speaking of agents, is it possible you spoke to mine?

Bess: I have no idea what you're talking about.

Tank: Uh-huh. So it's just a coincidence that Kassman's assistant decided to move my hotel, book me a spa massage, and then send me a fruit basket and... The last thing is just weird.

Bess: You needed a hotel change. And fruit baskets are nice. Everyone likes fruit. And baskets. But what is the weird thing? I'm worried.

Tank: A bouquet of mylar balloons. They have uplifting sayings on them. Like "We're your number one fan."

Bess: BALLOONS? WTF. Is Henry trolling me? That's weird and not very environmentally responsible.

Tank: So you pushed him to do this?

Bess: Henry and I text from time to time. We might have texted the other day.

Tank: I see how it is. But you don't have to worry about me, okay? I'm fine.

Bess: Come on. The new hotel kicks ass, right? Have you tried those croissants at the desk?

Tank: They're glorious. Still. I'm a big boy. You verified it yourself many times.

Bess: But never again.

Tank: Uh-huh. You said I'm your kryptonite. And I know how kryptonite works.

Bess: ?

Tank: Proximity. And now we're in the same neighborhood.

Bess: Go take a nap, Tank. Beat Philadelphia.

Tank: Later baby.

Bess: Later.

Tank: Later is better than never. See?

She doesn't reply, and I toss the phone aside. But texting with Bess was fun. And I'm already plotting how to get another chance to show her my big hunk of kryptonite.

Five hours later, I'm feeling more like the Hulk than Superman. There's two minutes left on the clock, and we're losing 1-0 to Philadelphia. Our offense is not creating enough scoring chances. They're too patient, which drives me up a tree.

Worse—the first line still can't find me when I'm open. After a week of intense practice, they're still completely confused by my style of play. When I'm open at the top of the circle, I'm somehow invisible to Castro, Campeau, and Drake.

"Coulda turned that into a goal," I growl at Castro before a third-period faceoff. "You have two shoulders. Check the right side once in a while."

"Who died and made you a forward?" the young wing spits. "Stay in your own lane."

Ugh. It's not like I don't understand the problem. They're young, and their captain is a different kind of D-man. O'Doul's a shut-down defenseman—a wall of "no." He's always behind the blue line, ready to stop whatever comes his way.

I'm not that guy. I'm an agent of chaos. I had twice as many points as O'Doul last year, and that's what this team needs—flexibility on the blue line. The GM and the coach thought so, anyway. That's the reason I'm here.

This logic has evaded my young teammates. They win the faceoff, dragging the puck toward the corner, and then passing it tidily amongst each other.

I move up, harassing the opponent and opening myself up for a shot. Again. No dice. Drake passes to Castro, instead. His angle is a hair's breadth off, and we get stripped.

It's the perfect storm. An opposing D-man tangles up Campeau in a blatantly illegal hit. There's no whistle. Castro lunges after his opponent but can't get there fast enough.

Our other defenseman—Anton Bayer, aka "Baby Bayer"—is perfectly positioned. But it's a three-man rush, and there's only so much he and the goalie can do. None of us can get there in time, and Philadelphia capitalizes on the chaos, lighting the lamp a split second before the buzzer goes off.

"*Les fuckés!*" Campeau shouts. His face is full of thunder. The guys on the bench all look miserable.

As we leave the ice, Castro looks like a bomb about to go off. That dude won't even look at me. His scowl leads us off the ice and down the chute to the locker room, past a dozen sports writers trying to make a big story out of a single early-season game.

"Tankiewicz, how'd it go?" one of them calls toward me.

"We'll get there!" I say cheerfully. Although I'd rather knee him in the nuts.

God, I need a shower and a drink. I strip off my sweaty gear and grab a towel. But then—because it's so much fun to be the new guy—I head in the wrong direction. I end up in the crowded anteroom instead of the showers, clutching a towel around my ass like an idiot.

Then it gets worse. Castro is standing there, head down, grumbling to a trainer. And what do I hear? "So fucking useless as a defenseman. I mean, the guy is so useless his own wife didn't want him anymore."

Anger rears up inside me. I reach out and grab the edge of his jersey, turning his body so he can see I'm standing right here. "Excuse me? You got issues to talk about, you do me the courtesy of saying it to my *face*."

Honestly, I couldn't have picked a worse time or place to behave aggressively to a fellow teammate. A dozen heads swivel. Half of them are journalists. And one of them is a certain redheaded agent with the prettiest blue eyes I've ever seen. Her mouth drops open in shock, and she stomps toward me.

"Are you *insane*?" Bess hisses. "Get your mitts off my player."

I drop my hand like a guilty child.

"Is this the story you want to read on the blogs tomorrow?" She somehow manages to yell at me in a sotto voice. It must be something you learn at agent school. "'Veteran Player Manhandles Younger Forward'? Are you fucking *crazy*?"

"Bess," Castro grunts. "Stop it."

She lets out a growl of outrage. "Don't escalate this, Jason."

"Shh. I won't." He puts a casual hand on her shoulder. "I was a dick first."

"What?" she squeaks. "How big a dick?"

Castro's brown eyes meet mine, and they look guilty. "Extra-large." He sighs. "The showers are around there—behind the trainer's table. Grab one before they're full."

I'm so angry I could explode. But I finally do the smart thing. I turn around and go.

THIRTEEN

Your Number One Fan

BESS

"GOOD GOD," I whisper under my breath. Even as I watch Tank disappear, my anger remains in the red zone.

I have a temper, too, but it doesn't show up very often. Teammate-on-teammate aggression makes me insane, and when Tank's hand yanked Jason Castro's jersey, I'd seen red.

It's my job to fight for my players. I don't mind playing the heavy. It's always better for an agent to yell in the locker room than for an athlete to do the same. Plus, people have been stereotyping me as the "fiery redhead" since I was small. I lean into this reputation sometimes, because you have to use what God has given you.

But *this* is why I can't sleep with a player. This is *exactly* why. There's no room in my life for divided loyalties.

"I was a dick," Castro repeats quietly. "I'm lucky he didn't punch me."

"Why?" I breathe. "What the hell did you say?"

Castro looks down at his skates. "I was venting, because that game sucked the big one. I said that Tank was so useless even his wife didn't need him anymore."

My heart squeezes. "*Jason,*" I whisper. "That's so cruel. What if you broke up with Heidi and your teammates *mocked* you about it?"

"I know," he says through gritted teeth. "I never meant for him to hear it."

That's when all the fight runs out of me. "The game sucked," I say, trying to find some way to empathize with my client. "You guys need more time. But where is the trust? And how are you going to build any with such a personal attack against a teammate? Your coach brought him on for a reason. Better start asking yourself why that is."

"Okay, Bess. Message received." He looks angry again, but probably at himself. Castro is smart. And while he's a bit of a grump sometimes, he's not a bad guy. "I'll apologize."

"Great idea," I say softly. "If he's smart, he'll apologize for getting in your face."

Castro shrugs, looking uncomfortable. "Gonna shower now."

"Fine. We'll catch up later."

He walks away, and I'm left standing here, feeling completely unsettled. The game *did* suck the big one, but there's nothing I can do about it.

I cut my losses and leave, winding my way through the bowels of the stadium until I reach the street. Traffic is a mess, and there are still dozens of spectators hoping to catch a taxi. I cross the street when the light changes and head home on foot. It's not a long walk, except I'm wearing a goddamn dress and cute little sandals again. Only because of Tank.

I don't plan to sleep with him again, but I got dressed up anyway. I'm wearing mascara, for fuck's sake. To a *hockey game*. That's how badly he scrambled my brain.

A thirty-year-old woman shouldn't be as confused as I am right now.

But lately I see Tank wherever I turn. Today I was minding my own business, reading the sports headlines, and there was a photograph of a sweaty Tank taking off his helmet after this morning's practice. "Rumors Circulate After Tankiewicz's Departure From Dallas," screamed the headline.

Some of the trashier blogs are still trying to tie his divorce to his trade. It's just clickbait. My own curiosity shames me.

None of it has a thing to do with me, I remind myself as I trudge through Brooklyn. He's not my client. And he isn't my boyfriend. It doesn't matter if I was half in love with him at twenty-one. It doesn't matter if I still find him more exciting than any man on Tinder. There's no fairy godmother who can wave all the obstacles away. I don't really believe in those fairytales that I love so much.

I make my own luck, and always have.

Looking for a distraction, I pull out my phone to see if Eric had any late-day questions for me. And sure enough, there's a text. *You had a delivery. The courier didn't say who this was from. But your name and our office address were on the card.*

There's a photo of a balloon bouquet. *I'm your number one fan*, each balloon reads.

Oh, Tank. You make it so hard to stay away from you.

I shove my phone in my bag and keep on walking.

The next day I sit down for a business meeting in Manhattan with a lip-balm company. Getting sponsorship deals for my clients is one of the ways I grow their paychecks. Last year I landed a lucrative wristwatch sponsorship for Jason Castro. I've also been talking to a menswear company about their hand-tailored trousers—the kind that fit over muscled hockey-player butts.

My job is pretty weird, in an awesome way.

Today's meeting is about beeswax lip balm, the trendiness of organics, and the many faces of sport. The female executive is eyeing an eight-by-ten glossy photo of Silas. She lets out a contented little sigh. "He'll do."

"Right?" I say, clapping my hands. "He has a handsome face and a lovely personality. You'll never regret working with the nicest goalie in sports."

The fact that he's dating a superstar goes unsaid, but it doesn't hurt Silas's appeal that his face has begun turning up on red carpets and in paparazzi shots. If the kid can earn an extra hundred grand stumping for organic lip balm, he should take it. Fame is mostly a pain in his ass.

"I'll send you a contract tomorrow," she says.

"Excellent. Can I bend your ear about one more thing?"

"Sure." She folds her hands on the desktop. "Although we've

found all the athletes we need at this point. We have a downhill skier, a marathoner, and now a hockey player."

"I get that. But I saw on your website that you're bringing out some tinted lip products this spring, so I thought you should see these ladies." I grab another folder out of my bag and quickly place four photos on the desk.

"These aren't professional headshots," she says, looking them over.

"You're right. Every one of these women is a professional hockey player. And here's the thing—these women are the most underpaid professional athletes in the world. Their salaries are around fifteen thousand dollars a year. It doesn't even cover their rent. You don't know their faces, because women's hockey is, like, the redheaded stepchild of the sports world."

She looks up at me, frowning. "Fifteen thousand dollars? That's criminal."

"The league is struggling. But think about the demographics. Hockey for young girls is growing faster than boys' hockey. And your products appeal to sporty girls, right? Besides—hiring these women for a single day's photoshoot will elevate a sport that the world needs to see. And it makes you guys look like heroes for supporting women's sports."

"Interesting," she says slowly.

"There's so much misogyny in hockey," I say. "But that will change. You could be a leader, and it won't cost you much. A female athlete costs less than an Instagram influencer. Think about it."

"I will," she promises. "May I keep these shots?"

"Absolutely. I wrote their names on the back. And if you go to my website, you can see all the women I represent."

I leave the meeting feeling pretty pleased with myself. Silas is getting his sponsorship, and I got to say my piece for women's hockey.

On the corner of Sixth Avenue, I watch the tourists swarm Radio City and wonder what else I should do with my day. I pull out my phone and text Henry Kassman. *Any chance we could grab a coffee? It's been too long.*

To my surprise, I get a response before I've walked a block. *Come meet with me, Bess. We need to talk.*

That sounds ominous. Henry and I usually communicate through hockey memes. But it's not like I'm going to turn the man down. He sends me an address on East 61st street, and I head right over there. It turns out to be an apartment building, and the doorman sends me up to the penthouse suite.

I've never been to Henry's home. I didn't even know the man had one. He basically lives in the office. Odd that he's here on a weekday afternoon.

When I knock on the door, it's opened by a smiling young woman in a nurse's uniform. "Come right this way. Henry!" she calls. "You have a visitor! Henry loves visitors."

"That is a lie," grumbles my mentor.

I follow her through a grand archway and into what appears to be a living room. Even though my senses are already pinging with worry, it's a jolt to see a hospital bed set up in the center of the big room. A bigger surprise is the grey-faced, skinny shell of a man with an oxygen tube at his nose and a weak smile. "Hello, Bess. Long time no see."

Pain and fear slice through me. It takes all my strength to force a smile. "It's great to see you, slacker."

"Sit, Bessie." He waves feebly at a chair. "We have things to discuss."

I walk over to the chair and sit down. It's way too quiet in here. And I know I'm not going to like whatever Henry has to say.

FOURTEEN

Everyone but Aunt Gertie

TANK

PUCKRAKERS BLOG

"Brooklyn Opener Ends in Disappointment"

That sound you just heard was Brooklyn's collective groan as the Bruisers failed to find the net during their entire home opener. Leo Trevi almost brought the magic on a breakaway during the second period, but the Philadelphia goalie made a highlight-reel save to deny him.

Only the brilliant netminding of Brooklyn's Mike Beacon—and some skilled defense from captain O'Doul—kept the damage to just two goals. The offensive effort was haphazard at best, and unable to capitalize on new trade Mark Tankiewicz's speed and maneuverability.

Things almost got ugly in the locker room afterward, when Tankiewicz's famous temper flared up at a forward. It's no wonder his teammates treat him like the Ebola virus when they're on the ice together.

Maybe it's too soon to call the Tankiewicz trade a disaster. But if the Tank can't make some friends and influence people, it's going to be a long season followed by a short flight for the veteran to some other team next year.

Practice lasts an eternity.

Or maybe it just seems that way, because Coach Worthington puts the same players together today—the same squad who lost together last night—and then spends two hours driving home all the ways our lack of communication lost the game.

"Don't look for Tankiewicz to stay on the blue line," he says. "He could be anywhere. Play the drill again."

He must have said it a hundred times already, basically pointing out why I'm supposed to be a different kind of defenseman than their hero, O'Doul. I would feel vindicated if I weren't so sweaty. And the irritation on the faces of all three forwards is pretty hard to miss.

I hate my life.

When we're finally done, I don't even try to make conversation with the exhausted men who'd endured that practice with me. I shower as fast as I can and then try to make my escape.

Unfortunately, I manage to leave the locker room area at the same time as Jason Castro.

"Hey," he says gruffly, as we both head for the glass tunnel that leads toward the main lobby and the street.

"Hey," is the only reply I can think of.

"If you're free the night after next, we're all putting together some furniture for Silas's girlfriend. She's moving in down the hall."

I blink in surprise, because it sounds like he's asking for my help. "The singer?" I ask after a beat.

"Right. She just bought Dave Beringer's apartment. So we could use one more set of hands. Delilah's buying pizza afterward."

"Oh. Sure. I'll bring some beer," I stammer.

"You know the address? 220 Water Street. We're meeting up at my place. Just tell the doorman that you're there to help with the move."

"You got it," I say as we step out onto the street. "I won't forget." But I wonder if somebody made him invite me, like it's a middle school birthday party.

He stops when we reach the sidewalk. "Look, I'm sorry about

that crack I made last night. That was egregious, and I shouldn't have taken my personal bullshit out on you."

Once again I'm startled, because it almost sounds like he means it. "Dude, don't worry about it. Especially because it was true. The wife has no use for me. Dallas, though? They should know better."

"Jesus." Castro chokes on his laughter. "What happened there? Did they fuck up their salary cap?"

"That's only part of it," I admit. "After last season, there was some unhealthy scapegoating. Palacio blamed everyone but his Aunt Gertie for losing that second-round game to L.A."

Castro sneers. "Is he as big a tool as he seems?"

I open my mouth to deny it, but then I realize I don't have to anymore. "Let's just say that if he's moving furniture and having pizza, I'm finding a reason I need to be anywhere else."

"Bummer. And you were co-captains?"

"Sure. On ice it's different, you know? You don't have to like a guy to play well together."

"Uh-huh." He looks like he doesn't believe me, though. He's twenty-four or twenty-five, and Brooklyn is the only big-league team he's ever played for. He doesn't know any different.

I'll have to remember that.

"Every interaction I had with Palacio," Castro says, "made me think he's a big bag of dicks."

"A big bag of dicks who can score," I point out.

"Can we beat them in January?"

"God, I hope so."

Castro grins. "Good. See you tomorrow." He turns on his Chuck T's and strides off toward Water Street.

On the walk back to the hotel, I check my texts. There's two of them, and I have this moment of happiness, because I'm expecting to maybe hear from Bess. Honestly, I'm like a school boy with a crush. I can't stop thinking about her, and I keep wondering when I'll get to see her again.

A month ago I would have told you that I was too jaded to have a hot fling so soon after the end of my marriage. Sex was just about the last thing on my mind. But this week it's practically all I think about.

Unfortunately, none of my messages are from her.

When I arrive at my hotel, the concierge offers me a fluffy croissant. I decline, because sometimes a guy needs some protein. "Do you have a recommendation for a Tex-Mex place that delivers?"

"Of course. This one is my favorite." He opens a desk drawer and then hands me a printed menu. "The pork tacos are divine."

"Thank you. Appreciate it." I take the menu and head upstairs. The bed in my room has been made, and my clothes are folded in a pile.

Maybe I could just live here forever. Then I wouldn't have to deal with the reality of my new life. I flop down on the bed to peruse the menu. I'm just about to place an order when someone knocks on my door.

That's weird. It's not like I have friends.

When I open the door, I'm stunned to find Bess Beringer standing there in tight black slacks and a flowing wine-colored blouse that shows a hint of cleavage. *Well, hello.* A single glimpse of her makes my body tighten. I've been thinking about her for *days.* Even when she yelled at me last night, it barely made a dent in my libido.

I'm about to make a sleazy crack about having a nooner when I notice her pinched expression and agitated body language. So I merely hold the door open wider.

"I fucked up," she says, stepping through the door.

"Okay? Is this about last night? 'Cause I'm over it already."

"No," she says, and her voice is so low that I start to worry.

"Come sit." I walk over to the sofa and perch on the arm, hoping I haven't upset her somehow. But I can't think of what I might have done. All I did was send her some campy balloons.

"You asked me yesterday if I'd prodded Henry Kassman about your setup in Brooklyn." She sits down heavily.

"Yeah?" I say lightly. "But I got a fruit basket out of it." I point at the desk near the window, where an orange and a gourmet granola bar are the only things I haven't already chowed.

"Well, I'm guilty. It was me who wrote him several lengthy texts about how you were struggling. Just because you're a veteran and a solid guy, doesn't mean you didn't need a lot more attention. I criticized the hotel location. I asked Kassman if he was paying attention." Her voice cracks.

"Okay, Bess. It's not that big of a deal."

"Yes, it is! He's my mentor," she says shakily. "I've never criticized him before. Not once. At least, I don't think I have."

"Is he angry?" I ask gently. "I'm sure he'll get over it."

"I stuck my foot in where I shouldn't have. He's *dying*, Tank." She whirls on me. "Did you know?"

"Oh. *Fuck*." My heart sinks. Poor Henry. "No, he hasn't told me a thing. But I wondered if something was up." Bess was right—it's not like Kassman to stay away. I've been in New York for a month already, and I haven't seen his face. "What's wrong with him? Is it cancer?"

She shakes her head violently. "Heart failure," she snarls. "That's it. Apparently your heart can just *stop working* for no reason at all."

"Oh, God." My mind whirls. "Could he maybe get a—"

"Transplant? No. I asked. He's not a good candidate for some reason." Her fists are clenched, and her brow is creased with anger. As if she plans to grab heart failure by both hands and knee it in the nuts.

"Bess," I whisper. "Take a breath."

"Why?" she shrieks. "I told a dying man that he was taking poor care of his client. I should have asked him if he was okay. I just *expected* him to live forever! And the worst part is that I am still thinking about myself! Who am I going to call when I'm confused about something in a contract?"

"I'll bet that doesn't happen often," I say soothingly.

"No. I haven't needed his help in five years," she grits out. "*Still*. Who am I going to meet for coffee when the gossip gets really good? Do you know what that man said to me just now?"

I shake my head, just letting her get it all out.

"He wants you to jump ship."

"Sorry?"

"He suggested I take over your account, which is a stupid idea.

I'm a busybody. I'm an awful human. He probably thinks I was trying to poach you all along."

"Nooo," I say softly, moving slowly closer to her on the sofa, the way you'd approach a feral cat. "He doesn't think that. He thinks you're the kind of woman who sees something wrong and tries to fix it."

She takes a shuddery breath. "Henry can't die. I won't let him." A fat tear squeezes out of one of her eyes. "Fuck. I never cry. *Never*. Nobody wants an agent who cries."

"Oh, I don't know about that," I whisper. I lift Bess and deposit her onto my lap. "You've had a shock. And everyone wants an agent who cares." I tuck her against my chest. She smells like lemons.

She hides her face in my neck and cries, her back shaking.

"Shh," I whisper. "I'm sorry for Henry. I don't want to lose him, either." Hell, my eyes feel hot, too. I've been with Henry for nine years. And I know what Bess means about feeling selfish. Because my next thought is: can't *one thing* in my life stay intact? Not even one?

I push that thought out of my mind. I kiss a tear off the corner of Bess's eye. And then I cuddle my future agent a little closer. I stroke her hair and wait. It takes her a while to stop crying, but eventually she relaxes against my body and sighs. The sun is shining brightly outside the floor-to-ceiling windows, splitting into a million diamonds of light on the river.

Strangely, I feel centered in a way that I haven't for weeks. Like a stone that's anchored in the river, while life rushes loudly by. I thought that rediscovering sex was Bess's big gift to me. And it was a pretty amazing gift. But this—providing comfort—is something else I once did well, too. I'd forgotten how this feels—holding someone you love in silence, just because they need it.

It's funny how I've missed this quiet pleasure. By the time we'd separated, it had been a long time since my ex and I had provided comfort to one another.

Bess takes another deep, slow breath, and her body's warmth slows down my heart rate. I can't resist stroking a hand down her back. I hold very still, hoping she won't get up and leave too soon.

I'm not ready.

FIFTEEN

What the Girl Wants

BESS

TANK, at some point, picks me up and carries me a short distance to the bed. He lies down and pulls me close again, pressing a warm hand against the small of my back.

Rolling closer, I cling a little more tightly to him. Is it horrible that Tank is the one I wanted to see right after I spoke to Henry? A week ago I would have locked myself into my bathroom and sobbed alone.

But here I am, pressing my face against Tank's sturdy shoulder, blotting my tears onto his T-shirt. I'm thirty years old and I've never been in a serious relationship with a man—the kind where you can turn to him when you're sad.

Tank and I aren't in a relationship, either. But now I know what that would feel like—strong arms and patient silence. I feel like I've been holding myself together for thirty years, and just for fifteen minutes I'm letting someone else do the holding.

I like it way too much.

Tank dozes off eventually, his arm still curled protectively around me. He has a game tonight, and most players nap before hitting the rink. I feel like a stowaway—catching a free ride on the warmth of his body and the comfort of his touch.

Sleep doesn't come for me. It feels wrong to slip away from this moment, with the sunshine on the river and the quiet rhythm of

Tank's breathing. I wonder if Henry feels like this when he looks out the penthouse window—like the afternoon sunshine is a commodity that's suddenly in short supply.

For me, Tank's embrace is that precious resource. It's not mine. I'm just borrowing it for an hour. Then I'll have to give it back and go on with my life.

Eventually, Tank stirs. I can tell when he wakes, because his breathing becomes quieter. He rolls toward me, kissing me gently on the temple. I reach up and stroke his jaw with my thumb. I don't want to talk right now, because only sad things will come out. So I lean in and kiss his neck instead. He smells like shower soap and clean T-shirts.

Tank presses another kiss to the side of my face. Then he ducks his head and trails his lips up my neck. We're still curled around one another, as if letting go would hurt.

So we don't. He clasps my face and pulls me into a kiss. A soft one. His green eyes lock onto mine, and then I wrap my arms around him and kiss him back. My body melts against his like a cat reclining in the sun.

For once, our kisses are slow and quiet. He savors my mouth until the taste of him is the only thing I know. Every languorous kiss is like another dose of a drug, softening the edges of my consciousness. I wish we could stay right here forever, where nothing is wrong and nobody is dying.

Because we're us, we don't stop at kissing. Tank's hands wander down my tummy. His fingers unzip my trousers. Then I kiss my way down his body, pushing his T-shirt out of the way and nibbling the skin just above the waistband of his athletic shorts.

I want to be *used* right now, I realize. I need to be selfless, because it feels wrong to be so healthy and alive.

Tank takes the hint, shoving his shorts down, taking his briefs with them. Not missing a beat, I bend right down and lick the length of his cock. He hisses, so I slip his tip between my lips and take his cockhead into my mouth.

"Fuck. Yes." He reaches down to gather my hair around his hand, probably so he can watch. I raise my eyes to his and give him an ambitious suck, hollowing my cheeks.

"*Jesus H,*" he sputters. "You have no idea how sexy you look right now. Take it, honey. *Fuck*. That's... Unngh." He rolls his hips to get me to take more.

I rarely do this for anyone. Ever since my first fling with Tank, I haven't had much interest in casual hookups. I'm more interested in finding someone to date. But nobody has made it past the third date in a long time.

With Tank it's different. *Rules? What rules?* I do whatever he asks, and then some. I run my fingertips over his sac, and he moans. I take him deep into my throat, and he starts panting.

"Slow down, girly. Or this will be over pretty fast," he rasps.

But I don't want to slow down. I like the sounds he's making, and the salty taste of him on my tongue. I suck him until I gag. And then I suck him some more.

"Bess," he grunts, tugging me off. "Get up here. I need to fuck you."

That's the magic word. *Need*. So I sit up quickly.

He tosses his T-shirt onto the floor, and now he's completely naked. Turning his attention to the delicate buttons on my blouse, he gently unbuttons each one. Every couple of buttons, I receive a hungry kiss.

Still feeling weepy and unsettled, I let him move me around like a puppet. His hands are warm and soothing as he peels my blouse off my shoulders and drops it onto a side table. "You're still wearing panties," he chides me.

He's right. And I'm still wearing my bra, too. We work together to strip them from my body, and soon they're on the floor.

"Damn," he whispers as I kneel on the bed beside him, my breasts bouncing free. "Look at me."

His green eyes are heated and glittering, his gaze making everything seem perfectly right. Like I was meant to be the temptress who knocks on his hotel room door in the middle of the day and then sucks his cock.

"Get over here." He tugs my very naked body onto his lap. As I straddle him, he pulls me against his chest and kisses me deeply.

I feel achy with desire as we meet, skin to skin. This is wrong in so many ways. Sex is a stupid way to grieve. I feel selfish and sad as our tongues meld again and again. I'm using Tank for comfort. And not just his hard body—although it is glorious. I need someone to hold me and make me feel loved.

He doesn't seem to mind the job, though. He braces my hips in his hands and slides his cock against my sensitive flesh. "Ride me, honey," he whispers.

I shake my head, because that's not what I want right now. Then I kiss him again and wrap my arms around his neck.

"Okay," he says against my mouth. "What the girl wants, the girl gets." In a serious feat of coordination, Tank rolls us both over with no break in the kissing. My no-sex-with-athletes policy is looking a little foolish right about now.

Or at least my no-sex-with-Tank policy. Nobody else tempts me like he does. Nobody else kisses like he does. I've never felt as worshipped as I do right this second. He clasps my hands and stares into my eyes like there's nobody else in the world except us.

Shamelessly, I part my legs for him.

He doesn't make me wait. With a hungry groan, he fills me. He brushes my hair off my face, dropping kisses everywhere as he slowly begins to move.

I lift my heels to his ass, holding him in place. Time slows. I hear the horn of a tugboat on the river. And the water's reflection sparkles on the white ceiling above us. "Don't stop," I breathe. "Never stop."

He doesn't. He picks up the pace. "You kill me," he grunts against my skin. "I'm trying to go slow, but you make me so fucking hard."

The praise warms me up inside. I'm helpless to enjoy the eager grind of his hips, and the weight of his green-eyed stare. "Faster," I beg.

Tank closes his eyes and groans. "You feel too good. I can't last forever." He lifts one of my knees, folding it under his arm, exposing more of me. Then he drops his head and sucks one of my nipples into his mouth.

I arch my back and moan, because he makes me feel so wild.

"Yeah," he grunts happily. "Oh, fuck."

His muscles lock as he groans loudly, and that's all it takes. I lift my hips and take what I need from him, shattering as he gives me one more deep thrust.

"That's a girl," he gasps. "Give it to me."

As if I could help it. I sink into the mattress and try to hold on to the bliss.

Tank collapses a moment later, rolling to his side and pulling me with him.

We lay there for a while—lazy and limp, curled up in the bed together, pretending that it's not midafternoon on a Tuesday. I'm in a post-sex coma, thinking only hazy thoughts. But they turn guilty as soon as my brain comes back online.

"Shh," he says.

"I didn't say anything."

"Yeah, but you're about to. Something about how we shouldn't have done that."

"Well, we shouldn't have," I point out, my face still buried in his neck.

"Hogwash."

I lift my face and glance at him. "Hogwash? Is that something people say in Texas?"

"Don't knock Texas," he says lazily. "God, I'm starving. Can I order you some Mexican food? It's an emergency situation."

"I already ate." Although it seems like a long time ago now. "Maybe just some guacamole and chips?"

"That's my girl." Tank strokes my back. "One more question?"

"Shoot."

"Will you be my agent?"

"What?" I sit up suddenly. That was *not* the question I was expecting. "No. I can't."

"Bess," he says softly, his hand cupping my hip. "It doesn't have to be today. I mean eventually."

"No way." I give my head a vigorous shake. "Did you miss the fact that we're naked right now?"

He lets out a guttural laugh. "I didn't miss a second of it. But it doesn't matter."

"Like hell," I insist. "Credibility is everything. 'Pay my client what he's worth' sounds a hell of a lot different than 'Pay my lover.' I mean, if we were *married*, that's —"

Oh shit. I realize two things in a big rush. The first is that I shouldn't have used the M word with Tank. I already know where he stands on that score. The second is that there's a brutally simple solution to this problem.

"Actually," I say, "I'm thinking about this all wrong. I will absolutely be your agent, if eventually that proves necessary."

His handsome face breaks into a warm smile — the kind that makes me feel all gooey inside. "Thank you, sweetheart." He runs a hand up my bare back. "I can count on one hand all the people in my life that I trust. And you're on this very short list. Don't make me confide in a stranger."

"I won't," I say, rolling off the bed. "You're right. We have a lot of history. When the time comes for you to find other representation, I'm happy to help. But I hope that day won't come very soon." I pick up my panties and hop into them. And then I grab my trousers.

"Wow, okay. Thank you for being flexible on this point. I thought I was going to have to win you over with some more hot loving." He gives me an adorably heated glance as I hook my bra.

"That's not necessary," I say with a sigh. "There will be no more hot loving."

"What? Of course there will."

"No way," I insist, putting on my blouse. "You were totally right — it makes more sense for me to be your agent than your hookup. From now on we're going to stick to the plan."

"Plan? What plan?" he sputters, running his hand through his sex-mussed hair.

"Smart decisions. Long-range goals. You need a place to live and a distraction-free life so you can concentrate on your game. I was never part of your Brooklyn plan, Tank. You know this."

"Well, sure, but..." He squints up at me. "That doesn't mean I'm not happy to see you."

That's the whole problem, isn't it? We're way too happy to see each other. But which Bess am I going to be? The one with the five-year plan? Or the one who throws everything overboard every time this man smiles at me?

"Your future agent is a smart girl." I'm rapidly buttoning my blouse now. "You said you trust me. That means you have to trust that I know what I'm doing."

"But—" He frowns, as if trying to find a hole in my logic.

Unfortunately for both of us, there isn't one. If there was, I would have found it already. My five-year plan—tucked securely into the briefcase that I'd dropped just inside his door a half hour ago—is quietly cheering me on.

"Eat some Tex-Mex. Rest up. Beat Tampa. You and I will talk soon."

"How soon?" he asks, still deliciously naked. I can't make eye contact with his abs, or I'll lose my resolve. Lust is fun, but it isn't everything. And this man is not in a place to love me.

"Soon," I lie. "Soonish." I give him a little wave, and then I make my exit.

SIXTEEN

That's a Lot of Muscle

BESS

FOR THE NEXT FORTY-EIGHT HOURS, the decision feels like a good one. In the first place, Tank and the rest of the Bruisers eke out a win against Tampa. So that's progress.

And I manage to get some much-needed distance from him. When Tank texts me a photo of himself in front of a bar called The Tank, I don't engage. I don't call him or flirt, even though I want to.

It's better to have a few heart pangs now than a bigger heartbreak later, right?

To put myself in the right mindset, I do some background research on Tank's career. His contract negotiation is still over a year away, which means that I can leave him in Henry's hands for a while longer.

When the time comes—and if Henry is out of the picture—I'll get Tank a good deal. I know Brooklyn's management team better than most. And I've already negotiated with them for an over-thirty player who's a challenge to the salary cap.

Speaking of Henry, I also do some frightening research on late-stage heart failure. The prevalent symptoms—besides shortness of breath—are pain and swelling. The man needs distraction, so I wander through Books are Magic in Cobble Hill and choose some titles that I think he'll appreciate. He likes thrillers and action. His books require at least one ugly plot twist and one major explosion. Bonus points if someone has to fly a helicopter without any training.

It soothes me to send Henry a gift. The man has more money than God and can buy his own books, but I want him to know that I'm thinking about him.

Meanwhile, I'm still catching up on all the little details that went astray while I took my long vacation. I take a day trip to see a young player who's just been traded to Pittsburgh. And while I'm on the train, I write up a proposal for an endorsement deal. I'm trying to get a national chain of chicken joints—called Chickie's—to sponsor some female hockey players.

The women are pro-bono clients, basically. There's so little money in women's hockey that I don't charge them to look over their paltry employment contracts. I only take a cut on whatever endorsement money I can win for them. Honestly, it would be more profitable to hunt for lost cash in the pockets of my jeans.

But I keep at it anyway. Raising the visibility of women's hockey is my hobby and my mission. Someday I'm going to make a few of these women rich. I don't know how, but it's going to happen. I'll probably be a hundred and one years old by then, but...

That makes me think about people who are a hundred and one, and how Henry isn't going to make it that long. And now I'm crying in the Quiet Car of the Amtrak train.

It's eight o'clock by the time I get back to Brooklyn. I drop my briefcase in my office, grab a gift bag that I've left waiting on my office chair, and head across the street. "Hello, Miguel!" I tell the doorman. "I'm here to see Delilah."

"Is it gonna be weird to see the apartment?" he asks. Delilah's new place used to be my brother's.

"I'm sure it looks completely different already."

"You'd be right," he says, waving me toward the elevator. "Go on up. The pizzas just got here."

"Yesssss." I give a fist pump and head for the shiny elevators.

When I reach the third floor, the hallway is full of cardboard moving boxes, plus Delilah's bodyguard. "Hi, Avivit," I say, giving her a wave. "I heard the pizza just got here."

She nods and then steps aside so I can reach the apartment door. Avivit is a woman of few words.

"Should I bring you a slice?"

"No, thank you. I don't eat when I'm on duty." She gives me a tiny smile.

"You know there's a dozen athletes literally standing between Delilah and trouble?" I pause, my hand on the door.

"That's a lot of muscle," she says. "But it's what's up here that counts." She points at her head, as her dark eyes dance.

"You make a very good point." And since my job is literally to prevent athletes from doing anything stupid, I should already know this.

When I step inside my brother's old apartment, the place is hardly recognizable. The living room has been furnished with sofas and chairs in bright, stylish colors.

And when I glance into the second bedroom, the weight bench and treadmill are long gone. They're being replaced by—

"Is that a giant telephone booth?" I ask the tangle of men who are trying to assemble it.

Several heads swivel in my direction. "It's a recording booth." Delilah pops out from behind a bright red panel. "It shipped in pieces."

"Lots of pieces," Castro says.

"Confusing pieces," Silas adds.

"Guys, let's eat pizza," Delilah says. "Maybe this will seem simpler after you eat."

Grumbling, the men lay down the various panels and boards they're holding. And to my surprise, Tank is one of those men.

My mouth flops open. I wasn't expecting to find him here, and I hadn't really prepared myself for the inevitable moment when I'd run into him again.

He gives me a quick wink. It takes me a second to realize that I'm blocking his way out of the room. I make an awkward sideways hop so he can get to the pizza boxes in the kitchen.

The other hockey players file past me, but my focus stays on

Tank. The way he's pushed the sleeves of his long-sleeved T-shirt up onto his forearms. The way he tilts his head to listen to Georgia as she hands him a plate. And the way he fills out a pair of jeans.

All hockey players have great asses. Hockey butts are muscular. That's why my clients all have to special-order their trousers.

Tank, though. One glance at him and I feel all stirred up inside. It's not just the muscles, either. It's the whole guy. And now it's hitting me that if I want to represent him someday, I'll have to wrestle everything I feel for him into submission and smother it with a pillow.

Or at least fake it really, really well.

And there's nobody to blame. I have feelings for a guy who can't return them. Lots of feelings. He's *that* guy to me—the bright, shiny goal that's just out of reach. The one that got away.

"Beer?" Delilah asks me. "Pizza?"

"Sure," I say, dragging my attention away from Tank. "But first, this is for you. Welcome to Brooklyn." I hand her my gift bag.

"Oh! You shouldn't have."

"Of course I should." I give her a quick hug. Silas is my client, and I see these two lovebirds all the time. And I love Delilah. She's literally a rock star, and yet she's one of the most modest, normal people I've ever met. "Open it. You know you want to."

She flashes me a smile and then pushes the tissue paper out of the way to pull a throw pillow out of the bag. "Oh, pretty! I love it! And now I won't get lost." She's looking at the pillow's front—it depicts a very tasteful map of Brooklyn.

"Turn it over."

She flips the pillow and then laughs. Because the reverse says, *Brooklyn: Fuggedaboutit.* "This is priceless. Thank you!"

"It's my pleasure."

"I thought you hated shopping."

"I hate it less when it's for other people."

Delilah smiles and shakes her head, like she can't figure me out. But it's true. Buying gifts for clients is easy. Shopping for myself always feels like a big commitment. It's the same with giving out advice. Figuring out someone else's bullshit is always easier than figuring out my own.

The rock star gives me another hug and then runs off to decide which of her new pieces of furniture deserves the pillow.

"Hey, boss. Want a slice?" Eric Bayer appears at my side.

"Maybe later," I tell my business partner. "Did you just come in?"

"They sent me out to grab some more beer at the store." He points at a stack of sixpacks. "Want one?"

"Sure," I say with a sigh. "I'd love one."

"Rough day?" He leads me to the windows and grabs a beer off one of the wide sills.

"I'm fine," I say quickly. "The train was quiet. I got that proposal done. Anything happen while I was gone?"

He opens a beer and hands it to me. "I got a call that was a little weird. I was hoping you'd be here tonight so I could tell you about it."

"A call?" I turn my body a few degrees so that I can't possibly stare at Tank. "From who?"

"There's this kid on a juniors team in Saskatchewan—a center with great foot speed and gaudy stats. He might go first round in the draft."

"Saskatchewan." I pull the name up from the depths of my memory. "Oistrok?"

"Damn." Eric blinks. "Good memory. That's the kid. He's a client of Henry Kassman's."

My heart aches a little just at the mention of Henry's name. "Yeah?"

"That's the weird thing. This kid called to ask me to represent him. Furthermore, he said it was Kassman's idea. What do you make of that?"

I can't help it. My eyes fill immediately with tears.

"Whoa, boss." Eric throws an arm around me. "What's wrong?"

"Henry is ill." I sniffle, swiping at my eyes. "It's serious. And I'm afraid we're going to get more of those calls. He's slowly shutting down his shop."

"Oh, hell." Eric grabs a napkin from a nearby coffee table and hands it to me. "I'm sorry. I know you two are close."

"I only found out this week." I blow my nose into the napkin. "Eric, you're going to get some clients. Be ready."

"Christ." He swigs his beer. "That's not how I wanted to recruit players."

"No kidding. But Henry feels strongly about his athletes having exactly the person they need. He wouldn't send you anyone if he didn't think it was a good fit."

"I barely know Henry Kassman," Eric points out. "I met him once before Clove died."

"Oh, but he knows me." I wave a dismissive hand. "And I talked you up the other day when I went to see him. I was so upset by how ill he looked that I couldn't shut up. Besides, he loves gossip. So I was telling him all the news from Brooklyn."

"Okay." Eric frowns. "Of course I'll help out this kid from Saskatoon."

"Where did you leave it with him?"

"First, I just asked to hear his story. I thought if I got him talking, the call might make more sense. It didn't, but I got to hear all about juniors hockey. The kid is smart. He's not very well-spoken, but he has a mature view of his own game."

"Well, that's something."

"Yeah, it's a start. I said I'd call him back tomorrow."

"Send him a contract in the morning. And then get right on a plane to go see him."

"Wow, okay. Of course." He sighs. "Have some pizza, Bess. Come on. Hang in there."

But Tank is standing near all the pizza, and I'm not even hungry. I just feel wrecked inside. My mentor is going to die before his time, and I'm hung up on a man I can't have.

I don't want Eric to know. I don't want *anyone* to know. I'm starting to realize that it's not really about my career. It's about my heart. If nobody knows how I feel, it might hurt less while I struggle to get over him.

And I have to get over him. It's the only thing to do.

SEVENTEEN

We Tried

TANK

I BITE into an excellent slice of pepperoni pizza and try not to stare at Bess. It isn't easy. She's giving me the brushoff this week, and I don't like it.

It's not like I don't understand where she's coming from. My life is a train wreck. If you look up "bitter man" in the dictionary, you'll probably find my picture.

But something special happens when we spend time together. I forget to be that angry guy. At first I thought it was just the sex. And lord knows my rusty libido needed a kick-start.

There's more to it, though. Bess is special. She has a lively energy that I didn't appreciate when we were younger. Or maybe I did, even if I never managed to articulate it. I remember heading back to New York after a road trip, counting the minutes until the plane touched down so I could flag a taxi and sprint to her little studio apartment in Midtown. Those memories are faded with time, and probably tinged with nostalgia for a moment in my life when everything was still on an upward trajectory.

But thirty-year-old Bess is even more interesting to me. I watch her laughing with Delilah, and then chatting with Eric. And I want to cross the room and kiss her hello. I want to hear whatever she's saying, because it's probably something sharp and funny.

I feel the pull. It's not just my libido that Bess has woken up. I feel her presence in the empty hollow in the center of my chest. Right where my heart is supposed to be.

As I watch, Bess's face crumples, and Eric puts his arm around her. And just like that, my appetite is *gone*. Bess looks so sad that I have to fight the impulse to walk over there and pull her into my arms.

She wouldn't want me to, though. *Fuck*.

I'm not the only one who notices. A worried frown crosses Castro's face. A minute or two later, he sets down his pizza to walk over to Bess and give her a one-armed hug. She smiles at him and then wipes her eyes one more time.

"Who is it?" Castro asks loudly. Then he starts to shadow box like a goofball. "I'll fuck him up, Bess. I mean, I lose every fight I've ever gotten into. But it's the thought that counts, right?"

She laughs. "Don't hurt your hands, fool. There's nobody who needs an ass-kicking, anyway. Thank the lord."

"You just let me know. I'll show him who's boss. I got the moves." Castro lifts an arm, strikes a ridiculous pose, and flexes his biceps until Bess laughs again.

Well, fine. If the kid tries to cheer up Bess when she's sad, I guess he can't be that bad.

I pick up my slice of pizza and try to catch Bess's eye. Does it make me an asshole to say I'm positive Bess is having as much trouble ignoring me as I am ignoring her?

"There's more pizza," Delilah says to me, opening another box. "Thanks for coming to help tonight. I've never furnished a home before. It's fun, but it's a lot of work."

"No kidding," I agree, dragging my attention off Bess. "If I ever find an apartment in Brooklyn, I'm going to hire somebody to buy everything for me."

"There's another solution," Patrick O'Doul says, grabbing a slice out of the new box. "I bought my apartment from two guys — a married couple. They were starting over on the West Coast, so I bought all their stuff. All the coffee cups, the towels, the butter dish. Everything."

"But they had *excellent* taste," Delilah points out. "Like, *Architectural Digest* taste. That's just lucky."

O'Doul looks at me and shrugs, as if to say, *I didn't even notice*.

I'm warming up to these guys, little by little. O'Doul seems like a solid enough captain. He teases his troops sometimes, but I haven't heard him be cruel to anyone. Not like Palacio was.

I guess there's one thing I don't miss about Texas.

"What kinda beer is this, anyway?" O'Doul asks, inspecting the six-pack I'd brought.

"What do you mean? It's Shiner Bock. Just one of the best beers in Texas."

"Texas," he says slowly, like the word doesn't feel right in his mouth.

"Dude, I know you hate Dallas. But don't hate on my excellent beer. Try one." I pull a bottle out of the pack and thrust it at O'Doul.

"Thanks, man." He gives me a serious nod. This is how I know I'm not one of the crew yet. He doesn't tease me. Until they're ragging on your taste in beer, the pattern on your tie, and your underwear-modeling career, you aren't really one of the team.

When O'Doul looks at me, he still sees a fight we had in 2017. I'd bet any amount of money on it. I'll bet I know which one, too — because he didn't win. There's no getting around it. I just have to ride out the awkwardness until these guys notice we're wearing the same jersey now.

"Hey, Mark?" Georgia reaches past me and plucks a slice of pepperoni out of the box. "Can I have a minute of your time?"

"Of course."

She beckons to me, and I follow her out of the kitchen area and into an alcove that has nothing in it except for some empty book-shelves hung on the brick walls.

"This building is killer," I say, trying not to sound jealous.

"Isn't it? Leo and I rent our place. But we love it here. Our apartment isn't this big, though." She wipes her mouth with a napkin. "Listen, I'm sorry to ask. But I'm getting a few questions from the media, and I wanted to check in with you."

"Questions about… My shitty performance against Philly? Or my divorce?"

She flinches. "That second thing. And it's only a couple more bloggers asking the same questions that Miranda did. We'd never comment on your marriage, unless you asked me to handle something. But I just wanted to ask you if there's anything I should know."

"So you want to know if any of the rumors are true?" It comes out sounding belligerent, which isn't really fair. Unlike some of the other people prying into my life, it's actually Georgia's job to ask if I'm going to create drama for the team.

She studies me with kind eyes. "I'm sorry to even ask, Mark. But if you had anything to tell me, I would hold it in the strictest of confidences."

"It's true that I punched my teammate. But there won't be any bombshells with regard to my divorce. It will be final soon, anyway. Before Halloween."

"Thank you for telling me," she says quietly. "That's pretty fast. Isn't it?" She winces. "I'm sorry. I don't know much about divorce."

"Me neither. But, yeah, I guess it is. My agent made me get a prenup all those years ago. So there's nothing to haggle over."

"And you don't have kids," she adds.

"Right," I say a little too quickly. "We don't even have a fucking dog."

"Okay. I'm sorry to pry," she says.

"No, I get it," I grumble. "Who's trying to kick up a story, anyway? And why now?"

"It's, uh, some Dallas blog. Nobody important."

I pull out my phone anyway. "Lone Star Hockey?"

"Tank." She puts a hand over the screen of my phone. "Don't read it."

"Why not? What could they possibly say about me?"

"It's not *you* they're writing about," she says quietly.

Wait. What? It takes a second until I understand. "They wrote something about Jordanna? Why?"

"It's nothing. There's photos of her dancing with someone at a team benefit."

A bitter laugh escapes me. "Really? At a hockey event?" I'd assumed she'd be happy to be free of the team. Then again, she's on the board of a children's charity that does an annual event with the team in September. "Whatever," I grumble. "She went with a date to some party. It isn't another player, right?"

Georgia shakes her head sadly. "Just some dude in a suit. They were speculating on who it was, and why she didn't follow you to New York."

I run my hands through my hair and sigh. "Yeah, okay. Thanks for telling me."

"You need anything, you come and find me, okay?" she says.

"Thanks." I stay in the alcove after she leaves. And I pull out my phone and head for that goddamn blog.

Sure enough, there's Jordanna dancing with some guy in a bow tie. He's looking at my ex-wife like he has big plans for her. But Jordanna looks mildly uncomfortable, if I'm honest. Like she can't quite fake it, and she's not sure she cares.

I squint for a few moments at a great photo of my ex-wife—her hand is on that guy's shoulder, and she looks pretty in a violet-colored dress—and I feel...nothing. It's as if every emotion I had for her got used up or dried out, until there was nothing left but dust.

And I'll bet she'd say the same about me. If our marriage had a tombstone, it would read, *We tried*. And if Jordanna has the energy to put on a ball gown and dance with some guy, there's really no reason why she shouldn't.

I leave the alcove to hunt down another slice of pizza.

After we eat, the guys take another crack at putting together Delilah's home recording studio. "Now that I'm actually reading the directions, I think we can figure this out," Silas says.

"Didn't I just suggest that a few minutes ago?" Bess asks, giving him a playful slap on the back of the head.

"Hush," Castro says. "It's hard for a man to admit he needs to read the instructions."

"Especially when he's naturally good with his hands," Silas says, smirking.

"TMI," Georgia says. "Somebody put me to work. Which piece goes on next?"

"All of them," O'Doul says, reading over Silas's shoulder. "But we need somebody inside this thing, applying pressure to the frame while we all screw in the panels."

"I'll do that," I volunteer, stepping into the center of the frame. "You guys can trap me inside where I won't be able to hear you mock my Texas beer."

Silas laughs. "Fine. Actually, we need two people, one to lean on each side."

"Bess will help," I say before anyone else gets a chance to speak up. "She's just standing there drinking a non-Texas beer."

She gives me a grumpy look. But then she puts down her beer and steps into the sound booth with me.

"Maybe we need one of these for the office," Bayer quips, a screwdriver in his hand. "Bess needs privacy for when she's dropping the hammer on the GMs during contract renegotiations."

"Good call." Bess turns her back to me, while O'Doul and Castro each lift a panel into place.

"I'll get the last one," the rookie Anton says. "Bess, if you use your tuchus to brace the end-piece, you can use a hand for each panel."

"Good idea," she says. "This backside should be good for something."

It's a reflex when I open my mouth to make a joke. Because I have quite a few uses for Bess's ass. But her glare silences me just in time.

One by one, the other players lift all six panels into place. As Silas fits the last panel in snugly, I'm closed inside the space with Bess. And it is quiet. I can't hear any voices outside.

"Hi," I whisper.

"Hi," she whispers back.

"Do you think this thing is actually soundproof? Because it might be the only way I can get you to talk to me."

"I'm sorry," she says in a low voice. "I shouldn't have come here tonight. You're bonding with your teammates."

"Don't be silly. You can crash my party any day, sweetheart.

But now I gotta know if they can hear us. Hey Castro!" I shout, because I can see him through the little window.

The young forward doesn't look up from his screwdriver.

"All right," I say. "We have privacy unless he's faking. Quick—tell me some team secrets."

Bess smiles in spite of herself. "Fine. On the night you get your first goal for Brooklyn, don't let them convince you that everyone celebrates by getting the Brooklyn Bridge tattooed on his ass."

I snort. "Like anyone would fall for that."

"I think Anton got one." Then she raises her voice. "But it's okay, you sweet summer child!" She waves at the young D-man through the window. "Chicks dig tattoos!"

Anton waves back, looking unconcerned.

"So this *is* soundproof," I say. "You can talk to me for real now. I know I'm your dirty little secret. But I'm fine with that. Because at least I like dirty secrets."

"Tank," she says with a sigh. "We can't be each other's dirty secret. I would never date a client."

"This again?" I argue, bracing one of the panels a little more firmly as someone screws it into the stud. "I didn't understand the deal I was making when I asked you to be my agent. I need to renegotiate our contract."

"No." She lifts her chin defiantly.

"But I'm your Kryptonite," I point out. "You should be fainting right now. I could carry you out of here and back to my hotel room."

Bess lifts her eyes to the ceiling. "That's not happening, stud. And I hope nobody can read lips."

"Let's see if they can." I turn my face a couple of degrees, so that I'm framed in the window. "Let's get naked again and have lots and lots of sex."

Since Bess's hands are busy bracing the panels, she has to resort to kicking me gently in the shin. "Stop that. It won't work, anyway."

"It's not nice to kick your client."

"That wasn't a real kick," she says, her bright eyes full of fire. "If I kicked you for real, you'd be crying right now."

"Uh-huh." My face cracks into a smile, which is something that only happens when Bess is nearby. I don't think I smiled for three months before she turned up. "But what are you going to do about it?"

"About what?" she asks.

"About *us*." I give her a hot glance. "You think you can just ignore me forever? I don't think I'm that good an actor."

"Tank," she says gently. "We're in a different place in life, you and me. I can't be your rebound girl. The sex is great—"

"*Amazing* is the word I'd choose," I break in. "And please don't feel guilty about us just because I'm a player. If you feel guilty, then I'll have to feel guilty. And I don't want to feel guilty because I really like spending time with you."

"It's not just the professional issues." She shakes her head. "I don't know what to think about the little...habit we're developing. You're on the rebound. You aren't thinking with your *brain*, Tank. Hell—you don't even use condoms."

Oh Jesus. Bess must think I'm an idiot. "Okay. Hold up. I'm really sorry about the condom thing."

"I'm covered, Tank. I am not going to get pregnant. But you're not in a place to—"

That's when Silas suddenly opens the door to the booth. "You kids okay in here?" he asks. "I think we've got it pretty tight now."

"Uh, great," I mumble, stepping out of the booth. Bess follows me, her eyes full of unresolved tension.

We need to finish our conversation, but obviously we'll need to do it somewhere else.

"Wow, I can't believe it's done!" Delilah cries, taking in the finished booth. "It looks amazing!"

"Take it for a trial run, honey," Silas says. "Grab your electric guitar and let 'er rip."

Delilah runs out of the room, coming back a few moments later with a guitar and a little amp. "I'm going to keep turning up the volume. Can you wave at me when you can hear the guitar?"

"Sure, babe." Silas plugs in her amp and then leaves the booth, closing her in there.

Delilah's smile shines through the window as she tunes up her guitar. *Can you hear this?* she mouths.

We all shake our heads. She's playing the guitar in earnest now.

"This is the worst concert ever," Georgia complains. "She's right there and I can't hear a thing."

Finally Delilah reaches a volume whereby we can hear it faintly outside the booth, and Silas waves with two hands to tell her.

"Wow," the singer says, opening the door. "I thought I was going to break my eardrums before you could hear it."

"Now play it out here," Georgia demands. "Please?"

"I thought we were headed to the wine bar?" Delilah says. "I promised to buy drinks."

"One song," Bayer demands.

"Okay, but I don't want to piss off the neighbors on the first day." She turns the volume down on her amp.

"But we *are* the neighbors," Castro reminds her. "I'd rather hear you play it live, then listen to Silas sing it in the shower."

"I'm still gonna sing it," the young goalie says. "Extra loud for you, homeboy." And then he beams as his girlfriend plays the opening chords to a song I don't know.

When I sneak a glance at Bess, she's smiling at the two of them with a look of pure delight on her face. And for a split second, I forget about all the bullshit in my life. My creaky heart warms up at the sight of Bess's smile.

She's under my skin, I realize with a start. Not that it's a welcome feeling. My shitty marriage had me feeling like I got dumped off a cliff. But Bess makes me want to get up and hike back to the top of the mountain.

If only Bess would let me.

Delilah starts singing. And it's a love song. She's got a handful of rapt hockey players tapping their feet and smiling.

Even I am not immune to its joys.

EIGHTEEN

They Don't Call Him the Tank for Nothing

BESS

I SHOULDN'T HAVE COME out to the wine bar. I'm not much of a drinker, but here I am on a barstool in the midst of happy couples, two glasses of chardonnay in and feeling pleasantly tipsy.

Tank was right. It's not easy to ignore him. One glass of wine made it tricky. Two makes it impossible. He's at the other end of the bar, talking to Eric, looking sexy as hell.

That settles it. I shouldn't drink when he and I are in the same zip code. It's hard enough to stay away from him when I'm sober.

"Bess, don't you think my face would look good in a shaving ad?" Anton Bayer asks, stroking his jaw. He yells down the bar to his cousin. "Hey, Eric! Why haven't you gotten me any endorsements, yet?"

Eric stops talking to Tank only long enough to fire back with: "Why haven't you scored any goals this year yet?"

Anton scowls and turns to me. "Bess, my agent is a hard-ass. I don't think he should be Employee of the Month anymore."

"I pay him extra for being a hard-ass," I say as I swirl the pretty wine in my glass. Wine is my best friend. If wine could get me pregnant, I'd marry it.

"Why don't hockey players get that many endorsements?" Castro asks. "Serious question. I mean—look at all the money they pay golfers and basketball stars. Hockey players are, like, so much hotter than that."

Inevitably, my eyes flick down the bar toward Tank, because Castro speaks the truth. But he's also missing the point. Even when I'm tipsy, I still know my sports business. "Hotness doesn't sell shoes, Castro. A kid can watch LeBron James win a game in his Nikes. And then he can wear those *same* shoes to school the next day. I don't see anyone walking around high school in skates."

"You would in Canada," Anton argues. "Totally normal."

"Uh-huh," I say, because we all have our own version of normal. "And how large is the population of Canada relative to the US?"

"Half the size?" he guesses.

"Eleven percent," I say, bursting his bubble. "That also explains the basketball phenomenon."

"But how do you explain golf?" Castro asks. "It's the least sexy sport in the world. And nobody wears golf shoes to high school."

"There are sixty million golfers around the world," I point out. "They buy five billion dollars' worth of equipment every year. Golf enthusiasts are four times as wealthy as average earners. And golf is growing by double digits in places like India and China."

"But golf doesn't have this face," Anton argues. He frames his admittedly handsome mug with his hands. "Maybe I should take up golf. Golf needs me."

"They do, buddy." I take another gulp of wine and wonder what Eric and Tank are discussing down there. And then Eric catches my eye and beckons.

Okay. I'll bite. Like I even need a reason to move closer to Tank. I'm so predictable. "S'cuse me, guys," I say, sliding off the barstool. I must look a little wobbly because Castro catches me and then straightens the angle of my wine glass. "Easy there, Bessie."

"I'm good," I insist, and then walk carefully towards Eric and the man with whom I'm trying not to have a fraught and confusing sexual relationship. "Hi, guys. What's shaking?"

Eric folds his arms across his chest and glances at the man next to him. The one who always makes my panties fall off. "Tank is seeking new representation."

"I'd heard that," I say slowly.

"He wants, uh…" Eric looks uncharacteristically uncomfortable. "He's asked me to represent him. Eventually. When Henry is no longer able."

"*Really.*" I glare at Tank, because this is a conversation we ought to be having in private. At least he has the good sense to look sheepish. "Can I speak to you for a moment, Mr. Tankiewicz?"

"Yes, ma'am," he says.

"Outside," I snap. I hand my wine glass to Eric and leave the bar. Anger makes me feel less tipsy. I have no trouble marching outside where I round the corner of the building to find a small vacant lot. I wait. Fuming.

Tank follows me, because he's not a stupid man.

Immediately, I light into him. "What the hell, Tank? Are you trying to do an end-run around me? That's some heavy-handed bullshit right there. I'm not twenty-one anymore. You can't manipulate me with a few kisses."

"Manipulate you?" he roars. "That's the pot calling out the kettle. You're the one who agreed to represent me just so you didn't have to make any tough choices about this thing we have." He waves a hand in the air between us.

"This *thing*?" I snort.

"Maybe you don't like my terminology." He puts one of his delicious arms up on the brick wall and looks me up and down, a possessive glint in his eye. And *goddamn it* why does that light me up? "But you sure as hell like me."

And then, just to prove the point, the asshole kisses me. It's a hot, angry kiss that curls my toes.

"Even if you're not willing to say so," he says at close range. "Even if it's unexpected." He kisses me *again*. "And even if it fucks up your five-year plan."

"Do *not* roll your eyes at my five-year plan." I put a hand on his chest and push. They don't call him the Tank for nothing. He doesn't budge.

"Yeah, guess what? Life grabbed my five-year plan, ripped it right down the center, threw both halves in my face. Then I went to a party in Brooklyn and found you. And you could barely string two sentences together because you were too busy remembering how amazing it is when we're alone together."

The next kiss doesn't even surprise me. He takes my mouth with arrogance and confidence and proves his point so well that I feel short on oxygen.

"You make me feel alive. You always did. You're the best thing about Brooklyn, Bess. The *only* thing I care about here. And I'll be damned if I let a little thing like agency representation stand in the way."

"But—" I pant. My brain is foggy. "You're—" I bite off my words, because I'm not ready to tell him the whole truth. *You're so dangerous to me.* Dangerous not just to my job, but to my stupid heart.

"Yeah." He chuckles. "I'm not that good at explaining it, either. But what we have is rare. The timing sucks. It's inconvenient. But I won't let you pretend like it's nothing. If you really can't stomach the idea of seeing me, at least have the guts to tell me to my face. Is it because you think I'm a cheater? You believe the gossip?"

"No." I give my head a firm shake. "Not that you ever set anyone straight on the gossip front."

"The world is not entitled to an accounting of my pain. And you don't owe the world an explanation, either. Are you ducking us because of your job? You think credibility is going to be a big problem?"

"Yes." *Among other things.*

"Well, how's that working for you?" He kisses me again. And the answer is obvious when I grip his shirt so that he won't stop. "Yeah, I thought so. That's why we need Eric as a buffer. Admit it. It's a great idea."

I growl instead. "You could have discussed it with me first."

"True." He shrugs. "But I wanted to run it past him first, in case he hates me, too."

"He wouldn't," I admit. Grudgingly.

"Well, good. Because I need you in my life. I want the whole Bess package, okay? You're the best in the business. So that means Eric will be, too. And I can't stay away from you. I don't even want to try. Maybe you're embarrassed to be seen with a bitter, rebounding hockey player with anger issues and a shitty reputation. You probably deserve better. But I'm a greedy asshole. And I meant it when I said you're the best thing to happen to me in a long time."

Oh dear. That little speech makes my inner Cinderella dust off her rags and preen. She really likes the sound of that.

And just as I'm trying to shove her back into the cupboard, a certain hot, ripped, irritating hockey player kisses me again. He steps into my space and pushes me up against the brick wall. All my senses are assaulted by the firm press of his body against mine, and by the taste of rich red wine and hungry man. He weaves his fingers into my hair and tilts my head to seal the deal.

Damn him. It's the best kind of kiss—breath-stealing and frustrating in a hundred wonderful ways. *I can't stay away from you,* he'd said. *I don't even want to try.*

We have that in common, then. Because I'm clinging to his shirt now and kissing him back.

Until someone clears his throat. Loudly.

We try to break apart, but it takes a moment, because neither of us is ready. Tank's kisses have melted my brain. And it's not like I really want to step back and squint at Eric, who is standing on the sidewalk looking amused.

"Eric..." I try. Words fail me. Some boss I am.

He waves a hand like I shouldn't bother. "I get it. Cone of silence. Your employee of the month already spotted you guys in a taxi together after Nate and Becca's party. You're not that stealthy. But Castro and Silas are inside wondering why you stormed out looking mad. So I promised I'd check on you."

Eric knew? For some reason that makes my face redden even more. "Thank you. I, uh, don't really date players."

"Except one," Tank says unhelpfully. Then he laughs.

"One mistake in nine years," I correct.

"At this point does it really still count as one?" he asks.

I just sigh.

"You kids figure it out," Eric says, turning back toward the corner of the building.

"Bess," Tank asks. "Will you let Eric represent me?"

Eric pauses to hear my answer.

"Yes." I sigh. "Sure. It's the right idea." Because my way was never going to work.

Someday Tank is going to break my heart, and if Eric is his agent, I won't have to sit across a conference room table and discuss contract clauses and pretend I'm not dying inside. He'll be Eric's problem instead. And I'll still get a cut.

"Awesome!" Tank pumps his fist. "I'm your second client after Baby Bayer, right?"

"Depends who signs first—you or the kid from Saskatchewan." Eric winks. "I'm gonna go finish my wine now, and also invent some reason why you two need to stand out here in a vacant lot." He's gone a second later.

Tank chuckles. "See? He doesn't care that we were just trying to eat each other's faces."

"I noticed that."

"Then why do you still sound grumpy?" Tank's eyes are twinkling.

"It's just a habit at this point." I can hear my five-year plan weeping. Spending time with Tank means forcing myself not to think about the future.

He leans in and kisses the corner of my mouth. "We have fun, Bess. Let's go home and have some more of it together. It doesn't have to be a life-changing kind of thing."

"Right," I whisper, looking into his clear green eyes. *That's the whole problem.* "I like your brand of fun." *But please don't break my heart.*

"My place or yours," he whispers. "We're going on a road trip tomorrow. I'm gonna need some quality time with you first."

"Yours," I say, still irritated at myself. My Tank moratorium lasted all of two days.

He takes my hand, threading our fingers. "Any reason we can't go now? Anyone you need to say goodbye to?"

"No." I shake my head. The press of his palm against mine makes me unreasonably happy.

"Let's get ice cream on the pier. It's on the way."

I follow him toward the water, pretending for a little while that fairytales are real.

NINETEEN

From: The Puckraker's Blog

"Tankiewicz Finds the Net for Brooklyn"

BREAKING his longest scoring drought—twelve games—Tankiewicz finally puts the biscuit in the basket for Brooklyn. With goals from Trevi as well as Drake, Brooklyn took the game over Buffalo, 3-1.

It's progress. But Tankiewicz had better make a whole lot more of it if he expects to put down roots in Brooklyn.

And it won't be long until the showdown in Dallas. Will old Sure Shot be ready in time?

Tank: Did you SEE that beautiful goal???

Bess: Yes baby. That's why I sent you a text last night that said NICE GOAL BABY in shouty caps. Didn't it come through?

Tank: It came through. But I just wanted to talk about it some more. Because did you SEE that beautiful goal? When Castro accidentally passed to nowhere but I got my stick on it anyway? And before you could say TANK IS A STUD, I put it in?

Bess: Gorgeous goal, hot stuff! I may have spilled my beer I was so excited.

Tank: Where did you spill it?

Bess: All over my naked breasts.

Tank: Really?

Bess: No. But the purpose of this conversation is stroking your ego, right? So I thought I'd just roll with it.

Tank: LOL! I'll take it.

Bess: :)

Tank: You were right, by the way. After the game, Castro told me I had to get the Brooklyn Bridge tattooed across my ass.

Bess: Well that's a good sign. If they're pranking you it means they like you now.

Tank: I got a goal. They like that at least.

Bess: What did you tell Castro about the tattoo?

Tank: I said, sure, buddy!

Tank: And, get this, I told him that if we connect on ten goals this season—in either direction—not only will I put the bridge on one ass cheek, I'll put his face on the other.

Bess: OMG. What did he say to that?

Tank: "Let's not get carried away." Honestly he looked terrified, which was the point. I told him I was just crazy enough to do it. And then I wondered aloud what the blogs would write about that.

Bess: You are an evil man.

Tank: Never bullshit a bullshitter. But enough about me. Let's talk about you. Specifically, I need to know if you're naked right now. Please say yes.

Bess: I'm sitting in my office waiting for a conference call. So that would be no.

Tank: Lie to me, baby! I miss you.

Bess: There's no need to lie. The next time we're in the same zip code again, you can make your dreams come true.

Tank: Now there's a plan I can get behind. Literally.

Bess: Indeed. Got to go now! Call starts in two minutes.

Tank: One more thing, hot stuff. Have you seen Henry again? I keep leaving voicemails, asking when I can visit. He texts me back, but I can't get a phone call. I just want to talk to the old codger.

Bess: Same. I sent him a present but when I asked to visit he shot me down. Now go beat Florida.

Tank: Maybe you should send me a few motivational photographs to improve my game.

Bess: A good workout followed by a protein drink and then a nap would improve it more.

Tank: Says you.

Bess: I am a professional. I know things. Get some rest! I'll be watching tonight.

TWENTY

A Day Late and a Dollar Short

TANK

November

SLOWLY, I inch toward greatness. I grab an assist in our game against Chicago. And then another goal a week later.

But it's a slog. And what's worse? It's a *job*. I used to play hockey because I loved it and couldn't imagine doing anything else.

I guess I still can't imagine doing anything else. I'm too deep inside my own head, though. And on the nights when I can't see Bess, I'm lonely.

As autumn drags on, I keep asking Henry Kassman when I can visit or at least call. He keeps saying, "Soon, but not today." And I try not to care.

Then, on an unseasonably warm weekday, my phone rings as I'm walking away from a restaurant where I'd eaten a late lunch. When I answer, there he is. *Finally.*

"Tankiewicz," Henry growls into my ear. "How are you, boy?"

I stop in my tracks on the sidewalk so I can listen a little more carefully. I didn't know how much I needed to hear this man's voice. "I'm okay, Henry. I'm doing fine for a guy whose life is still blowing up all over the place."

"How was practice today?" he asks, taking a wheezy breath in between the words. The sound of it makes my chest tighten in sympathy.

"Fine," I say quickly, wondering if he's okay to talk on the phone.

"Fine," he echoes. "Don't give me that bullshit. Tell me the truth."

I smile in spite of myself. "Practice? It was mediocre in parts and dreadful in others. Coach is still yelling at guys who can't adapt to my style of play. And when I try to adapt to theirs, Coach yells at me instead."

Kassman laughs, as if I've said something funny. "It's early in the season, Tank." He takes another audibly difficult breath. "I say this every year, because you're always in need of hearing it. But you still have time."

I make a grumpy noise, because I don't really believe him. Every frustrated look on the coach's face feels like another nail in my coffin. I need to impress that man or I'm going to be traded again.

"Got something for you," Kassman wheezes. "Wasn't sure how to put this, because I've never given a man his divorce decree before. But your papers are here and executed."

Whoa. "It's done?"

"Done," he says.

"I don't have to sign?"

"Nope. The judge signed, and that's that. I'm gonna send 'em to you by courier I guess."

"Nah—keep them," I say quickly. "You can give them to me when you let me visit."

"I'm so sorry, kid," he says quietly.

"Don't be. I'm fine."

"I know you are. But nobody enjoys failure. I have my own divorce to prove it. And it's not easy to start over in a new city alone. I'll bet the gossip is a drag."

I grunt, because he's right. This very morning I'd seen another rumor of my infidelity on Twitter, of all places. "People say I cheated."

"People are *idiots*." Henry's voice sounds stronger all of a sudden. "They don't know you. Just remember that. They don't know Mark Tankiewicz at all. Say it."

"They don't know me at all," I repeat. And he's right. It helps to say it out loud. "Who writes shit on Twitter about people they've never met? Who has the goddamned time to spend on that?"

"Assholes," he says firmly. "Who needs 'em."

"Not me," I say, feeling better already.

"You find an apartment yet?"

"No." I laugh. "I haven't even tried. The new hotel your assistant found for me is so nice. I may never leave."

"Find a place, Tank. Try to make New York your home."

As if that would even be possible. The only time I feel like myself is when I'm hanging out with Bess and we're grabbing dinner or watching TV or rolling around in her bed. We're not a typical couple. I'm a cynical pain in the butt, and half the time we're in separate cities. But I still look forward to every hour we spend together.

"If you can't find a place in DUMBO, try the Heights or Manhattan. I'd help you look if I could."

"I'll take care of it," I say, just to make him happy. "When am I visiting you?"

"Don't come here," he says with a wheezy sigh. "It's fucking depressing. Bess Beringer came up here, and I scared the poor thing to death. And that woman doesn't scare easy. You know Bess, right?"

"I know Bess," I say, smiling as I walk down Front Street.

"She's a great agent. Great person. You need another agent, Tank."

"Someday," I say lightly. There's no way I'm going to discuss those plans with him. It's morbid.

"Find an apartment, then. Soon. Get a cat."

"A cat?" I laugh out loud. "What for?"

"Even grumpy men deserve pets. A cat won't take any shit from you. But it will still be happy to see you, even if he won't show it."

"You are full of advice today."

"And now you are obligated to listen to it," he growls. "If I kick off before we speak again, you'll regret not listening."

"I'm listening," I promise. I'd say anything to stop the talk about dying. I'm nowhere near ready for Henry to go.

"Good," he rasps. "Now go home and call the realtor."

"Fine," I grumble. "Text me a date when I can stop by, though. I'm heading to California for a three-game road trip. But after that, I'm around for a while. I'll bring you lunch or something and you can give me my divorce papers."

"All right, kid." He sighs. "Soon."

"I'm gonna hold you to it."

After that, I let him off the phone. He'd sounded exhausted, and I feel blue. I head towards the team headquarters, where I have an appointment. And I try to summon some enthusiasm for calling the real estate broker.

When I pause at the next stoplight, I check my phone and see a new message that grabs all my attention. It's from Patrick O'Doul, of all people, and the subject is *Apartment for rent*.

No way! Thanks, universe.

I open that sucker immediately. It's addressed to both me and the Finnish kid—Ivo Halla. *Hey guys—Ari and I are almost ready to rent out the studio, starting December 1st. I don't know if either of you are still looking for a place to live, but before I tell the whole world, I want to offer it to my teammates first. Rent is $3,900 a month. If one of you is interested, please stop by tonight. I'm home. —P.*

Whoa.

On my way, I reply immediately. And then I turn on my heel and reverse my steps toward Water Street.

He'd sent the message only ninety minutes ago. It takes me five minutes to literally run over there. When I get to the front desk, I have to stop to catch my breath before I ask the doorman to buzz me upstairs.

The guy picks up the phone, but before he speaks to anyone, Ivo Halla appears from the direction of the elevator banks. He's smiling, of course.

When he spots me, his smile slides off. "Ah, nej," he says. "Sorry."

Patrick O'Doul appears behind him, and when he sees me he winces.

"Hey, men," I say as lightly as I can manage. But is this the worst day, or what? "I'm too late, huh?"

"It wasn't supposed to be a race. I didn't know if either of you was still looking."

"It's fine," I say quickly. "I haven't even started looking. I gotta get on that."

O'Doul shakes Halla's hand and waves goodbye. The kid lopes out the door looking as happy as I've ever seen him. Which is, to be fair, always pretty happy.

"Dude, I'm sorry," O'Doul says again. "I wasn't even sure if he could read my email."

"There's always Google translate," I say drily.

O'Doul shakes his head. "He just signed the lease without reading it and handed me a check."

"He's a good kid," I say, looking out the door where he'd disappeared. "And it's no big deal. I could have gotten here quicker, but…" I actually laugh, because I'm a fucking mess right now. "I just got off the phone with my agent, who's dying. He called to tell me that my divorce papers are ready."

Now O'Doul looks really uncomfortable. "That's terrible. I work with Tommy Povich. If you need somebody eventually, I could…"

"Nah, it's okay. I'm going to work with Eric Bayer."

O'Doul's eyes widen. "Really? That's cool of you, man. His first client. He's gonna be really good at that job."

"Yeah, great guy." Not like I'm worried. Bess will have my back, anyway.

"You want to grab a beer or something?" O'Doul asks, rubbing the whiskers on his chin. "I could tell Ari that I'm stepping out for an hour."

For a moment, the invitation tugs at my brittle soul. O'Doul isn't a bad guy. He might even be a good guy. But I don't think I can sit in a bar and make small talk today. He doesn't really want me to say yes, either. He's just doing his job as captain to make my grumpy ass feel welcome.

"Can I take a rain check? I got this appointment I've been dodging for a month now." It's the truth, too. How convenient.

"Let me guess—Doc Mulvey? The team shrink?"

"That's the guy," I grunt. Most teams have a psychiatrist who every player must visit a couple times a season. It's a pain in the ass.

"Say hi for me," O'Doul says with a wink. "I love that guy."

See? I knew Brooklyn was bonkers. Nobody *likes* seeing the team shrink. "Will do."

"And we'll get a beer next week, you and me."

"Thanks. Good plan. See you tomorrow." Next week it won't be different, though. I'll find another excuse.

We say our goodbyes, and then I head toward the shrink's office.

Doctor Mulvey is an aging Brooklyn hipster. He's wearing a black plaid shirt over a white tee, and a beanie. And then there's his carefully tailored mustache and beard. If he wants us to meditate together, I'm outta here.

"Nice of you to keep your appointment this time," he says, standing up to shake my hand.

"Sorry. I've been busy busting my ass at the rink."

"Let's talk about your busted ass," he says, settling into his chair, and picking up his...knitting? Seriously? The doctor slides one needle against the other, then wraps the yarn around it. "How is the adjustment coming?"

"Rocky," I admit, because this man already knows. He has all our stats, and probably a file containing my life story. "I'm a different kind of player than the team is used to. They're fighting my style."

"Uh-huh," he says, calmly making another stitch. "What about the rest of your life? Have you found a place to live?"

"Not yet. I had a lead on something, but it fell through."

"What kind of place are you looking for?"

"Um..." It's not like I've given this a lot of thought. "One bedroom. Maybe two. I guess even a studio would be fine." My mom will probably visit later in the season. But we're not very close. She'll stay at a hotel. "Why? Do you live in the neighbor-hood? If you know anybody who's trying to rent..."

"Sorry." Dr. Mulvey shakes his head. "But it's interesting to me that you haven't narrowed down your search."

"I've just been busy."

"You're very busy," he agrees. "But that's what real estate agents are for. Do you feel overwhelmed?"

"Well, sure. Who wouldn't? New city. New team. Bad on-ice dynamics. Of course I'm overwhelmed."

Dr. Mulvey sets down his knitting and looks me in the eye. "Anyone would be. And that's why you're having so much trouble visualizing."

"Sorry?"

"You don't have a picture in your mind of the apartment you need. Brooklyn doesn't look anything like Dallas, right?"

"Right," I agree. "Exactly. That's why it's hard to start looking."

His piercing eyes bore into me. "Your on-ice problem is just the same, I think."

"Uh, what?" I thought we were talking about apartments.

"You said the team was struggling to adapt to your style of play."

"Right—they want me on the blue line like O'Doul. It's a failure of imagination."

"Exactly," he says again. And then he gives me an evil grin. "Your imagination."

"What? No. That's not what I meant." And this is why everyone hates the team shrink. They talk you in circles.

"It's all about visualization," he says. "If you can't visualize connecting the pass, you can't connect the pass. If you can't visu-alize your life in Brooklyn, you can't make a life in Brooklyn."

"I connect passes all the time," I say irritably.

"Of course you do. That's muscle memory and training. But you've forgotten that visualization matters. If you can flex this muscle again, your teamwork will smooth right out."

"You lost me," I grunt.

"How old were you when you started hockey?"

Oh brother. They always want to talk about your childhood. "I was six."

"Did the six-year-old Mark ever stand around with a toy stick, pretending to score the winning goal for... Who was your team?"

I laugh. "Well, sure. And we rooted for Vancouver. That's where my dad grew up."

"Kids are really good at visualization," the shrink says with a shrug. "When you were six, you could picture it. But it would be years before you'd have the strength and muscle control to score a winning goal, right?"

"Yeah. Sure."

"So there you are, moving up through the ranks of club hockey and college hockey. Then straight to the majors. All that training and muscle development and skill. Your trip to greatness was smoother than some other guys face."

"It was," I admit. "Thanks to hard work and a healthy dose of luck."

He nods. "You never slacked off on the hard work. But lately it feels like your luck is a little slippery, no?"

"Maybe," I concede.

"Your wife leaves you. Then you get traded to a team that doesn't appreciate you."

This is a trap. You can't trash-talk your teammates to a guy who knows them better than you do. "There are days when that seems true."

He smiles. "It's been a long time since you had to employ visualization, Mark. But I think it can really help you. I'm going to give you some exercises."

"Great," I say, because it sounds like he might let me out of this room soon if I agree.

His smile widens. "The trick, though, is that you actually have to do them."

"Sure. You mean, like, sitting around and trying to picture Castro passing to me when I'm open?"

"Exactly like that." He flips to a fresh page on his legal pad and clicks his pen. "You'll start with just five minutes. You'll close your eyes and play a mental film for yourself. A repetitive highlight reel, basically."

Fucking Brooklyn. I knew meditation would come up. "Okay."

"I need you to humor me." He's scribbling on the page. "I'll send you an email tonight with complete instructions. Then you'll come and see me again in two weeks. We'll talk about how it's going."

Oof. "Sure thing."

He puts the pen down. "Getting traded is very disruptive, Mark. Everyone knows that."

"Uh-huh." They know it. But if it doesn't work out, they'll just trade you again anyway.

"You can make this work. I can help you."

"Thanks," I say tightly. I shake his hand and leave his claustrophobic little office.

Visualization. What a crock.

I'm halfway up the block when I realize he didn't make me talk about my divorce. So that's a small mercy. Although I could have poked a giant hole in his visualization theories.

Early on, Jordanna and I spent a whole lot of time visualizing what our happy future together should look like. A house full of kids. A big, loud family like the one she grew up in. We were really good at visualizing. So good at it that we bought a big house in the suburbs, with a big backyard that was just waiting for a sandbox and a swing set.

And it didn't do a lick of good. Visualization is a big load of bullshit. Nobody knows that better than me.

TWENTY-ONE

Who's with Me?

BESS

"WE HAVE TO GET UP," I tell Tank as the clock ticks past eight a.m.

It's not that I'm eager to break the spell. We've just made sleepy love in my bed, and, given the choice, I'd never get up. But now the sun is shining down on us, and I need to shower and head into my office. This working girl has to review several contracts and return about a hundred phone calls.

Prince Charming is a busy man, too. "You have to go to practice, and then get on the jet," I remind him.

"So you say," he mumbles. His hand is a steady weight on my hip, and his solid back is pressed against my chest. "Your bed is my favorite place in the world, though. I really don't want to leave."

My heart doubles in size, of course. "But we can't always have what we want."

Tank runs a hand down my thigh, and it feels dreamy. "Should I order some breakfast from the deli? I brought my gym clothes with me so that I could go straight to practice."

"Yeah," I say softly. "Of course." I'd have breakfast with Tank every day, given the choice.

"There's no chance you have eggs and bacon in that little refrigerator of yours, right?"

"Nope," I say cheerfully. "When I told you I don't cook, I wasn't kidding."

"But that means different things to different people," he points out. "I can't manage a crown roast, but I cook eggs all the time."

And now I feel incompetent, and I hate feeling incompetent. "I've never been much of a breakfast person."

"What's not to like about breakfast?"

"It's too early in the day," I say, even though meal timing isn't really my issue.

My lack of skill in the kitchen is directly related to my shitty childhood. I'd gone hungry in the mornings because I'd been too afraid of my father to ask for things like cereal and milk when we ran out. Dave and I had *never* woken him up. We knew better. I remember tiptoeing around the house before school, my brother trying to tame the knots in my hair with an old brush of my mother's. He'd done his best. But we'd been little kids when my mother died of a drug overdose, and my dad hadn't cared enough to step up and run a household.

Those memories are grim, and I keep them to myself. Tank knows that Dave is my only family, but I've never discussed why. Tank likes spending time with me because we have fun. My past isn't fun, though. He doesn't want to hear about my harrowing childhood.

"What do you want from the deli?" Tank asks, finally sitting up.

"Scrambled egg, bacon, and cheese on a roll. Large coffee."

He snorts. "That sounds like a girl who enjoys breakfast."

"Once in a while, I guess."

He slaps me playfully on the butt as I head into the shower. When I'm just about finished under the life-giving spray of hot water, the bathroom door opens. "Can I hop in after you?"

"Of course." I step out, and he hands me my towel.

Our hips brush as we trade places in my tiny bathroom, and Tank takes the opportunity to press a kiss to my neck. "Open the door if the deli guys buzz, okay?"

"Yeah," I say, feeling suddenly shy. I like the closeness a little too much, and I don't want him to read it on my face.

After getting dressed, and texting Eric that I'm running late, I go into my miniature kitchen to pour two glasses of orange juice.

Breakfasting with Tank feels so domestic. Hell, I'll sign up for a class on cooking eggs if it meant spending more time with him.

I wonder if that's a thing? *Cooking for domestic dummies*. Maybe he'd enroll with me.

Although it sounds a little pushy. Like I'm planning a life with him. But you can't rush a man who's just getting out of a terrible relationship. *Hey, now that your divorce is final, let's talk about the future.* On the other hand, I can't avoid wishing for things. And that feels a little dishonest, too.

So I really can't win.

Tank is singing in the shower. I recognize the song as "Aint No Man" by the Avett Brothers. He doesn't know all the words, so he has to improvise with some "bop bop" here and there.

I can't help but smile as Tank hits the high notes. And my hungry heart wants to know—if he's comfortable enough with me to sing in my shower, does that mean we're on the road to a long-term relationship?

I don't know how to turn off that part of me that's always looking for a sign.

A knock on my door distracts me. God, I love New York. Delivery is so fast. I run over and flip the lock and open the door.

Only to find Jason Castro and Anton Bayer standing there.

"Hi," I squeak. "I thought you were the deli guy."

"No! I got—" Castro starts.

"Bop bop boppy bop," sings Tank from the bathroom.

Castro blanches. He opens his mouth to continue. And then closes it again.

I can almost see the synapses connecting behind his eyes. Surprise morphs into a darker expression as the truth slowly dawns.

This is partly why I don't have a personal life. I spend all my time trying to make sure that thirty-five athletes believe they're the center of my world. And they are. Usually.

The sound of the shower cuts off. "Is the food here, baby?" Tank's voice calls.

"Um..." Words fail me, because I'm busy watching my clients' eyes widen even further. "That's, uh..." My jaw slams shut, because I'm just making things worse. We all know whose voice that is. "Is there an emergency of some kind?" I ask, trying to redirect the conversation. This pair never turns up at my door.

"Um..." Castro echoes. He doesn't know what to say, either.

"He got a call from *Sports Illustrated*," Anton says. "They want him for the body issue."

I blink, hoping Tank stays in the bathroom so this doesn't get any more awkward. "Congratulations," I say haltingly.

"Thanks," Castro says slowly, his eyes darting over my shoulder. "I, uh, wondered what you thought. Georgia says it's up to me. But will it help me land future endorsements, or hurt because I'm doing it for free?"

"It will help!" I say brightly. "Let's talk about it later today."

"We're heading out on a road trip," Castro says. "That's why I..." He clears his throat. "We'll talk on the phone, maybe."

"Sorry, Bess," Anton has the good nature to say. "I didn't know you and Tank were..."

My face is in flames when Eric comes into view on the landing behind the players. "I'm sorry, boss. I tried to stop them. I knew you were keeping it on the lowdown."

"Wait. This is an ongoing thing?" Castro asks. "Since when?"

"Pretty sure that's none of our business, man," Anton says with a grin.

"Nine years ago!" Tank helpfully supplies from somewhere behind me. When I glance over my shoulder, he's standing in the doorway to my bedroom, a towel wrapped around his waist. "And then September."

"Yeah. We met a long time ago," I stammer.

Castro's eyes narrow. "You told me you don't date players."

"Guys," Eric says quietly. "I'm going downstairs. Who's with me?"

Nobody moves.

"Tank is the only player I've ever dated," I say, feeling the need to explain myself. I can almost feel Jane Pines looking over my shoulder, whispering, *I told you so.*

"I'm *that* irresistible," Tank says from the bedroom.

"Does your brother know?" Castro asks.

"No!" I yelp. "It hasn't come up. God, don't—" I stop myself before I say something snippy to my client. "It's private," I say in a low voice.

"Okay. Sorry." He sighs. "The whole thing is none of my business."

"Rightio!" says Tank from the bedroom.

The door buzzer goes off, and I leap a foot into the air, because I'm standing right beside it.

"Sounds like your food is here," Eric says. "Come on, boys. Let's let the lady have breakfast."

"Can I call you when you land?" I ask Castro. "We'll talk about your photo op."

"Sure," he says quickly. "No problem." He follows Eric and Anton down the stairs.

Tank emerges from my bedroom in workout clothes, just in time to tip the deliveryman. I close the door and lean against it like I'm trying to shut out the world.

"You okay?" Tank asks, pulling food items out of the paper bag and setting them on the coffee table that I finally purchased with Rebecca's help.

"Yup," I say quickly.

He looks up, studying me with those clear green eyes. "I'm sorry, Bess. I know you're a private person."

I sit down beside him on the sofa and sigh. "That's a nice way of putting it. 'Private person' sounds better than 'paranoid and prudish.'"

"You didn't do anything wrong," he says.

"I know." It's true, even if my terrified heart doesn't always believe it.

"Plus, I'm totally worth it." He hands me a cup of coffee and then gives me a sexy smile.

"You really are," I say quietly, and that feels even bigger than telling the whole world that Tank and I spend our free time together. I don't usually tell Tank how I feel, because I'm afraid I won't hear the same words back.

He sets his coffee down. "I'm gonna miss you when I'm gone, you know."

My heart does a happy dance. "Same."

"You're off to Vermont tomorrow, right?"

"Eventually." He pulls me in for a hug, and I sink luxuriously into it. "I guess I have to tell my brother that you and I have been hanging out. Because those boys are going to gossip. It's only a matter of time."

He chuckles, and I love the feel of his laughter against my chest. Making Tank laugh is basically my second favorite hobby. After stripping him naked. "Should I watch my back? Is Dave going to come for me?"

"Probably not."

"Can you put better odds on it? I need to plan my month." He kisses my forehead.

"Fifteen percent chance he kills you. Twenty percent of a maiming. Sixty percent chance you just get the stink eye for eternity."

"And the remaining five percent?"

"Survey error."

He laughs again. "Let's eat these sandwiches while they're still hot, okay? Might as well have a good meal before I die."

"Good idea."

"Did you happen to see who won the Caps game last night?" he asks.

"Philly. And Toronto took the Canes."

"Really?" His eyes widen as he bites his sandwich.

I describe how the defense suffered, giving Toronto too many scoring opportunities, while he nods along. And I try not to fall any more in love than I already am.

TWENTY-TWO

Bad Juju

TANK

ON THE ROAD, we have a morning off in Anaheim, so Coach puts an "optional" morning skate on the schedule.

If you're me, that shit isn't optional. The new guy who isn't setting the world on fire yet can't take the morning off. So I show up, skate hard, and then hit the weight room at the hotel where we're staying.

Hotel workout rooms are a pretty mixed bag. Sometimes you find four pitiful stationary bikes and a handful of dumbbells. But this is California, where people care about fitness, and the place is equipped with two solid benches and two squat racks, both with a perfectly adequate number of plates.

I claim a squat rack and fish out my phone to put on some tunes. When you're the first guy into the weight room, you get to pick the music. It's one of those unwritten rules of the gym, along with wiping your sweat off the bench and replacing the weights on the rack when you're done.

Moving my body feels good. I don't think I could have made it through the last five months without skates, weights, and sweat. Today I've got "Aint No Man" by the Avett Brothers on the Bluetooth speakers, because that song always reminds me to keep my chin up.

So it doesn't sit well with me when Anton—the young

150

defenseman—starts trash-talking my music while we're taking turns on the squat rack. "What is this…Texas music? I'm not sure we can have Texas music in the gym. It's bad juju. We got that Dallas game coming up in January. We gotta stay sharp."

I let out a beastly grunt as I rise out of my last squat, and then let the barbell drop onto the supports with a clang. "Fuck." That set almost killed me, and it makes me feel old. "Pretty sure the Avett Brothers are from North Carolina. Which is nowhere near Texas."

Anton towels off his hands and then shakes his head. "I hear a Texas twang. It's a fact."

"Uh-huh." I roll my eyes.

"Say—you don't have those little green underwear anymore, right?"

"Sorry?" I lean over to stretch out my quads.

"Those tiny green underwear from that ad you shot? I think you gotta burn them. It's the only way to get the Texas out of you."

"Burn them? You're insane." I'm ninety percent sure I don't have any of the underwear from that old photo shoot anymore. But I don't want to give these idiots the satisfaction.

"We're very superstitious," Castro says from the bench press. "An underwear bonfire exorcism wouldn't be crazy at all around here. It's just, like, Tuesday, you know?"

"I hear the Texas twang," Anton insists. "It's giving me the heebie-jeebies."

"Don't *touch* that speaker," I grumble.

My playlist moves on to a different song, and thankfully Anton shuts up. The room is getting a little crowded, and I'm grateful to be almost done with my workout. The music shifts to "I and Love and You." It's another great Avett Brothers song, and it's about moving to Brooklyn, oddly enough.

The funny thing is that I always liked this song, even before the chorus became my reality. Life is weird.

"Now *this* is music," Anton says. "Hear that, guys? This is a band that belongs in Brooklyn."

"Oh, for fuck's sake." I should probably keep my mouth shut, but I just can't. "It's the same band."

"What?"

"It's the *same band*—the one you decided was Texas music." I lift a forty-pound plate off the barbell and return it to the rack.

"Nah," Anton says, shaking his big head. "No twang."

"What?"

"It can't be. I know twang, and I don't hear twang."

"The boy *knows* twang," Castro says from the opposite corner, where he's stretching. "He can feel the twang in his *thang*."

These goofballs can choose their own music, because I'm out of here. "Y'all have a good day."

"Oh God! He just y'alled us," Anton hoots. "We're gonna lose to Dallas if he doesn't cut that shit out. First the twang and now the y'all."

"Later!" I call over my shoulder as I head for the showers.

"You better look for that underwear!" Anton calls after me. "Don't jinx us, y'all!"

I take a long, long shower in the hotel's luxurious locker room. But when I come out, there aren't any towels. I could swear I grabbed one off a stack on the counter, hanging it on the hook before I got into the shower. But now I'm dripping on the floor and there's not a towel in sight. "What the hell?"

The only towel in the room is slung around Castro's hips. He's standing by a locker, shaking out his shirt. "You know he's kidding, right?"

"What? Who?" I'm distracted because I'm still trying to solve the towel mystery.

"Anton. He's a music hound. He plays the guitar and goes to every concert he can find. He was just putting you on with that Texas thing."

"*Oh*." For a split second I feel only annoyance. I fell for that shit? But then I realize something important. If Anton and Castro are pranking me, that's a good sign. You don't prank a teammate that you hate. "Wait. Did you take all the towels?"

"Towels?" Castro says innocently. "There are some paper towels in there, I think." He points to a wall-mounted dispenser.

Because I'm a little slow, I actually walk over to the dispenser, if only to mop up the water I've dripped on the floor.

It's empty.

"Fuck you," I grumble, and Castro laughs. So I do the only reasonable thing, which is to stalk over to him, grip the edge of the towel he's wearing, and yank it off his body.

Castro, bare-assed now, just snorts. "I was done with that anyway."

"Good thing." I dry myself off as best I can with his wet towel. "Did you really take the paper towels out of the dispenser? That's pro-level. I hope you'll put 'em back, though, so that some under-paid hotel worker isn't cleaning up after your little prank."

"Don't you worry." Castro opens his locker and shows me a tower of towels—cotton on the bottom, paper on top. "I left the toilet paper in the stalls. Once I watched a player try to dry himself off with TP. It disintegrates, you know? He was picking little pieces out of his underwear for days."

I shake my head. The prank could have been worse, I guess. If I wasn't willing to grab his towel, I probably would have walked back into the weight room buck-ass naked for a workout towel.

We get dressed in silence for a few minutes. Right until Castro opens his yawp and says, "So. You and Bess, huh? What exactly are your intentions?"

"My—" I let out a chuckle. "What are you, her dad? And is this 1955? Where do you get off asking me that?"

It comes out sounding snippy, and I fully expect Castro to get mad. But he just sits down on the bench and calmly levels me with a brown-eyed stare "You got to stop thinking of me as a young punk who doesn't know things. And you really shouldn't blow off my question. Bess doesn't date players."

"Yeah, except for this one. And I bet she wouldn't be super-excited about you discussing it behind her back."

He doesn't even flinch. "But she *really* doesn't date players. She says she needs to be able to go anywhere with us in any situation and never have to wonder if people will whisper about her. She says that's the only way she can do her job."

"I get that," I say testily. "Except she's not *my* agent. And obvi-ously she's made a different choice this time. So maybe you shouldn't question it."

"But that's just the thing," Castro presses. "She *did* make a different choice. She broke her own rule for you. And that means something. Something big."

There's a bad joke in there somewhere about *something big*. But I let it go. I would never embarrass Bess. And she wouldn't like this conversation at all.

"She likes you," Castro says. "She *really* likes you. That's what I'm saying. So I hope you're worth it. Are you gonna treat her right?"

The question makes me bristle, but I won't give him the satisfaction of letting it show. "Aw." I chuckle. "Thanks so much for asking. I'm glad you guys are so loyal to Bess. But, yeah. Bess is special to me." It's a hundred percent true, too. I'm startled by how I feel about her. Lately I'm wearing a silly grin half the time, because she put it there. It's not just the sex, either. She's made me feel like my fun self again. Like everything in the world isn't so fucking complicated.

"She doesn't need anyone fucking around on her," Castro says.

"Oh man. I thought we were having a moment, and you had to go and ruin it. Not that it's any of your business, but I never cheated on anybody. Don't believe everything you read. I'm good to Bess, and I was good to her way back when flip phones were still popular."

He frowns. "I know the bloggers don't care about a little thing like the truth. I'm not an idiot. But I do know this—Bess wouldn't take a chance on you if it didn't matter to her. But you're this bitter guy who just got divorced. Last night you told Jimbo never to get married."

"Yeah, and I was *kidding*. That kid is twenty, and I'm sure he's smart enough not to marry someone who will divorce his ass and then still text seven times during dinner to ask him how to flip a circuit breaker in the garage of the home you bought in the neighborhood *she chose* even though it gave you a shitty commute."

And now I'm in a piss-poor mood again. *Thanks, kid.*

Castro shrugs. "I don't begrudge you the pain. I've known loss, and it isn't pretty. But please don't make it Bess's problem. I'm very protective of her. We all are."

"Because she's your teammate's sister." That's why I'm getting the extended remix version of this speech.

"It's more than that. She's been through a lot."

"Uh-huh," I agree, even if I don't know exactly what he's referring to. "Dave is her only family, right?"

"Maybe." He scratches his chin. "Their dad might still be alive somewhere. But he wouldn't dare enter a room if Dave is around. Or me, for that matter. Bess used to be his punching bag. Even when she was only yay high." He holds his hand down by the floor.

I do a poor job of keeping the surprise off my face, because Bess never mentioned her father to me. "She grew up with her grandparents."

"*Eventually*," he corrects me. "Not until Dave was fourteen. He realized he couldn't always be there to step in front of his father's fist. And he was sick of watching his little sister get bruised. And burned, too. There's a scar on her arm." He touches the inside of his elbow. "Cigarette burn. That's one of the ways her dad kept her in line."

Something goes wrong in my stomach. I know that scar. I've kissed that scar. But I never asked Bess where it came from.

"Eventually, Dave landed on a strategy—he breaks his own face with a wrench." Castro taps his cheek. "Two bones. Just so someone would report their dad to social services."

I honestly might vomit if he says anything more. I've spent the last couple of months whining about my trade, and my divorce. Then turning to Bess to cheer my sorry ass up. Meanwhile, she's cheerfully putting up with my bullshit after barely surviving childhood? I kind of want to punch myself right now.

"Anyway..." Castro shrugs as he pulls on his socks. "Bess has already had her fair share of difficulty. If you bring her any more, I will end you. And so will Dave."

"Yeah," I grit out. "Message received."

But he's not even done. "Dave had it worse, I guess. Their mom died of a drug overdose when Bess was still little. Dave found their mom on the living room floor after he got home from kindergarten. Bess was screaming her head off in her crib for hours."

I'm all out of words. I just stare at him, trying to picture Dave Beringer at five, standing next to his mother's dead body.

Castro stands up and zips his jeans. "I said my piece. Just don't let her down. She deserves the world."

"I know." Of course she does. And I'm suddenly craving her so bad. I wonder how many hours are left in this day before I can sneak off to my hotel room and call her, just to hear her voice. She's on her way to Vermont, though. She said the phone service is spotty up there. So we might not connect.

But I hope we do. Missing Bess on the road is a familiar feeling. Back when I was twenty-three and watching my teammates hook up, I'd been so lonely for her.

I never told her, though. I still haven't.

Castro leaves, and I stay there for a while, sitting on the fancy spa bench. It's dawning on me that Bess must not have wanted me to know about her childhood. It's the only explanation for why she's never said a word about it.

And I don't know what to do with this realization. Was it pride that kept her from telling me? Or did she think I wouldn't care? The truth is that I've never given her the chance to confide in me. We were so young the first time we met. I remember wanting to impress her. I was trying to impress the whole world.

It worked, I guess. We impressed the hell out of each other on a regular basis. But I'm not that kid anymore. I've figured out that impressing people only goes so far. Now I need more.

I've seen that scar on Bess's arm so many times. Yet I never asked how she got it. Maybe I didn't want to ruin the fun. But now we're past that, aren't we? Bess means a lot to me. If she'll talk to me about her past, I'm ready to listen.

I told Bess that being together didn't have to be a "life-changing thing." But somehow it already is.

Can a jaded divorcé fall in love again? Maybe this one already did.

TWENTY-THREE

That's Not an Ax

BESS

"AND THEN CINDERELLA accidentally turned into a mouse. The end."

My niece looks up at me with her little pink mouth open in surprise. "No, Aunt Best! Read it for real."

"I did, you stinker." I close the book. "Three times. We're both going to get in big trouble if you don't go to bed soon. Your daddy is going to give us both a spanking."

"No. Daddy not do that." Nicole grins at me, showing off a perfect set of tiny teeth.

"Of course not," I whisper. Spankings are just a fiction to Nicole. "But it's still bedtime." Not that I'm much of a disciplinarian, either. My niece is wearing pink, striped pajamas that make her short legs look like sausages. She's so cute and cuddly that I would honestly sit in this rocking chair all night and hold her. And this adorable little scamp is dragging out her bedtime to epic proportions because she knows I'm a huge softie.

But Zara is making dinner downstairs. So I rise from the rocking chair, hugging Nicole tightly. She wraps her arms around me, too. It will be a struggle to let go of her. "Sleep with the angels, baby."

"Night, Best."

And now I have actual tears in my eyes. I hope she never stops calling me that. I'm so smitten it's ridiculous. I have to force myself to set her down in the crib. One of the sides is removed, because at two and a half, my baby is not so much of a baby anymore.

I cover her with the blanket and ruffle the coppery curls near her face. "Night, angel. I'll see you in the morning."

"I climb on your bed?"

"Of course." And lord help me, that will probably happen at six thirty. But that's why I'm here. I moved eight hundred miles just to be more available for six thirty wakeups with this child, in this house. I give her one more kiss on her satin cheek, and then make myself leave the room.

Slowly I descend the stairs, taking a moment to put on my game face. I've decided that I need to tell my brother about Tank, because I don't want him to hear it as gossip.

Honestly, it's not a big deal. Dave is vaguely aware that there are occasionally men in my life. And I'm thirty freaking years old. Although he does have a classic "nobody is good enough for my baby sister" complex. So that'll be fun.

I dread talking about Tank, though. Because Dave will ask me if it's serious, and I'll have to say no. And if he asks me whether I want something serious with Tank, I don't know what I'll say. Because I do want more. But you can't always have the things you want.

In the kitchen, I find Zara but not Dave. She's adding cream to a pan full of crumbled...

"Is that sausage?" I ask. "It smells good."

"Sure is. We buy it from a farmer in Tuxbury."

"And what do you use it for?"

"This is going over pasta, with some garlic, peas, and chives in a white sauce."

My stomach rumbles. "Can I help with dinner?"

Zara gives me a smile. "Probably not. No offense." My lack of cooking skills is widely known. "How about you pour a couple mugs of that hot cider and take one out to the lumberjack outside?"

"Sure. But you could put me to work setting the table or something."

"It's handled, Bess. You did the hard work of putting that kid to bed. Have some cider and make sure Dave doesn't remove any important body parts while he's splitting wood."

"Okay. I won't spike his, then."

"Good idea." She picks up a ramekin full of chopped herbs and adds them to the pan with the sausage. Her cooking smells wonderful, and I'll bet it's something I could learn to do if I just put in the time.

The other morning when Tank asked me why I don't cook, I flat out lied. It's not that I don't have any interest. It's just that putting food on the table was always a fraught issue when I was young. There was never enough of it. My father couldn't be bothered. And then my grandmother complained about how much we ate.

Dave used to heat up cans of soup and stew for me. I think he mastered Kraft dinners at some point, because I remember watching him sprinkle packets of powdered cheese over pasta.

"Hey, Zara?" I ask spontaneously.

"Hmm?" my sister-in-law asks as she pours the pasta into boiling water.

"Someday will you teach me to cook a few things? Just to get me started."

"Sure!" She throws a smile over her shoulder. "That would be fun."

"Thanks," I say gruffly. And then I reheat the cider for Dave and myself. Because even a dummy like me can use the microwave.

Outside, the evening is cool, and the light is gone. Dave is splitting wood in the glow of the porch light. It gets dark early in Vermont in November. But I love the cool, crisp air and the scent of pine on the breeze.

While my brother does hard physical labor, I'm sipping a mug of cider and thinking deep thoughts about what I might want to learn how to cook.

Life is good.

Dave stands another log on a wide, flat stump. Then he lifts the ax high and splits it with one sharp blow.

I cackle. "I swear this is better entertainment than a playoffs game. Who knew you'd turn into a lumberjack with an ax?"

"Not an ax. A maul."

"What's the difference?"

"A maul is heavier and duller than an ax. It splits the wood by force, not blade sharpness."

I crack up again. "Who knew, big brother? Who knew."

"You go ahead and have your fun." He flashes me a smile. The stupid man doesn't even care that I'm teasing him. That's how much he loves Vermont. "Want to try it?"

"Are you kidding? I'd probably lose a limb."

"Nah. Come here. Quick, before we have to go in for dinner."

Reluctantly, I set down the mug of cider and stand next to Dave.

He hands me the maul with a grin that says he knows I'm nervous but also too stubborn to say so. "Let gravity do all the work. So long as you keep your eye on the log, and your body out of the way, there's nothing to it."

I lift the maul overhead. It's kind of heavy, but I don't complain. Then—taking care with my aim—I let it fall to the cut end of the log.

I'm too tentative. Instead of splitting the log neatly in two, the maul just sticks into the log's top. When I tug on the handle, the log lifts with the maul's blade.

Now it's Dave's turn to laugh. He takes the maul from my hand, aims, and brings the whole mess down onto the stump with a bang. The log splits neatly away from the maul. "Try again."

"No. My drink is getting cold."

"Dare you."

"Asshole!"

He cracks up again. Neither of us will ever refuse a dare. Bravery was our sibling code. Because it took an act of bravery just to walk through the door every night. We had the kind of childhood that people don't talk about in polite company.

When I watch my brother stacking all those wedges of wood

he's just split, I feel like I can see two different people. There's the happy father splitting wood for his new wife and their three fireplaces. And there's the frightened boy who's desperate enough to break his own face to save us both.

The back door opens. "Dinner in five minutes!" Zara calls out before disappearing inside again.

I stand up quickly, because when someone calls you to dinner, you go.

"Hang on," he says. "There's something I have to tell you."

My stomach dips, and I don't even know why.

Dave turns to me with a smile. "We're having another baby in May."

Oh.

"A *baby*," I echo. "Oh, wow." It takes a second for the news to sink in. I don't know why I hadn't seen it coming.

"Yeah, my teammates were right on target with their teasing." He chuckles. "This time it's a little boy."

"Oh! Congratulations!" The guys in Brooklyn had some kind of pool going to bet on how soon after Dave's retirement he and Zara would have a second child. It's funny when a cliché comes true.

But my insides are swimming in turmoil.

The existence of my brother's first child had been a huge shock. For two years after his first tryst with Zara, Dave hadn't known he had a child with her. That drama is over now, and I'm happy for them.

So why do I feel so gutted right now? "Congratulations," I choke out.

"Thank you," he says quietly.

"In May," I say slowly, turning it over in my mind. While I'm watching the playoffs, my brother will be welcoming his baby son into the world. This time he'll be there at the hospital, encouraging Zara to push.

Then I'll go to the Baby Gap and buy one of everything from the baby boy side of the store. I'll fly up here to hold my nephew, who I will love the moment I lay eyes upon him.

And when I go back home to my quiet Brooklyn apartment, my

yearning for a family of my own will become even more clawing and desperate than it already is.

"Bess? Hey."

"Mmm?" I manage to look up eventually.

"Are you okay?" My brother is frowning at me.

"Perfectly," I say quickly. "Of course."

"We should go inside, then."

"Right!" I say, blinking. I grab my mug and head into the house, already wondering how long I'll have to wait before the Baby Gap puts out the spring and summer collections.

The guest room is perfectly comfortable, and the house is quiet, but when I eventually turn in for the night, I can't sleep. I lie in bed, my head a whirl of tangled thoughts. It occurs to me at some point that this bedroom will probably become the baby's room. I picture Zara tiptoeing in here to check on her sleeping infant. Then I picture my brother doing the same thing.

I don't know why Zara's second pregnancy is hitting me so hard. Even before tonight, I'd wanted what they have. Nothing has changed, except for the better.

So why is it suddenly so difficult to breathe?

"Richie," I say into the phone the next morning. "Take a breath."

"But the coach hates me," the young defenseman whines into my ear. "How many days are left before the trade deadline?"

"Lots of days," I say soothingly. "Your job is not to try to guess what the coach is thinking. You can't control the coaching staff. You can't control your teammates. You can only control Richie Kristov. Open up your workout plan. Then go to the gym and get busy." I glance up and give Zara an apologetic smile. It's her morning off from work, and the two of us are sitting on her coffee shop's new patio for breakfast and gossip.

"Okay," he says with a sigh. "You're right. I'll stick to the plan."

"That's the way to do it," I promise him. "Go drink a protein shake. Make yourself a to-do list of healthy habits and get busy. I'm counting on you."

After a few more pats on the head, he finally signs off.

"Sorry!" I tell Zara. "That was just—"

"It's fine," she says. "You're so patient with them when they panic."

"They just need someone to listen," I say, putting my phone away. I grab my giant latte in two hands and gulp it straight into my soul. "So tell me everything. When is the baby due?" I force my mouth to make a smile shape. I don't know why it's difficult. Another baby in my life to snuggle? Sign me up.

Zara cocks her head. "May. The week before Memorial Day."

"Oh! A summer baby. Great timing."

"Yeah. Now I have a question for you." Zara sets her cup down.

"Hmm?"

"How much did it cost you to ask me that question?"

Shit. I lift my giant mug and try to drown myself in it.

"I'm worried about you," Zara says quietly.

"Whatever for?"

She gives me a look of mild disdain and picks up her cup of half-decaf again. "Because you're not happy."

"Who's perfectly happy? I'm happy enough."

Zara shakes her head slowly. "You are very good at faking it. But I know you want more than what you have. How's *your* life plan going?"

"It's…going," I hedge. "Slowly." The truth is that Tank has derailed all my planning. And I hadn't even had the courage last night to tell my brother I was dating him.

Zara looks me in the eye. "Bess, it's time we had a performance review. Here's what we're going to do. I'm going to be your agent."

"What?"

"That kid Richie Kristov has you, right? Well, you have *me*. I'll be the voice on the phone who asks for a full accounting. Now tell me—have you been dating? Wasn't that Chapter One of your plan?"

"I did a little dating, yes."

"I see," Zara says. She gives me a sage nod, but her eyes twinkle. "Well, that's a good start. You'll keep it up, right? You can't make the right guy appear. But you can control your own attack."

"Oh my *God*, Zara. You're a little too good at this."

She cackles. "Now let's talk about Chapter Four."

Oh, hell. Sharing my five-year plan with her was a tactical error. "I have made no progress on Chapter Four."

"But you told me two months ago that you were going to make the first appointment. What happened there?"

The appointment she's referring to is another secret of mine. I'd decided to make preliminary inquiries with a fertility specialist, just in case I decided to have a child without a man in my life.

"I'm not ready for that, as it turns out. Other, uh, things have kept me busy."

Zara's dark eyes double in size. "*Really*. What things?"

I look over both shoulders to make sure my brother hasn't snuck up on us somehow. I'm dying to get this off my chest. "There's this guy. He's terrific. But he's not in the right stage of life to settle down."

She leans forward. "What stage is he in?"

"The just-got-divorced stage," I admit at a near-whisper. "He said he's never getting married again."

"Does he have kids?" Zara whispers back.

I shake my head. "They were married for—" I do the math. "Five years. Or almost six."

"Well…" Zara cocks her head. "Did they not want kids?"

"Maybe," I say, because the truth is I have no idea. Tank doesn't like to talk about his divorce, and I sure don't like to pry into his marriage.

"So you don't really know where he stands on kids."

"No," I have to admit. "But if he doesn't want marriage, it's pretty safe to assume he doesn't want kids."

"But you do," Zara points out. "Do you love him? Does he love you?"

"You *know* these are tricky questions, right?" I fire back at my sister-in-law.

She laughs. "Yeah, Bess. As your agent, it's my job to ask the tricky questions. In fact, do you have a sheet of paper? I'm going to have to ask you to make one of those decision charts."

"A decision tree?" I ask drily.

"Yes!" She claps. "So, the first question is whether or not you love this guy."

"I'm not writing that down," I grumble.

"So you do love him." Zara grins.

"I didn't say that."

"You didn't have to. It's written all over your face."

Well, damn it. I suppose it probably is. "I have never told him so, but he is exactly the kind of man I could love. He's a good guy, even if he's a little gruff on the outside. Actually I like that about him. He doesn't suffer fools."

"And yet he likes you," Zara says. "When the grumpy man smiles at you, it's like watching the sun come out."

I feel a little pain in my chest, right in the center of my breast bone. Because she's right. The idea that Tank would choose me over any other woman makes me feel all squishy inside.

"Next question. Do you two have a lot of chemistry? Is the sex good?"

"Check and check."

"Excellent! So the baby-making sex would be a good time."

"Zara," I hiss. "You can't talk about baby-making sex when you're having babies with my brother. That's got to stay in the cone of silence."

"Fine. Moving on. Is he a good provider? If you two decided to make a go of it, would you be able to step back from your job and not starve because he's a sculptor or a professional mime or something?"

I laugh out loud. "Do you really see me with a mime?"

"There's a sexy version of anything, Bess. Mimes are very expressive, and I'd bet they're good with their hands. But they don't earn well. And a divorced mime..." She shakes her head.

I think of Tank's hands and let out a little sigh. "Money wouldn't be an issue. He's a professional athlete."

"Oh." Zara sits back in her chair. "Well. Why didn't you say so? I would have skipped over the sex and money questions at the same time. But I thought players were off limits to you?"

"They're supposed to be," I mumble. "And he's very good with his hands. I have it bad, Z. He's everything I've ever wanted in a man. You can skip right down to the big questions, because this player can't be easily disqualified."

"Ah." She folds her hands. "Then the only question that matters is this one—would you marry him if he asked tomorrow?"

Oh boy. There's a reason I don't sit around indulging in this kind of fantasy. Because that's an easy one. "Without hesitation."

"Oh, wow." Zara puts a hand over her heart. "So your heart is, like, *play ball*, but you're afraid that his divorce puts him on the bench forever?"

"In the dugout, sweetie. If you're going with the baseball analogies."

"What is his sport, anyway? I need a visual."

I just shake my head.

"Ooh, hockey!"

"I didn't say that!" I squawk.

"You'd tell me if it wasn't hockey." She shrugs. "Besides, hockey players are the hottest. And you're pretty far gone for this guy. I hate to break it to you, but the decision tree is pretty clear, honey. You have to poll him on his feelings. You have to ask him if he thinks you guys could ever be on the same page."

I feel sick just trying to imagine this conversation. "He'd hate that. It's too soon."

"Is it?" Zara challenges me. "You have a lot of feelings for him. And it's only going to get harder to hold it all in."

It's already hard. She's right. "What if I ask, and he runs? Maybe I should wait a little longer. It's only been six months since she kicked him to the curb. The ink on his divorce is barely dry."

Zara reaches across the table and covers my hand with hers. "You might be right. But please consider giving yourself some kind of deadline. You sat here this summer and told me you wanted to have a baby. That you were willing to uproot your whole life and take a big business risk to focus on your family. Don't let this guy stand in your way if he can't ever be The One."

I look down into my empty coffee cup and swallow hard. "Okay," I promise.

"What's that? I couldn't hear you?" Zara cups a hand around her ear.

"Okay," I repeat grumpily. "I won't let this guy stand in the way of my plans. I will try to find a way to talk to him about the future. And if he says he doesn't love me, I will let go of that dream."

"Hot damn." Zara punches the air with her fists, one at a time. "I'm good at this. Running other people's lives is so exciting! I never knew."

"Oh, you totally knew," her brother Benito says, walking past our table. "You've been bossing me around since birth."

"He had it coming," she says without turning around. Then she gives me a huge smile. "What color is his hair?"

"What?" It takes me a second to realize she means Tank's. "It's brown, why?"

"Maybe it doesn't matter, but I read an article about the genetics of red hair. Supposedly, globalization means that gingers will go extinct within a hundred years."

"Shut the front door," I say. "That's ridiculous."

Zara shrugs. "Apparently it isn't. Redheads are only two percent of the population, and only four to five percent carry the gene. But I'm doing my share, Bess. I'm here to carry on the line with your brother."

"My people are grateful."

"Step up, Bess," she says, teasing me. "Do your part."

"I'll try," I promise.

TWENTY-FOUR

I Want Tex-Mex

TANK

COME OVER AT SEVEN? *We can order Indian Food.*

Sitting on the weight bench in the gym, I pump my fist. I've been waiting for Bess's text all day, and when it finally arrives, I'm elated. It's been eight long days since I've seen her.

"Something happen? What did I miss?" Silas Kelly is watching me with a grin on his face. He crosses the room and drops down onto a mat to stretch.

"Aw, it's nothing," I say, tucking my phone under the bench and leaning back for another set of warm-up presses.

"I think I made that same face a half hour ago when Delilah said she'd be home tonight by eight." Silas folds himself in half as he says this, because goalies are all made of rubber.

"Yeah," I grunt. "It's been a long road trip."

"TV, takeout food, and sex," Silas says. "That's what everyone on the team will be doing tonight."

"Not me," Anton says, strutting into the room. "I'm too tired to find a playmate. I'm going to be face down on the sofa, watching reruns and shoving Doritos into my facehole."

"Sexy," Silas teases.

I do another light set of presses and then sit up again. I return Bess's text. **What if you leave the food to me?** *I want Tex-Mex. I'll* *make it happen*. And then I add, ***Can't wait to see you***. Because it's a hundred percent true.

Rationally, I know it's way too soon to jump into a relationship. When I told Bess I was never getting married again, I meant it.

But a few hours later I'm standing outside her apartment building at five minutes to seven, pressing the buzzer like a junkie who needs his next fix. And it's hard to remember why I shouldn't go all in with Bess. Spending time with her is the brightest part of my week.

The door latch releases, and I enter the building and jog up the stairs.

"You're early!" she calls from the bedroom when I push open her apartment door.

"Sorry! Just a couple minutes."

"Oh, I don't care. I just like to bust your chops." She appears in the doorway, wearing tight jeans and a Colorado Avalanche T-shirt, and my heart thumps a little harder.

"Missed you," I blurt out.

Her expression softens. "Same here."

"How was your trip to Vermont?"

"It was good. They always are. What did you bring?" She eyes my two large shopping bags — one in either hand. "How hungry are you, anyway?"

"*Very* hungry," I drawl, giving her tight T-shirt a very apprecia-tive glance. "I can't decide what I want first."

She gives me a shy smile. "Let me know when you figure it out."

I carry my bags into her tiny kitchen and set them on the counter. It occurs to me that I should get the dinner started before I seduce and debauch her. I take out a rotisserie chicken, a bunch of tortillas, sauces, toppings and various cheeses. And then I take out the pan that I bought to cook in, because Bess doesn't own pots and pans. It's hilarious.

I'm preheating the oven when she comes in, her face full of questions. "What are you doing?"

"Making enchiladas. I can't find any in New York that taste how I like."

"Really? I'll bet there's authentic Mexican food somewhere in New York."

"That's the problem. I don't *want* authentic Mexican," I tell her. "I want Texas Tex-Mex, with gooey yellow cheese all over it." My stomach rumbles at the thought. "Want to help?"

"Sure," Bess says. "But I'm the kind of girl who helps by setting the table and keeping the beer cold. If you ask me to dice an onion, be prepared to provide detailed instructions."

"We all have our strengths. Can you shred up this chicken meat?"

"I can probably manage that." She grabs a breast and pulls off the skin. "How, uh, small should the pieces be? I don't know what I'm doing."

"It couldn't matter less." I put down the package of tortillas I was unwrapping and pull her close. "I don't care if you can't even boil water."

She kisses me on the jaw. "That's nice of you to say, because it's a little embarrassing. I notice you brought your own pan. Smart man."

"Haters gonna hate, Bess. Fuck 'em."

"Did you just become the only thirty-two-year-old man to quote Taylor Swift?" She lifts her pretty face and studies me.

"Maybe I did. The girl has a point with that song. Now get back to work, or dinner will never be finished."

After assembling my ingredients, I roll shredded chicken, cheese, and beans into a dozen tortillas. I place them in a tidy row in the baking pan. Then I drizzle two whole packages of enchilada sauce everywhere, followed by loads of yellow cheese and some diced chilis. I cover the pan and slide it into the oven.

When I look up, Bess is watching me with a soft expression on her face. "What?" I ask. "Did I do something funny?"

"Not in the least." Her eyes flick away. "When I told you I can't cook, I meant I *really* can't cook. I can't even scramble an egg. It's pathetic."

"No it isn't," I say quietly, leaning over to kiss her jaw. "I like you just the way you are. Scars and all."

Bess swallows hard. Her eyes hold mine, like she's trying to figure something out. "Wow."

"Wow, what?"

"I'm just…happy to see you. And I *really* like the sight of you in my kitchen, making dinner like it's no big deal. I know I'm not supposed to bring it up, but your ex-wife must be stark-raving mad. That's all I have to say about that."

Something inside my chest loosens. "Do you know what we're supposed to do now?" I ask, stepping closer.

She shakes her head, and her big blue eyes look up into mine.

"Right after I set the timer, we'll have forty minutes to kill," I whisper. "So I'm going to need to kiss you, nice and slow. And then take you to bed and show you how much I missed you."

Bess shivers. "What are you waiting for, then?"

"Not a damn thing." I thread my fingers into her hair and kiss her.

Bess eats three enchiladas, which is almost as many as I do. She's finishing up her beer when I ask if she wants to watch a movie.

"Maybe," she hedges. "But there's something I need to ask you first. It's uncomfortable for me, though."

"Okay?" I take a gulp of beer. "Ask me. Anything."

She sets her bottle on the coffee table. "This thing that we have is perfect. I don't need to change anything right now. I'll never tell you that your schedule is a drag, because mine is a drag, too. I'm just really happy to see you when you're in Brooklyn."

"Same to you, lady." But I'm a little lost. "And we already discussed our parameters, right? You're all the woman I need. You should have seen me counting the minutes until I could climb the stairs and peel you out of my rival's T-shirt."

She gives me a happy smile. "I may have worn that just to taunt you a little."

"I noticed."

"This is a good color on a redhead, though."

"Oh, for fuck's sake."

She smiles again, but then it fades as she takes a deep breath. "When I moved to Brooklyn, it was because I wanted to think about my future. My personal life, not my business. I hired Eric so that I could eventually spend more time on me and less time on the road. That won't happen for a while, though. It's a long-term plan."

"Yeah. Sounds like a great goal."

"And then there's you, and you weren't part of my plan. But I care about you and I am willing to make space in my plan for you. So much space." She gives me a nervous smile, and I really don't know where this is going. "You just got out of a marriage, and the timing of my question sucks. But someday I'll need to know if you could trust someone again and share your life. And, if so, am I the kind of girl you could love?"

"Bess—" Hell, does she really not think she's lovable?

She silences me by raising her hand. "You don't need to answer. In fact, it's too soon. But this is the question of my heart. I'm falling pretty hard, here. So if you just see me as a good time, I need to know that. I'm thirty, Tank. Eventually, I'll run out of time."

"Out of time," I echo as my heart drops hard and fast. Now I understand where this conversation is headed. "You want to have kids." The last word practically gets stuck in my throat.

"Eventually," she repeats. "I have a few years, though. Five, probably."

"Five," I repeat stupidly.

The problem is that I already know how this works. And five years isn't enough. That's sixty months of potential disappointment, followed by tears, and distance, and regret.

For some guys, no amount of time is enough.

Suddenly, the living room is too damn small. I grab my plate off the coffee table and stand up quickly. I carry it into the kitchen and rinse it off. I know I shouldn't have left the room. But a familiar chill is wrapping itself around my heart.

I rinse that fucking plate very carefully and tuck it into the dishwasher. *So this is how it ends.* This is why I can't fall for anyone. I should have known this would happen.

Bess is waiting for me when I come back, a shattered look on her face. "I knew it was too soon. I knew it, and I asked anyway because…" She swallows hard. "Never mind. I'm sorry to ruin a nice evening," she says quietly. "But it wouldn't be fair for me to have an agenda and not mention it. Say something."

I walk over and sit down beside her. But I feel cold inside. My heart already resembles the same lump of granite that it became at the end of my marriage. For a while there I'd thought Bess had chased it away.

But I was fooling myself. She can't fix this for me. And I'm an asshole to ever think she could.

"Honey," I rasp. "Having a family isn't in the cards for me."

"I see," she chokes out. She's trying not to get upset. And I'm trying not to howl at the sky.

Her disappointment is like a knife through the tattered remains of my heart. "It's not you, okay? I just can't go there. My marriage was…not good." A stronger man would provide all the gory details. Then again, the end result would be the same. So I don't really see the point.

"I know," she grits out. "You told me, and I didn't listen."

"This is *not* your fault." I stand up again. "I should go, Bess. I'm sorry I'm not the kind of man you can make a future with. I wish I was that guy." And why the hell did I not see this coming? "I'm sorry," I repeat. "You didn't do a thing wrong. And you deserve better."

So, so much better.

"You have to do what you have to do," she says in a low voice. "I knew it might come to this." Her face is red, but she doesn't cry. Instead, she lifts her chin and straightens her spine. That look of determination is something I've always loved about her. But now I realize she looks that way because she's had a lot of practice at facing disappointment.

And I can't believe I'm the kind of asshole who's only brought her more.

She doesn't say anything further. She just regards me with an expression that dares me to disappoint her again with more of my shitty apologies.

I walk behind the couch and grab my jacket off the hook on the wall. Then I lean down and drop a kiss onto the top of her head.

She smells like lemons. I can't believe I'm walking away from her right now. I don't want to.

But I can't give her what she wants. And every moment I linger in her life, I'm preventing her from going after the future she desires.

So I do it. I leave. Three seconds later I'm jogging down the staircase of her apartment building. When I hit the bottom I wrench the door open and rush out onto the sidewalk, breathing hard. I'm wearing sneakers, so it's easy enough to just break into a jog and head toward the path along the river.

There's no distance that's far enough, though. Some troubles just can't be outrun.

TWENTY-FIVE

The Trouble with Grumpy Defensemen

BESS

December

THE NEXT MONTH is difficult for me. I watch a lot of hockey and eat a lot of ice cream. But I do it alone. The Bruisers are winning, which is nice. But I avoid their games, choosing other times and places to see my clients.

Eric is gentle with me at work. He really deserves that plaque on our office wall. He and Alex invite me over for dinner a couple times, which is lovely. I get to eat gourmet food and snuggle Rosie in the midst of their obvious domestic bliss.

Zara is taking it hard, though. "I guess I'm not cut out to be your agent," she says, her voice full of regret. "How do you do this? What do you say to your clients when they don't get what they want?"

"I tell them to dig deep and go after the next opportunity."

"But I don't think we're ready for that step," Zara muses. "First we eat all the carbs and watch Bridget Jones's Diary on repeat."

"Carbs?"

"I'm sympathy eating. For two," she explains.

God, I love Zara.

And I suppose there's a silver lining to breaking up with Tank.

Now I don't have to tell my brother that I've been dating a hockey player.

I do, however, tell my girlfriends. Over margaritas, I fill Becca and Georgia in on the fact that I'm in love with him, but that we are not together.

It's a good decision, too. Because the moment I share my pain, these two circle the wagons. Every week they invite me out somewhere new. They've more or less adopted me, and I am grateful.

That's how I come to sit one weeknight in a brand-new massage chair at Becca's newly opened salon. Georgia and Becca flank me on either side. And at my feet, a nail technician fills a foot bath with ginger-scented water. Meanwhile, the salon manager hands me a flute of Prosecco.

"Thank you!" I say as cheerfully as I can. "I think I could become a convert, here."

"See?" Georgia says. "I love getting a pedicure, but it doesn't have a thing to do with the way my nails look."

"I get it," I say, relaxing against the leather. "I was a doubter like you. But I'm coming around." A sip of bubbly wine helps, too. Not that my mood is easy to improve these days.

"That's why you have me, babycakes," Becca adds. "To save you both from a lifetime of imperfect toes."

"I'm just here for the foot massage and the wine," Georgia says with a shrug.

"And the gossip," Becca adds. "Don't overlook my true purpose in life."

"I like how you think." This is just what I need, too. Soft lighting, classical guitar music on the sound system, and the company of women. "Remind me how you decided to buy this place? It's so pretty now." The glass tiles sparkle beneath the paint job and the new upholstery.

"We used to come here in the middle of the day," Georgia explains. "When work was stressful, we'd run in here on our lunch break, because we knew we'd be alone."

"I mean, can you imagine hockey players coming here?" Becca adds, sipping her wine. "It was always our little oasis."

"But that was before Becca turned this place into an *actual* oasis," Georgia adds. "The old decor was a little shabby. We didn't mind. But this is so much better. Becca picked out all that glass tile herself."

"You've got game. But it's risky to buy a place that's going out of business." Although it seems to be doing fine tonight. When I walked through the door, every manicure table up front was occupied.

"Yes and no," Becca says. "There was a citywide scandal that shut down a whole bunch of nail salons. Apparently they weren't paying their workers a fair wage. When I told Nate how upset I was at the loss of our favorite spot, he didn't even hesitate. '*Buy it,*' he said. 'Renovate. Raise the prices and reopen. You can hire back everyone who worked there at a fair price.'"

"Genius," I say as the technician eases my feet into the warm, bubbling water.

"I'm not used to thinking like a billionaire," Becca says. "But Nate feels good about investing in this neighborhood. And it doesn't even feel like an indulgence, because I have nine people on the payroll, here, including the new manager, who's a single mom. Ooh! Xue!" She waves to a young woman. "Over here!"

The young woman sashays toward us in impossibly high heels —the kind that I could never walk in. "Would you like a strawberry dipped in dark chocolate?" she asks, leaning down to offer each of us a treat.

"Oh my goodness." Georgia reaches for one. "Becca's influence is everywhere."

"Damn straight." Becca takes a berry, too.

As I reach for mine, I'm hit with the Cinderella tingles. This is my life—pedicures and bubbly wine. I'm still lonely for Tank, but I refuse to work late into the night, hunched over my phone. The five-year plan is back on. I can nurture female friendships without a man. I'm in a good place.

Tonight, anyway.

"Becca for president" I say as I bite the juicy end off the strawberry. I can feel my sadness lifting by a tiny amount. "Are you sure that bright purple toes are a good idea, though?" The technician is shaking the bottle of polish that Becca chose for me.

"Purple is the right move," Becca says seriously. "No boring toes on my watch. Plus, it's the Bruisers color. I had that shade specially mixed. Now I need Georgia to tell me how worried I should be about the upcoming game against Dallas. Did practice go okay today?"

"It went fine. We're going to beat Phoenix this weekend. And that will build confidence before Dallas."

"You've got Castro back in the lineup," I say between bites of strawberry and dark chocolate. Castro had a muscle pull, but it turned out to be no big deal. "The doctor cleared him."

"Excellent. That deserves a toast. To healthy men and smooth ice!" Becca angles her glass first toward mine and then Georgia's. We all toast.

"Crikey is healthy, too," Georgia adds. "And…" She turns to me, hesitating. "Am I allowed to talk about hot, grumpy defensemen?"

"Go ahead," I say. "Hot, grumpy defensemen are my living."

"Okay. Then here's the skinny on the blue-liners," Georgia says. "Loneliness must be good for defensive strategy, because Tank has been playing like a beast these past few games. Our offense is still a little baffled by him, but the other D-men are coming around. Anton has figured out how to work with him. And now I think Coach is going to try O'Doul and Tank on shift together."

Becca whistles under her breath. "They could be an unstoppable pair. The dream team."

"Right?" I agree, and my voice only wobbles a little. Even though I'm hurt, I want the best for Tank. That's how you know you love someone.

Isn't clarity a bitch? On the one hand, I regret trying to have a relationship chat with Tank before he was ready. On the other hand, his reaction taught me everything I needed to know about my own feelings.

It was possible that a little more time might have sorted him out, but it was just as likely that he'd never see himself as a relationship guy again. It hurts, but I needed to know that. Waiting around and hiding my feelings wasn't ever going to end well.

"Tell me more gossip," I say, begging for a change of topic. "How's Leo doing? Are you spending Christmas with his family?"

"Oh, definitely," Georgia says. "I love his family. Except lately his mother can't go an hour without asking when we plan to have kids."

"Oh, brother," Becca groans. "Nate's mom has been dropping some hints, too. And we've only been married a few months."

"Shouldn't we be taking bets?" I ask. "Which of you two is going to be first?"

"Georgia is," Becca says. "Leo has been angling since ten minutes after they got married. And Georgia doesn't hate the idea, either. Trust me."

"We're still negotiating the number, though," Georgia says. "I'm an only child, so I think one or two kids is plenty. But Leo thinks three is the minimum."

"Leo just wants to have lots of baby-making sex," Becca points out.

Georgia snorts. "Leo's appetites are great, that's true. But isn't baby-making sex the same as any other nookie?"

"No way," Becca argues. "I mean, I haven't *had* any baby-making sex, so I'm just guessing here, but there should be trumpets and an angel choir. If you're making a human life, that has to be beautiful."

"The angel choir might mess with my concentration," Georgia says, and I choke on a sip of Prosecco.

"You okay?"

"Sure." I cough. And then I blurt out my strange question. "I wonder if the choir shows up at the fertility clinic I went to yesterday."

There's a stunned silence. "Omigod. Hello, mic drop!" Georgia yelps. "Are you having a baby? Did we bet on the wrong horse here?" She waves a hand over the three of us in our massage chairs.

Even the woman who's buffing my cuticles looks up in surprise.

"I'm investigating the possibility," I admit. "This was just a preliminary consultation. But I've been thinking about it a long time. And if Tank and I aren't going to be together, maybe it's time to take matters into my own hands." The idea of going back to Tinder makes me want to curl up in a ball and howl.

"Wow," Becca says. "You are impressive. So how does it work? Do you have to have a bunch of tests?"

"There will be a couple of tests. But then there are choices to make. IVF versus artificial insemination. IVF sounds a little intimidating, honestly. You have to inject yourself with a drug."

Becca shivers. "I hate needles. But I guess I could stab one into my own butt if it meant I could have a baby."

"Thigh," I correct. "And I hear there's no angel choir."

Becca reaches over and squeezes my hand. "I just want to slap Tank."

"And then give him a firm shake," Georgia agrees.

"He can't help it," I say, jumping to his defense. "The man's wife asked him to move out, and that was only seven months ago. He's not over it."

"He's not," Georgia says quietly. "Some people never get over it. Maybe you two are star-crossed."

"It sucks," Becca says. "And if you need someone to go to the clinic with you, I'm there."

"You're the best. Seriously. Getting pregnant in a doctor's office does seem kind of weird and lonely."

"When you're holding a baby it won't seem weird, and it won't be lonely," Georgia points out.

She's totally right. "When I think of myself rocking a baby, it all seems worth it." We'll be a small team of two players. "I really want a baby."

"Does Dave know you're doing this?" Georgia asks.

"Not yet. Zara does, though. And the second I decide to go through with it, he'll be my first call." I can't predict how he'll react, either. He loves his child, and he'd want me to have one, too. But he'll probably worry about me.

"We'll be your second call," Becca says, draining her Prosecco.

"And then we can start looking for a bigger apartment for you. I can't work my magic in that rental you've got now."

"Okay. It's a deal."

The nail technician begins stroking Bruisers purple onto my big toenail, and—for a moment—all is right with the world.

TWENTY-SIX

Woo Woo Shit

TANK

"NICE GOAL LAST NIGHT."

"Thanks. Every goal counts." Grudgingly, I take my seat in front of Doc Mulvey. These sessions continue to be a waste of time, but the shrink is paid to talk to me, so here I am.

"So—did you visualize that goal ahead of time?"

I snort. "You know I didn't. What is your point?"

The goal in question was the result of a messy rebound. The puck shook loose in front of the net after getting momentarily stuck in the goalie's shin pad. Then the goalie's own teammate overskated the puck while trying to clear it.

I pounced on it like a cat on a stunned mouse, poking it toward the net. And it only worked because my opponent blocked his goalie's view of me. It's what we call an ugly goal, and Doc Mulvey knows this.

"My point is—how are those visualization exercises going?"

After a moment's indecision, I decide to level with him. "I gave up on that pretty fast. It just wasn't working for me. After a few minutes sitting there with my eyes closed, I get sleepy. Or my mind wanders. I find myself visualizing my sushi order instead of the rink."

"Uh-huh. So you don't believe that visualization can help you?"

"No, sir. I guess I don't."

"Hmm. When we're young, we do tend to believe visualization works. So if you feel this way now, then you probably feel that visualization has failed you. Humor me, okay? Tell me about a time when you were visualizing hard, and nothing turned out like you planned."

"Uh, okay. How about my marriage?" Jordanna and I visualized our future together with so much gusto that we bought a five-bedroom house, intending to fill it with little Tankiewiczs.

Spoiler alert: there aren't any little Tanks in the world.

"That's a good answer. Your wife said 'until death do us part,' but then asked you to move out."

"Exactly," I agree, because it's easier than going into detail. "The way you look at it, every failed marriage is a failure of visualization. Do I sound like a shrink now?"

He ignores the jab. "Failed visualization and failed teamwork. Last night your ugly goal put a score on the board. But it wasn't the kind of teamwork a player dreams about, right?"

"Although it still counts," I point out.

"*Go Brooklyn*," he agrees. "But I'm still a believer it's all connected, Mark. If you can't visualize the kind of teamwork that gets your production up, then you're closed off from that success. And the reason you can't visualize it is because other people on your team have let you down so badly. Including your wife."

"Whatever. Fine. I'm willing to accept some of the blame. But only up to a point." My teammates have been particularly cool to me lately. Because I let Bess down. I don't know what they've heard, exactly. But the chill factor is real. "It's pretty hard to picture a day when I'm on the same wavelength as this team."

"Mmm," he says, maddeningly. "But when you're open to the universe, you're open to the puck finding your stick."

"That is some really woo woo shit, Doc Mulvey."

He laughs. "And I *love* woo woo shit. I was that kid who stood in the middle of my basement holding a plastic light saber, trying to feel the force."

"Yeah?" I laugh. "Fine, me too. But that's every little boy."

"Here's the thing, though." He leans forward in his chair. "*Did* you feel the force?"

I blink. He's right, damn it. As a kid, I'd stood there, eyes closed, knowing to my bones that my X-Wing fighter was parked beside me in the sand and feeling an unexplained energy ripple through my body "Sure, I felt it. But not since I was seven."

"Try again, Mark," Doc Mulvey whispers. "Humor us both. Try to feel it again. Whether you call it the force, or luck, or meditation. Try to see yourself at one with this team. Your stick is that light saber, okay? And there's a magnet inside it that draws the puck whenever you're ready."

I do my best not to roll my eyes. *Sure, pal.*

"Feel the force, man. What do you really have to lose?

When my thirty-minute session is up, I swing by the locker room to grab my gym bag.

The only guy around is Jason Castro. The moment he sees it's me, he shoves his ear buds into his ears and makes himself busy with his phone.

I don't like it, but I don't even blame him. He'd warned me not to hurt Bess, but I did anyway. I deeply regret it, but nobody cares.

If there's a silver lining, it's that Bess isn't my agent. Thank God for Eric. If I had to chat with Bess about hiring a New York accountant or finding an apartment I would probably lose my mind.

I might be losing it anyway. It kills me to know that she's right here in Brooklyn, yet I can't see her. I should have known that it would turn out this way. None of this is her fault. It's all mine. She asked me for the one thing I couldn't give.

It's lunchtime, so I take myself out to eat. As I'm finishing up, my phone buzzes with a text, and I have a knee-jerk moment of optimism, wondering if it's from Bess.

As if. It's from Henry Kassman. *Got something for you. Come visit.*

Finally, I reply. *This afternoon?*

Sure, he says, as if he hasn't steered me away every other time I've asked.

Instead of taking a nap, I catch the ferry across the river and walk up the East Side to Kassman's fancy apartment building.

The moment after I enter Henry's penthouse, I understand why Bess ended up in my hotel room that afternoon, crying her eyes out all over my T-shirt. Even from fifteen paces I can see that Henry Kassman looks dreadful. He's horribly thin, and his skin is gray. He's wearing pajamas in the middle of the day, which is just plain wrong.

Now I want to cry, too.

"Tank, my boy," Henry says in a slow, thready voice. "You're looking well."

I take a deep breath and man up. "You flatter me, Kassman."

"Nah. Everyone looks well compared to me." He takes an audible breath just to finish the sentence. "Take the compliment."

I pull a chair a little closer to his hospital bed and sit down, and the silence threatens to choke us both. What do you say to a man who's dying? "Is there anything at all I can do for you? Any of your favorite foods you need me to fetch?"

"Not a thing," he wheezes. "Unless you've got any decent gossip. It's boring being old and sick."

"Huh. Okay. This year I think I *am* the gossip."

"This too shall pass." He removes a folder from the table by his bed and hands it to me. "These are for you."

I flip open the cover, and I'm staring down at a set of documents that I'd forgotten about. "*Final* decree of divorce," I blurt. What's the proper reaction to receiving one's divorce decree? If there's a right way to feel, I don't know what it is.

I'm failing at this, too.

"Yeah. You don't even have to sign it. Sorry, kid," Henry says.

"No, I'm really okay." I remove the paper from the folder, fold it into quarters and tuck it into my jacket pocket.

"Take care of that," Henry says, pointing at my pocket. "You'll need it if you get remarried."

I laugh suddenly. "No chance of that."

"You say that now, but..." He gives me a fond smile. "You know how after a disappointment some coaches say: 'We're having a rebuilding year'? Well, this is a rebuilding year for you, personally."

"I might need more than one year."

"You have time," he says. And that's a refrain between us. It has been for years.

Henry first approached me when I was a teenager playing juniors hockey. My father had left the family by that point. I was the man of the house, and I had a giant ego at seventeen. I thought I was going to go directly from juniors to playing beside my idols in the NHL.

I was really good at *visualizing*. The team shrink would have loved it.

Henry knew better. When I was nineteen, he talked me into applying for college. "Go to school. Play some hockey. Gain forty pounds of muscle. Skate faster. And get an education. You have time. The big leagues will still be there when you're ready."

It had worked out just like he'd said, too. I'd made it to the Show at twenty-three, without bouncing around in the minors.

"Did you find an apartment yet?" he asks eventually.

"No, but I got a guy working on it for me." Finally.

Henry clicks his tongue. "I wish I could help you with that. I'm sorry to abandon you."

"You *never* did," I say as my throat grows thick. "Not once."

"Gotta get yourself another agent, son. A while ago I told Bess Beringer she should take you on as a client. She had all those opinions about what you needed in order to settle in."

"Yeah." I swallow hard, thinking of Bess. "Actually, I'm gonna go with Eric Bayer."

Henry tilts his head and seems to consider this. "He's a good man. Not so much experience, though. You and Bess don't get along?"

I force my face into a smile. "Oh, we get along. We got along too well. But she's not exactly speaking to me at the moment."

"Oh dear. You sly dog," Henry says, and then he coughs. "Wait a minute. Didn't you and Bess have something together some years ago? Wasn't that you?"

"Ancient history, but yeah. She was working for you back then. You weren't supposed to know about it."

"Ah, well. I did know." He leans back against the pillows. "I'd forgotten all about it, and now I wonder if I did you two a disservice."

"How so?"

He closes his eyes. "I heard the rumors. Couple of players made some jokes, you know? And I felt bad for Bess because she seemed like the kind of girl who wouldn't like people talking about her. I didn't know what to do about it, though, because I didn't like the idea of telling a young woman how to run her life." He opens his eyes and stares at the ceiling, as if deep in thought. "So I asked Pines to give her some perspective."

"Oh." I try and fail to keep the disappointment out of my voice.

"Pines is a great agent, but she's a little…"

"Bitchy?" I supply, because I'm not over that woman telling Bess that she was a whore.

"*Acidic* is the word I was looking for. Anyway. I didn't know what to do. I guess I could have ignored the whole thing."

"Maybe," I agree, wishing he had. But he hadn't meant to make Bess feel bad, and it's not like I'd banged down her door to tell her I loved her after she'd dropped me. Nope. I was too stupid to do that.

Still am.

But our little tragedy wasn't Henry Kassman's fault. "Bess still feels it's unprofessional to date a player. And we're not together anymore. So don't tease her, okay?"

"Not even a little?" Henry asks. "I don't get much entertainment."

"Tease her as much as you want, Henry. But not about this."

"Fine," he grumbles. "I can see you two as a nice couple. You both have a lot of spirit. I know I shouldn't hand a man his divorce papers and then press him about his love life, but…"

"Don't rush me, old man. And Bess and I aren't meant to be. I don't think I'm meant to be with anyone. I can't go through it all again."

Henry makes an impatient noise. "If I'm still here a year from now, I'm gonna ask you again. I bet you'll be singing a different tune."

"You go ahead and ask me. In fact, I'll set a reminder in my phone," I say, because I can't bear the thought of Henry dying. "But my answer will be the same. Bess wants a marriage and a family, and I can't give that to her."

"That's bullshit, Tank." He folds his hands over his belly. "I bet you didn't even tell her why your marriage to Jordanna fell apart."

"It fell apart for the same reason all marriages fall apart—a lot of disappointment and not enough love." I will never get over the sound of my wife crying night after night in the bathroom, where she thought I couldn't hear her.

It wrecks a guy.

"That's oversimplifying things," Henry scolds me. "You got to bring the dark stuff out into the sunlight, or it won't ever go away. You want someone to spend your life with? There's no reason you shouldn't have that. You're healthy. You're still rich, thanks to the prenup this old man made you sign. You're not bad looking. And your new team is *just* about to figure out how to use your best skills on the ice. Any second now."

I snicker. "Sure they are."

"And most importantly…" He reaches over and lays a hand on my elbow. "You're a good man, Tank. I have always thought so. And I always will."

Fuck me. My eyes get hot. "Thank you, Henry. And right back at you."

"I have one more document for you. But this one you have to sign." He reaches for the bedside table again and grabs another folder, opening it and handing it to me.

"What's this?" There are only a few lines of text on the page.

Dear Henry Kassman,

You are hereby fired as my agent.

Although the stated terms of our original contract do not require an explanation, only a waiting period of thirty days, and a settling of accounts pursuant to a very boring paragraph on page four, I feel the need to explain myself. I have already heard your best jokes, and I am tired of steak dinners and red wine. So let's just end this thing amicably.

Sincerely,

Mark Tankiewicz

P.S. I still regret the million dollars you got me for shooting those underwear ads.

Slapping a hand over my mouth, I laugh. But, damn it, my throat is tight. I don't want to sign this paper. Ever. And it kills me that his last professional act for me was making the fucking thing funny, so I wouldn't feel so guilty that I'm living and he's...

I inhale carefully through my nose, controlling myself. "Why do we need this?"

"So nobody has to second guess Bess and Eric's right to represent you." Henry hands me a pen. "This is really for them. That's why you have to sign."

I quickly scribble my name on the line and hand it back to him. My throat is a desert, and my sinuses feel prickly.

A nurse comes into the room, announcing that Henry needs medication and a bath. So—after extracting a promise from him that I can come back next week—I show myself out.

It isn't until I'm taking deep, cleansing breaths in the elevator that I realize something. Signing that document to separate my business from Henry's hurt me a hell of a lot worse than taking delivery of my divorce decree.

"It's a rebuilding year," I say to nobody as I leave the building and head for the ferry.

I'm crossing the East River toward Brooklyn when my phone rings again. The caller ID says BERINGER & ASSOCIATES, and my stupid heart gives a kick just seeing Bess's name. But the caller is Eric. Of course it is.

"Hey, Tank," he says. "Are you nearby, perchance?"

"On the ferry back to Brooklyn. Why?"

"We've got to get you out of that hotel. Last week I slipped a C-note to the concierge at 220 Water, and asked him to tip me off if any apartments came up for lease or sale."

I give a low whistle. "Smart man."

"I'm feeling pretty smart already, because Miguel just called me to say there's a Corcoran realtor showing a two-bedroom right now. So I speed-dialed another realtor at Corcoran, and got him to find the listing in their system. It isn't even on the website yet. But if you jog over here..."

"Yeah! Dude. Thank you. Give me fifteen minutes."

The second the ferry docks, I don't stop running until I arrive in front of the Million Dollar Dorm, as the guys refer to it. Hell, it doesn't even matter if the apartment is a wreck. I'll buy it anyway, before the other buyer gets a chance.

Eric waves me into the lobby, introducing me to a young broker named Wilson. Then he high-fives the concierge and ushers me toward the elevator banks.

"Sorry to hustle you," Eric says as the elevator doors open. "But things in this building tend to move fast."

"Don't apologize. If the price isn't egregious, I could move fast, too."

Wilson grins like a guy who's just won the lottery. He's about to earn a fat commission for fifteen minutes' work. "It's a second-floor unit," the kid says. "But this building has great windows, and I'm sure the light will still be adequate."

"We'll have to see," I say, because I don't want to sound like a sucker. But I'm all in. I want to walk a block and a half to practice and live in the same building as my teammates.

Not that I'd repeat this aloud, but I'm honestly starting to trust some of them.

The doors slide open again, and I follow Wilson out of the elevator. At the end of a long hall, we arrive at Apartment 212. Wilson tries the door. It's locked, so he knocks.

When it swings open, another realtor is standing there, clipboard in hand, irritated look on her face. "This unit isn't even on the website yet."

"But it's already in the database," Wilson says, widening the door and stepping inside. "And I'm watching this building for my client."

Eric and I exchange amused glances. Our boy Wilson has some hustle. I like him already.

And the apartment is great, too. It's got the same wide-plank wood floors and brick walls as Delilah's place. I'm standing in a generous living room, and I can see into the kitchen. It isn't as flashy as Delilah's, but it's fine.

"Nice bathroom," Eric says from down the hall. "And this must be the master." He pokes his head into another room. I follow him, and when the door swings open, I catch a glimpse of a gorgeous bedroom.

"There's an en suite bathroom," the listing agent says. "You might as well take a look, but don't crowd my client. She's checking out the second bedroom."

"We're not crowding anyone, Lily," Wilson argues. "Go ahead, sir."

I've forgotten how odd it is to inspect a stranger's home. There are family photos on the wall, and I feel a twinge of guilt when I open the closet in the master bedroom to check its size.

"Why are they moving?" Eric asks, perhaps just to make conversation.

"There's a second baby coming," the listing agent sniffs. "They need more space."

Ah. I think back to the day when Jordanna and I found our house in the Dallas suburbs. She'd been so excited. "Four upstairs bedrooms!" she'd gushed. "And that yard!"

She'd been mentally filling the place with children. I had, too. We'd had no idea what we were in for. Years of disappointment, followed by a bitter divorce.

I'm lost in thought as I step into the other bedroom. The walls are pink, and a fluffy rug dampens the sound of my footsteps. *They have a little girl*, my brain says.

It takes me a moment to register the other apartment-hunter in the room.

It's Bess. She's standing very still, looking at a framed painting of a mother polar bear cuddling her fuzzy little infant.

My heart stops beating for a long second, before thumping wildly back to life. She hasn't spotted me yet, so I drink her in. Bess isn't a big person, but there's something so vivid about the way she carries herself. Neck straight. Shoulders back. Ready to take on anything.

She's so beautiful, it hurts to look at her.

"Tank?" Eric calls from the hall. "Did you—" Bess's chin whips toward us just as Eric appears in the doorway. "Oh," Eric says quietly. "Hell. Hi, Bess."

Her eyes widen, and for a moment, nobody speaks.

"Um. I'll just…" Eric backs out of the bedroom and leaves the two of us.

"What are you doing here?" she whispers.

"The same thing you are, I guess." It's so quiet, I can hear the pink clock ticking on the nightstand. "I'm sure Eric had no idea you were looking at this place."

"I didn't tell him."

There's another awkward silence, and I want to ask her how she is. I want to tell her how much I miss her. I want to close the distance between us in three quick strides and kiss that perfect mouth.

"I'll go," I say instead. "This place is perfect for you. And I only need one bedroom."

"So you mentioned," she says with a sigh.

And that's my opening. My cue to blurt out the whole fucking story—right here in front of the crib and the fluffy stuffed bear on the rocking chair. I could tell her how much effort and trouble I'd gone through to try to have a family.

But then I'd have to tell her how bad it hurts to fail. Most people don't have any idea what that's like. Does Bess want to know how every one of Jordanna's monthly periods became times of mourning? Or how I didn't even care if I ever had sex again, so long as I could stop letting Jordanna down?

Whoever owns this apartment probably has no clue how lucky they are. *Another baby on the way.* Do they know that you can try for five years and come away with nothing?

"I probably can't afford this place," Bess says quietly. "It's a stretch. This building is so bid up."

"You can too afford it," I argue. She probably makes more than a half million a year.

Slowly, she shakes her head. "I'm a coward. My five-year plan looks great on paper. But those leaps of faith look different when the sticker price is almost two million bucks. And that's before the cost of IVF, and a procedure called egg retrieval, and private preschool." She shivers.

The drugs aren't that bad, but egg retrieval is just as tricky as it sounds. I don't say this aloud. If I start spilling my guts, I'll never stop.

We can't have this conversation in front of a crib that some stranger put together on his day off. The apartment owner probably has no idea how it feels to fail at the basic manly art of impregnating your wife. To spend fifty thousand dollars on specialists who give you a sterile cup and a pitying look as they point you toward the privacy of a room where you're supposed to flip through some porn and unload some of your low sperm count jizz into a sterile cup.

My slap shot is fifty miles an hour. I can bench 350 and squat 475. But near the end of my marriage, there had been a night when I'd felt like the weakest man on the planet. My wife had wanted to try it again the natural way, and I physically couldn't do it.

"What are you thinking about right now?" Bess asks, and I realize we've been standing in an uncomfortable silence.

"I was thinking…" So many ugly things. "You should buy this place. Pink isn't really my color."

"Really? That's what you were thinking?" Disappointment crosses her face. "I think we're done here. I'm outie."

She scoots past me, a fiery angel. I can't hear what she says to the startled brokers in the living room, but the door opens and closes a moment later.

Fuck. I leave the baby's room, my neck hot with shame. I fucked that up, and pretty much everything that happened before it.

I can do better. I *will* do better. Right now.

Eric is waiting with a worried look in the living room. "Nice place," he says, rubbing the back of his neck.

"What do you think?" Wilson asks, ever hopeful.

I think I owe Bess a giant apology. "One of us will make an offer tonight. Let me have your card."

The other broker frowns at me from across the room. "I'm going to have photos up on the website tomorrow. This place will go fast."

"I don't doubt it. That's why you'll hear from either Bess or myself tonight." There's a testy edge to my voice, and I just don't care. "Thank you all for your time."

And at that, I'm gone.

TWENTY-SEVEN

Normal is a Stretch

BESS

HOW WAS THE APARTMENT? Zara's text asks me.

Expensive, I reply, just so she won't ask a follow-up question. I need time alone here on my couch, preferably curled up into a ball. Preferably with a cocktail. Too bad I didn't stock up ahead of this little crisis.

Of all the people in the world it had to be Mark Tankiewicz who'd walked into that bedroom-turned-nursery. Like I haven't spent the last three weeks trying to erase him from my brain. *Damn* it.

If I bought that place, I'd always remember the soft expression that took over his face as I turned to look at him. And then I'd remember the hardened one that replaced it a moment later.

Even if my expensive new reproductive endocrinologist gets me pregnant on the first try, I'd stand in that room rocking my baby girl or boy and wonder why Tank didn't want to be there, too.

Who could lead a normal life under those conditions? Although "normal" is a stretch for me already. "He can have that apartment," I grumble aloud. He can turn the second bedroom into a man cave with a wet bar and a TV the size of a highway billboard.

I'll live someplace else. Like Finland. I hear Finland is a nice country to raise a child. I could learn Finnish and scout goalie talent all over Copenhagen.

No. Not Copenhagen. That's in Denmark. Oslo? No. Helsinki!

There's a knock on my door, sudden and loud. Who the Helsinki could that be?

"Eric," I call from my ball on the sofa. Today I could have done with a stupider employee. Goddamn him for sniffing out that listing just as quickly as I did. "Eric, I'm fine. I don't need company. And you don't have to apologize for doing your job."

He knocks again. Men are so freaking stubborn.

I heave myself off the couch and open the damn door so he can see that I'm not drowning in tears and ice cream and tequila. Not yet, anyway.

But it's Tank standing there. "Shit. Eric let you in the front door?"

"Yeah."

"I'll fire him tomorrow."

"Then *you'll* have to be my agent, because Kassman made me fire *him* today."

"Never," I hiss.

"Can I come in? I need to say my piece."

"No, you really don't. Every time we're alone together, the same thing happens. And I can't ride that train anymore. I went off birth control, too. So my apartment is officially a danger zone for you."

"Honey, it isn't," he says, his voice full of gravel. "There are things I have to tell you. And if you don't let me in, I'm gonna have to shout them through your door, which is probably going to embarrass both of us. So for the sake of the neighborhood, it's best if you invite me in."

Help. I'm weakening. "Will it change anything?"

"Doubt it."

My heart sinks all over again, and I make a move to close the door.

"Bess." He catches the door before I can close it. "I love you."

"What?" My eyes fill immediately with tears. "That's just cruel."

"I know, baby. But sometimes life is a little cruel, and I need you to know why I walked away from you."

All the fight goes out of me. I step back and let Tank into the room. After closing the door, he walks over to the sofa, sitting down.

But I don't follow. I stand here, arms crossed, because it hurts to look at him. I didn't know I'd be seeing Tank tonight. If I had, I would have put on some emotional armor. Or at least a nicer T-shirt.

And slammed a shot of tequila.

"You asked me if I could ever get married again and have a family," he says, his green eyes studying me.

"I recall."

"The answer is no, but not for lack of trying. I spent five years trying to give Jordanna a baby. After lots of old-fashioned sex, we did six rounds of IVF. She got pregnant twice and miscarried."

"Oh," I gasp. Oh *hell*.

"Those injections you were talking about? I'm a pro at those. I'm also a pro at making eye contact with the fertility specialist who's delivering bad news. And I'm a pro at going to practice the next day and pretending like everything is fine when my teammate announces that he and his wife are having twins, while my wife is at home crying."

"Oh," I say again. I feel like a giant idiot right now. Because it never once occurred to me that Tank wanted kids and couldn't have them. On the other hand, there was a simple reason for why I hadn't known. "Why didn't you say so?" I squeak. "I just spent a whole month thinking I wasn't...enough for you."

"No, baby," he says, dropping his head. "You're everything to me. But I couldn't man up and tell you."

"You didn't trust me," I say in a low voice. "I was ready to trust you completely."

"Were you?" He gets up and crosses to me. Then he gently grasps my hand, rotating my arm until the scar on the inside of my elbow shows. "Then how'd you get this scar?"

I look down at the evil mark, and feel my chest flush with embarrassment. I remember lying about it to him. I hadn't even thought twice about it. "Okay." I sigh. "Maybe you have a couple of good points."

"Sit with me, honey." He gives my hand a little squeeze. "Let's talk."

Chastened, I follow him to the sofa and sit down. I feel all torn up inside. And it doesn't help that he's close enough to touch, or that I can smell the lovely scent of him. Like clean towels and spicy aftershave.

"Bess, you deserve everything. You really do. But I can't try again. It was..." He sighs. "I don't mean to be melodramatic. But it was torture every month when we failed. We'd both get depressed. And that was just the start of it. Depression gives way to blame and mistrust. And so much dread. I cannot get back on that tilt-a-whirl."

"Shit." I'm still trying to wrap my head around five years of brutal disappointment. That's a lot of praying not to get your period. That's a lot of trying to reassure each other that it will all turn out okay.

"And then when she got pregnant—twice..." He swallows roughly. "That was even worse. We got so hopeful. It seemed like we'd finally make it. And then..." He slowly shakes his head. "Brutal. And nobody understands. They say, 'You're young, you can try again.'"

"Oh, God." I think I'd murder anyone who said that to me.

"Yeah. There's no way for me to leave that experience behind. I cannot go joyfully into the future with you, knowing that history will just repeat itself."

"But..." I'm still catching up. And there's a lot to this story that I don't understand. "What about sperm donors? What about adoption?"

"She wanted *our* baby. And since neither of us had any significant health problems, that seemed reasonable. Even after a few failures, we thought we'd succeed. But we never did. And I was stubborn, too. I thought there's no reason why I can't have what everybody else has."

"Did they know..." I stop myself before asking *who* had the trouble. "Did the doctors determine why you had so much trouble?"

"Not exactly. I have, uh, not the highest sperm count." He

looks away. "But IVF still should have worked for us. And most miscarriages are mysterious. After all those years, doctors were still saying that we had a lot of bad luck. But at a certain point you start blaming each other."

"Oh." My eyes are leaking. I hadn't noticed until water started dripping off my face.

He reaches over and brushes a tear off my cheekbone. "Eventually you get burnt out. All the love and optimism gets used up, and you can't remember why you wanted this thing together in the first place. Everything stops making sense."

I can't stand the distance between us anymore. So I lean over and put my head against his chest, and he wraps an arm around me. I can feel his steady heartbeat against my face, and it calms me.

We stop talking for a little while, and I try to take it all in. I never gave infertility very much thought. I don't know anyone who's struggled with it.

Or—wait—I guess I probably do. It wouldn't be an easy topic to bring up in casual conversation. Tank just led me to the edge of his own personal abyss, showed me how deep his fault-lines run. And I had never seen them before. I never even knew they were there.

Tank strokes my hair as the light fades from my apartment. It feels so good to lean against this man that I love. I don't want to let him go. I don't know if I even can.

"How did it end?" I ask suddenly. "How did you know it was time to give up?"

He lets out a sigh, and I feel a little guilty for asking. "After Jordanna's last failed IVF, we agreed that we weren't going to try that again. I should have felt better, but I just didn't. And then right after my season ended, Coach had a lavish party for his fortieth wedding anniversary. Right in the middle of it, he and his wife held a recommitment ceremony. We all stood around with our glasses of champagne, and they read these vows to each other..."

Tank swallows, and I can feel myself holding my breath.

"And Coach says to his wife—'Honey, we've been through some really big fights, and some really bad times, but I always knew that you were the one for me. I always knew we were bigger than our troubles.' Afterward, I realized there was no way I could give that kind of speech to my wife. I wasn't the only one who thought so. On the way home from that party, Jordanna asked me to move out."

"Oh, ouch," I gasp. "I'm so sorry."

"I'm all right," he says gently. "I know I should have told you all of this before and saved you the grief. But things were so good. And I just didn't want to relive the whole thing, and let you know how badly I'd failed. It's embarrassing to me."

"It's okay," I say quickly. He's right—things had been good between us. "We had so much fun."

"We did. I felt like a new man. I *was* a new man. For the first time in a long time, I felt like I was enough for somebody."

"You *are* enough. Jesus." I take a deep, shuddery breath, because I realize it's really true. "Tank, I need you more than I need to have kids. What if it was just the two of us?"

"Whoa, now." He lets out a whoosh of air. "That's not an easy decision. You're not allowed to make that decision right after I tell you my horror story. Because your luck is not my luck. And what about your five-year plan?"

I make a grumpy noise. "I've spent my whole career telling athletes they need to have a five-year plan. And I spent the last year telling myself that I needed one. And it's all bullshit."

"Nah," he says. "You don't really believe that. How can you get what you want if you can't articulate it?"

"But there's such a thing as too much planning. I didn't count on falling in love with you. I'm ready to tear the whole thing in half right now, and make a new one. With you. Because I do not want you to walk out my door and say, 'Let's be just friends.'"

His hand freezes on my head. "Bess. Careful. I will not let you change your whole vision for the future just because I can't have kids."

"Maybe I won't be able to conceive a child, either. We have no idea. And I care about you too much to let that be an obstacle."

"You say that now. But let's just say that a year goes by and you're holding your brother's new little red-headed baby. What's going to be going through your mind?"

Well, hell. That exact scenario is headed my way, and the truth is that I'll be insanely jealous. I know I will. And Tank knows it, too, because he's probably been in exactly that same situation more times than I can count.

"There's lots of ways of having a baby," I say softly.

He pinches the bridge of his nose. "But I can't say for sure that I'll ever be ready to try *any* of them. I need to stay off that carnival ride. You don't want that man, Bess—the one who gets depressed every time you get your period."

My stomach hurts as I realize he's right. My gaze falls on the book that's sitting on my coffee table. It's called *Safeguarding Your Fertility*. I stand up and pluck it off the table.

"Don't move that on my account," he says. "I've read that thing cover to cover."

But I am moving it on his account. I cross the room and chuck it into the recycling bin.

"Bess," he warns. "You might decide you want that after all."

"Then I'll buy another copy," I insist. Tank is more important to me than that book. My gut made the decision the moment I opened my door and saw him standing there. He's not ready to hear it, but it's true.

Tank's not the only one with a shitty story. I have a lifetime's practice at overcoming bad situations and appreciating the good things in life. Cinderella doesn't get her prince and then immediately set her sights on a nursery full of princelings. That bitch knows to be grateful.

"What if we just put a moratorium on big decisions?" I ask him. "What if we order takeout food and watch hockey and go back to where we were before I made everything complicated?"

Tank puts an arm around me as I sit down on the couch. "Is that fair to you? You're the one who said that every time we're alone together the result is always the same."

"I left out the part about how good it is, though. Every time we're alone together I'm happy."

"Me too." Tank takes a shaky breath. "I've missed you like crazy, honey. So much that it hurts."

"That's important, Tank." I lean in and take a deep whiff of his clean scent. He pulls me closer to his chest, which is exactly what I needed him to do. "I understand your hesitation. You don't want to be responsible for changing my big plans. Too late. Sorry. You can't make me stop caring about you. You can't make me stop wanting you."

"Well, I'm a lucky guy, then." He eases me off his body, and for a moment I'm disappointed. But then he lays me down on the couch, and covers me with his delectable self. "I just want you to know one thing," he says quietly.

"What?" I'm drowning in his serious green eyes.

"If I could, I'd give you everything. A baby. *All* the babies." He smiles down at me. "I love you, Bess. I like your quick mind. I love your sense of humor. I want you in my life, even if it's selfish."

"It's not," I whisper. "Because I want it, too."

Just as my poor, battered heart is trying to understand this wonderful reversal of fortune, Tank kisses me. It's a very serious kiss—slow and intentional and full of new promises. I moan into the firm press of his lips, because I missed him so much.

His fingers weave into my hair as he kisses me again. I'm all in for this kiss. I catch his head in my hands and sigh against his mouth. "Need you," I whisper as his lips trail off to tickle my jaw and then kiss the spot below my ear.

I close my eyes as his lips move down to caress my neck. And I feel lucky.

His arms close around me, and we stay in this nice place for a while, kissing slowly. Remembering how much we need each other. It lasts until Tank's phone rings from somewhere in the vicinity of his back pocket.

I'm so eager to ignore it that I slide a hand down his hard stomach and over the bulge in his jeans. He chuckles happily as the ringing stops. He's unbuttoning my blouse as it starts up again.

"Is that someone important?" I sigh between kisses.

"It's my agent," he grumbles. "If you would have taken me on as a client, Eric wouldn't be calling when I'm trying to kiss you."

The phone rings again, and I push him off me. "Answer the man or silence your phone before I throw it across the room. I can't work in these conditions."

Tank sits up, tugs his phone out of his pocket and taps the screen. "This better be important."

Since we're lying so close together, I can hear Eric's voice respond. "It's not like I really want to disturb you. And please don't tell me what you're up to at the moment, because whether it's good or bad I really don't want to know. But I need to remind you that Wilson is waiting to hear about the apartment. Those realtors aren't going to sit around and sip tea while you two decide whether or not to buy it. They're probably working the phones as we speak."

Tank groans. "Okay, man. You're right. Can I call you back in ten minutes?"

"Of course."

TWENTY-EIGHT

No Picket Fences

TANK

AFTER I SET down the phone, Bess and I gaze at each other for a moment, trying to take it all in. "So much for your moratorium on big decisions," I say slowly. "Is one of us buying that apartment?"

"You are," Bess say immediately. "It isn't even a question. I already have a place to live. That place gives me sticker shock, but you could make a cash offer. They'd have to say yes."

I lean down and kiss the side of Bess's face, because I can't stop touching her. But I feel uneasy about this. "I would step aside if you wanted that place. You still might decide you need a two bedroom."

"Nope." She gives her head a slow shake. "The moratorium on big decisions is still in force. Buying that apartment would be a huge decision for me. But for you, not so much. *Take* it, Tank. If someone else snaps it up while you and I are tiptoeing around each other, that will be a travesty."

I let out a grunt of agreement. But it makes me all kinds of uncomfortable that Bess would throw away her plans to be with me. "I'll call Wilson, the realtor."

"You do that. I'm going to order some Indian food. You want your usual?"

"Yes," I say easily. Because I'm a selfish man, and I *do* want the usual. I want Bess's usual smile, and the pleasure of eating dinner with her and then taking her to bed.

She has no idea how much she means to me. And I intend to prove it. But first I call Eric back, and together we make a cash offer at the asking price, just like Bess suggested.

After I hang up, we eat Indian food and drink a bottle of cheap white wine that Bess had in her kitchen. "You'll need furniture," Bess says. "I'm not sure Eric will be much help. He's not very interested in home furnishings."

"You can help me, then." It takes all my willpower not to add: *and why don't you just move in with me?* But I'm not going there, not yet anyway. In the first place, we're not supposed to make big decisions. And more importantly, I need Bess to take her time and really think through what she's giving up if we stay together.

Having kids, or not, is a huge decision.

"I *cannot* help you with furniture," Bess scoffs. "Look around yourself. Is this the home of someone who knows anything about home fashion?"

"I like the new rug and the pillows," I say, noticing them for the first time.

"Yeah, me too. Becca picked them out. She made me buy them. My toenails are Brooklyn Bruisers purple right now, because Rebecca redecorated my feet as well."

"What a handy friend," I say, pulling Bess into my lap. "Tell me again why you chose this apartment."

"The commute. Duh." She loops an arm around my neck, and now I have everything.

"The commute rocks," I agree. "But I have a theory about you and this place. About why you chose a cheap walk-up with no doorman."

"A theory? You think I'm afraid of doormen? Or their shiny gold buttons?"

I shake my head. "I listen to the calls you have with players. You're always telling them to work hard and dream big."

"Uh-huh. That's, like, day one at agent school."

"But I don't know if you do the same thing for yourself. You've definitely got the hard work part down. Nobody works harder than you."

She runs a hand through my hair. "Thank you. That's a nice thing to say."

"It's true, though. I just wonder why the *dream big* part is so hard for you. You got an apartment that's good enough, but not great. You fly coach. You buy cheap wine, even though you could afford the nicer stuff."

"I'm not a connoisseur," she sniffs. "Expensive wine would be wasted on me."

"No," I argue, tracing a path across her nose, where there's a light smattering of freckles. "You spend a lot of energy making sure your athletes get all the best things in life. But you deserve those things, too, you know. I'm a simple guy. I like hockey and Tex-Mex. But I want to treat you to another dinner at Sparks, okay? Soon. Just the two of us."

"Okay," she whispers, and her smile wobbles. "That's a lovely idea."

"If we're going to be together, let's enjoy it. Let's have fun. No holding back. When I got on a plane to New York, I didn't expect to find you here. And maybe I could have handled everything better. But I love you, and I want you to know that you deserve the world."

"Tank." Bess blinks. Her eyes look a little red. "Wow. That's the nicest thing anyone has ever said to me."

"Can you forgive me for not explaining why I freaked out before?"

"Yes." She gives me a watery smile. "I already have." She tucks her cheek onto my shoulder and sighs.

We stay here a while in silence. And I feel more peace than I have in weeks.

Eventually, Bess speaks up again. "L.A. Is playing Vegas right now. Want to watch some hockey? That's what I was going to do before you showed up."

I wrap my arms around her and then stand up quickly. Bess squeaks with surprise. "That's not what we're doing."

"No? Why."

"Because I've got something better for you to *do*, if you catch my drift."

I take Bess right to bed, because I can't wait any longer. I peel off her clothing and kiss her everywhere until she's whimpering and begging, and I'm shaking with need. When I take myself in hand and nudge her knees apart, I feel pure gratitude as I slide home. Her tight body grips me, and she makes a low sound of satisfaction.

My body flashes with heat as I begin the age-old dance. Bess has no idea how she freed me from the mind-fuck that sex had become for me. "I love you," I whisper as her heels dig into my ass. She lets out a keening moan and wraps her arms around me. "I love you," I repeat as I immediately pick up the pace.

"Oh, Tank... me too." Bess sighs.

I smile as I sink into our kiss, because I already know she loves me. I already knew, even as I tried to leave her. "I love you," I murmur as I slow my strokes to try to delay my gratification. Bess isn't having it, though. She arches her back and takes me deeper. She doesn't want to let go. Neither do I.

"Love you...so much," she gasps as her body grips me tightly. She takes one more deep breath and shivers as she comes.

"Do you want me to go back on the pill?" she asks much later.

We're curled up together after several rounds of lovemaking. We're having the kind of soul-bearing conversation you can only have at midnight in the pitch dark, naked and sated and raw.

"You have to make that call yourself," I tell her. "It's your body. You should do whatever makes you comfortable. I can use condoms if you'd like. You probably thought I was an idiot for never thinking about them before."

"I thought you were so used to married sex that you didn't remember what it was like to be single. And I knew I had us covered."

"*So used to married sex,*" I repeat slowly. "Not in a good way. I stopped caring about sex."

"Why?"

It isn't easy to talk about this. But hiding my pain from Bess has only caused us more of it. "At one point I asked the team doctor for Viagra."

"What? No way."

I run a finger across the swell of her breast. "And after the third round of failed IVF, she wanted to try naturally again. And the pressure really got to me. If it was day fourteen, I'd get psyched out."

Bess groans. "Okay, we're *never* going there. I'm thinking all kinds of judgmental things about your ex right now."

"As do I sometimes. But it wasn't all on her. There's a lot of cultural bullshit wrapped up in being a man. My day job is, like, the essence of masculinity. But I'd go home from the manly art of hockey to a wife who blamed my body for failing to get her pregnant. And then I made the mistake of telling a teammate that we were struggling with infertility…"

Bess grips my hand a little more tightly when I break off the sentence. And I guess I owe her the whole story.

"Palacio caught wind of it. And that man lives his life just looking for weaknesses that he can exploit."

Bess sits up. "He was a dick about it? About *that?*"

"He'd be a dick about anything, Bess. It wasn't even personal."

"That's why you punched him," she whispers. "It didn't have a thing to do with his wife or your wife."

Slowly, I shake my head. "You're right. He started chirping at me all the time in the locker room. Like—how could Sure Shot be my nickname if I couldn't get my wife pregnant?"

Bess makes a low noise of rage.

"One day I'd had enough. I leveled him in front of the whole team."

"He had it coming!" Her body is full of tension now. Like she might leap from the bed and go after him.

I slide my palm down her knee, and give her leg a reassuring squeeze. "It's okay now, baby. But you can see why I wasn't too keen to explain why I punched the guy."

"I get it, Tank." She flops down on the mattress again. "I get why it happened, and why you can't go through that hell again. And whatever we are to each other, I don't ever want us to be like that. We can't be all about having a child. We have to just be us and see where that leads."

My heart gives a squeeze of pure hope. "Nothing makes me happier than coming home to you, honey. I'm happy to be on your team. But we have to take it slow, because you're the one with a five-year plan that includes a pink nursery and a picket fence."

"There are no picket fences in Brooklyn," Bess says, poking me in the belly.

"What's the Brooklyn equivalent of a picket fence?"

"Twenty-five-thousand-dollar preschool tuition," she says.

"Twenty... Did you say twenty-five *grand?*" That can't be right.

"It's true. There's a Manhattan preschool that gets forty. They have ten times as many applicants as they can handle."

"What a scam."

"Right? You'll have a home office in your new apartment. Or a TV room. Paint that pink room another color," Bess says. "Anything but Dallas green."

I laugh and her hair tickles my bare chest. "Seriously, can you and Eric find me a decorator? Someone to pick out some furniture, have the place painted, and remind me to buy things like towels and a bath mat."

"Of course."

"I need a bed. It should be enormous. The more space to roll around with you, the better."

"Did you see that shower in the master bedroom?" Bess asks, her smooth hand stroking my chest.

"No, I didn't make it that far."

"It was spectacular. There were three shower heads and a marble bench."

"*Nice*. I can't wait to try it out. You can add that to your five-year plan."

"Oh, I will." She settles against me. And then she falls asleep in my arms.

TWENTY-NINE

What If

TANK

LIFE IS GOOD AGAIN. Really good.

After a brief negotiation, Eric and Wilson agree on a closing date for the apartment in the Million Dollar Dorm. In three short weeks I'll be leaving the hotel for my new place.

Even better—Bess is back in my life full time. She attends two home games in a row—against New York and D.C. We win both of them.

The second victory was especially sweet. Castro passed to me in the third period—finding my stick after a beautiful deke that sent our opponent's eyes in the wrong direction. All it took was an airborne shot to the upper left corner of the net. The lamp lit, and ten thousand Brooklyn fans yelled my name.

"That was beautiful," O'Doul said afterward.

"Nice job, *Sure Shot*," someone added.

It was hard to hate the nickname under the circumstances.

The following night, I take Bess out for a steak dinner at Sparks. She orders the filet mignon and the creamed spinach, just like she did all those years ago. And I indulge in a pricey bottle of red.

"Have you been back here without me?" I ask her as the candle flickers between us on the white linen table cloth.

"No," she admits with a sultry little smile. "But even so—" She

211

leans close to whisper in my ear. "Every time I have creamed spinach, I get really turned on."

I laugh so loudly that people turn and stare. I order a sinful dessert that Bess picks out, and we eat it together.

When we finally emerge from the restaurant, there's a limo waiting to pick us up. "Hop in, baby?" I ask, opening the door for her. "This time I won't have to convince you to come back to my hotel room, right?"

"If I recall," she says, sliding onto a leather seat, "you didn't have to do much arm-twisting that first time, either."

We make out like teenagers all the way back to Brooklyn. In my hotel room, Bess strips me down and gives me a back rub in the middle of the bed, while the Manhattan lights twinkle in the distance. "Are you going to miss this view?" she asks as her hands do amazing things to my shoulder muscles.

"No," I say quickly. "I need a kitchen and some more space. Besides, I want to live across the street from you."

Soft lips meet the back of my neck. I close my eyes and let out a happy sigh. Spending time with Bess is everything I didn't know I needed. I still don't deserve her. But I'm learning to live with the guilt.

And Bess is happy, too. I can't deny how she lights up when we're together. Or how sweet and happy she looks as she falls asleep in my arms. Sometimes I lie awake just listening to her breathe in the dark. And I wouldn't trade the sleepy weight of her against my body for anything.

Now she stretches out on top of my bare back and lets out a contented sigh. "The decorator wants to know if you prefer light-colored towels or dark. I told her you wouldn't have a preference."

"True story," I grunt. "As long as I can dry off my hiney with them, it's all good."

"This designer is fantastically efficient. The day you move in, the delivery trucks are going to descend. By cocktail hour you'll have an apartment that's more comfortably furnished than any other in New York."

"Mmm." I reach back and catch Bess's hand in mine. "Have I told you what I want to do first in that new apartment?"

"I believe you've mentioned it several times."

I grin against the pillow. "Good. The first thing I'm going to do is cook Tex-Mex."

"Wait a minute!" Bess sputters. "I thought the first thing you were going to do is *me*, in that shower."

"That's what we're doing while the enchiladas bake."

I can feel Bess's laughter against my back. "Fine. I guess I can't argue with that. Now roll over."

She slides off my body, and I do as she asks. "Why am I the only one who's naked?" I complain as I look up at her in the dark. She's wearing a Bruisers T-shirt and panties.

"No whining." She leans down and begins to kiss a trail down my chest.

By the time she nears my cock, I'm hard and waiting for the first brush of her lips. Bess doesn't make me wait. She takes me in hand and licks a slow path up my shaft until I make a desperate noise. My fingers find their way into her hair. With a bossy grip, I pull her closer to my cock.

Bess gives a muffled chuckle as she takes me into the wet heaven of her mouth.

"Fuck yes," I groan, my hand tightening on her hair. "Take more. Take all of it."

But she takes her time, weighing me against her tongue, teasing my thighs with silken fingertips. Slowly, she tightens her lips, and I let out a hot gasp as she finally begins to take long, lovely pulls with her sweet mouth.

I relax against the bed, trying not to get too riled up too soon. But she's relentless—licking and sucking and stroking my sac with soft hands. "Baby," I warn. "You're going to make me come."

"Mmm," she purrs, looking up at me with bedroom eyes.

"Honey," I gasp, clenching my muscles against the urge to come. "Come here. I need you. Take off that shirt."

Bess sits up and shucks off her T-shirt and bra. *God*, the view. Waves of hair tumble down to frame her pale breasts.

"Touch yourself," I rasp. This is the stuff of fantasies, and I can't get enough.

Bess drops one hand to stroke my cock, and uses the other one to cup her breast and pinch her nipple. Then she tips her head back and lets out a hot sigh.

"Come here," I order. "Lose the panties."

She disobeys me. Dropping down one more time, she swallows my cock to the back of her throat and moans. This time I don't have enough willpower to hold back. When she looks up at me again—heat in her eyes, bare breasts bouncing against my thighs as she works me over—I just lose it. My hips buck and I let out a shout of satisfaction as I come inside her decadent mouth.

"Goddamn." I'm still panting when Bess returns from the bathroom a few minutes later. I have an arm thrown over my eyes, and my chest is heaving. "That was fun. But it's gonna take me a while to recover."

"Take as much time as you need," Bess says, climbing into bed. "Because I got my period a few hours ago, and I'm off the roster for a few days."

"Oh." I roll my sated body towards hers, my arms reaching out to pull her in. "You feel okay?" I trail a hand across the smooth skin of her belly.

"Sure. Advil is a miracle drug." She makes herself comfortable, lying beside me, an arm over my chest. "I'm sleepy. And you're my favorite pillow." She kisses my chin.

I stroke her back and hold her close. Bess seems perfectly content right now, but I'm suddenly awake and on edge. *Day one of the cycle.* My big, dumb head can't forget how this works. *I wonder if I'm scheduled to be in town on day fourteen.* I seriously feel the impulse to climb out of bed and check the travel schedule.

I don't do it. But that familiar voice is *right* there, at the front of my consciousness. I wonder if Bess will do the same math, too. If she'll come to bed naked on the fourteenth night, feeling hopeful.

She wouldn't bring it up, of course. She knows the drill, and she wouldn't willingly put me in that position. But it's easy to imagine a scenario where we're both secretly hoping for a happy little surprise.

I mean—what if it just *happened*? Then Bess would never have to make any sacrifices for me. What if—just once—my swimmers made contact the same way that other guys' do every flipping day.

What if Bess is one of those women who gets pregnant on the first try, never miscarries, and never even gets morning sickness?

What if. What if. What if.

I could drive myself crazy like this. No, it's worse than that. I could drive us *both* crazy.

Closing my eyes, I force myself to take a slow breath. My happiness feels more tenuous than it did an hour ago. *We're not doing this*, I remind myself. Yet I don't know how to silence that little voice in my head that whispers: *Wouldn't it be funny if Bess got pregnant?*

That little voice isn't going anywhere. But that doesn't mean I have to listen to it. That's my new job, isn't it? Shutting off that voice and being happy with what I have.

She's sleeping now. She's unbothered by getting her period. This is not a tragedy. It's just a Thursday. I need to keep telling myself that.

There's a book pregnant women read called *What to Expect*. My ex-wife bought a copy about ten minutes after her first ill-fated positive pregnancy test. That book is probably on a shelf somewhere in my old house in Dallas. We never really needed it.

Instead, I need a book called *How to Stop Expecting*.

I wish the apartment I was buying only had one bedroom in it. It's like I'm saving the other one for a ghost.

THIRTY

Big Ideas

BESS

January

THE DALLAS GAME is three days away, and the team has already left town. They're playing Colorado first, but everyone in my life is focused on Dallas. And I mean everyone.

Jason Castro is blowing up my phone to ask if I have an opinion about which brand of strawberry jam is the luckiest one in Texas. And my brother won't stop texting, asking how practice has been going.

"Do you think the Dallas offense looked a little shaky in last night's game?" Eric asks me as I close my laptop on my desk.

"Definitely," I lie, just to make him feel better. I need to get out of the office for a few minutes and think about something else. "Where's that Ringborn contract? I'm going to make a post office run and pick up some coffee."

"Oh, awesome. Can I have a double espresso and a cookie?" He hands me an express envelope and a five-dollar bill.

"You can have a single espresso, because you're already jumpy. Stop watching videos of Dallas and proofread the Chickie's contract."

Eric grunts. "There's no reason to restrict my caffeine intake while I'm combing through the fine print. That's a bad strategy."

"Fine. I'll bring you a triple espresso if you stop talking about the Dallas game for the rest of the day."

"Deal." He opens the contract file.

"I'll be about an hour, though," I warn. "I'm meeting the girls for coffee."

His head snaps up. "You mean Rebecca? Does she have any news about—"

I hold up a hand. "What did we just talk about?"

Eric clamps his jaws together and waves me out of the room. "Go already. Come back with coffee. And some news."

"Can't guarantee the news. But I will bring you that cookie."

He gives me a smile and turns back to his work.

I head outside, pulling my coat tightly around me as the Water Street breeze hits me full force. It's January, and the wind off the river is icy.

When I pull out my phone to check the time, I see that my brother has called again. He's also sent a text. *How are things looking for the Dallas game?*

Not you, too! After I let out a groan, though, I realize I need to talk to Dave. So I tap on his name and return his call.

"Hey, Bessie!" he says after picking up on the first ring. "How's business? Do you think my boys are ready?"

"I'm sure they are. But don't ask, okay? There are eighty-two games this season, but everyone is wound a little too tightly about this one."

"But how is practice going?" he asks.

"Great," I promise him. "There's something else I wanted to talk to you about, though."

"Yeah? Do you have some intel on the Dallas injuries?"

"No, blockhead. It's not about hockey."

"Oh," he says, and I can hear him wondering what could possibly matter more than hockey. "What, then?"

I take a deep breath and then let it out. "I'm dating someone."

"Dating someone," he echoes. And then he's silent for a moment. "Nice. Can I meet him? I promise not to punch whoever it is. But I might need to threaten him just a little bit, so he understands that I'm lethal if he's not good to you."

That's more or less what I expected him to say, so I let out an uncomfortable chuckle. "It's possible you punched him already at least once."

"What?" Dave yelps. There's a brief silence, and I can practically hear him doing the math. "You are *not* dating a hockey player. You can't mean that. I haven't really punched anyone, except Robbie Oswald in the fourth grade."

"It's not Robbie Oswald," I say with a sigh. "Dave, I'm dating a perfectly nice hockey player here in Brooklyn."

Dave actually moans. "I have to kill one of my *teammates*?"

"You don't have to kill anyone. And he was never your teammate. It's Mark Tankiewicz. The trade from—"

"*Dallas?*" Dave's horror practically radiates through the phone. "Bess, nooooo."

I sigh. This is exactly why I haven't ever gotten around to telling him about Tank. Dave has a very fierce Big Brother Mode. When it kicks in, we're eleven and fourteen again. I know Dave can't really help his reaction. And Big Brother Mode saved my life at one point so I try not to get too irritated.

It doesn't always work.

"You don't know Tank," I say as gently as I can. "But I've known him for almost ten years. We were briefly together when I worked for Henry Kassman."

"How nice a guy could he be?" Dave grunts. "He's from Dallas."

"He's from Washington state," I correct. "By way of Dallas. And cut it out, because I like him very much. Also? I'm thirty years old. You don't get a say."

Dave falls into an unhappy silence, which means I can hear Zara in the background. "Are you getting on Bess's case? Let me talk to her."

"Tell Zara I'll call her tonight," I say, because I'm crossing under the Manhattan bridge, and both the post office and Brooklyn's best cookie shop are in view. "I have a meeting in five minutes."

"That's why you dropped this bomb right now!" Dave says. "Because you have a meeting in five minutes."

"Seems like a pretty good decision," I say drily. "The only acceptable response to me telling you that I'm happy is for you to say, 'That's great, and I can't wait to meet him.'"

Dave sighs. "That's great," he says woodenly. "I can't wait to meet him."

I laugh out loud. "Nice try. Maybe practice it in a mirror. Later, big brother."

"Later. I love you," he says, his voice sullen.

"Back at you." I disconnect the call and shake my head. I run into the post office and drop off my express-mail envelope, and then hurry over to the coffee shop where the company is not quite so judgmental.

The moment I walk in the door, Becca beckons me toward a table in the corner. After I sit down, she says, "Bess, thank you for coming. I am taking on a big project, and I am going to need some of your wisdom."

"Does it have to do with my nail color?" I ask, shedding my coat.

She shakes her head. "This is bigger than nail color. Can you keep a secret?"

"Of course!"

"Let the girl buy her coffee first!" Georgia hollers. "What if they sell out of ginger cookies?"

"I don't mind," I say. "Just as long as we don't have to talk about the Dallas game."

The women make matching faces. "That topic is strictly verboten," Georgia agrees.

"Nate can't shut up about it, either," Becca says. "The players must be so stressed out. Especially Tank."

"He's..." I don't even know what to say, because Tank seems stressed, too. On the one hand, he's been loving and wonderful since our Come to Jesus conversation ten days ago. But he's a little quiet, too. I can only hope that Dallas is the reason. "I thought we weren't going to talk about it."

"Right," Becca says, clutching a folder to her chest. "Let's talk about my pet project, instead. It was actually you who gave me this idea, and I haven't been able to let it go."

"Me?"

"Yes, you. And then my husband, who's still trying to teach me to think like a billionaire. I must be getting better at it, because I'm about to bring professional women's hockey to Brooklyn."

I let out an honest-to-God fangirl shriek. "You're kidding! Becca, don't tease me."

"Oh, I'm not. See?" She opens the folder and pushes it toward me. There's a page full of sketches with various logos and team names. *The Brooklyn Bottle Rockets. The Brooklyn Beasties. The Brooklyn Breakaway.* "What do you think?"

"Wow," I breathe. "This is everything! Are you buying out one of the women's teams?" Women's pro hockey is so small—just five teams—and every one of them is hanging on by their fingernails.

"Nope." She shakes her head. "I want to fund a new one. It would be the first women's team to enjoy the training staff and facilities of a men's pro team. It won't be a moneymaker, but that's not even the point. Nate's original goal was to bring excellent hockey to Brooklyn. And that's what we're doing, right?"

"You're...wow." For a long moment I can't even speak. I'm just so overwhelmed with excitement and gratitude. "Can I help?" I squeak. "I mean—you can totally say no. But there will be so much work to do. And I have so many ideas. So many!" I'm starting to sound a little manic, but I can't hold it back. "This could be big for women's hockey."

Rebecca reaches over and puts her hands on my shoulders. "Yes, you can help. Breathe, Bess. This is going to be a slow build."

"Okay." I take a breath. "Where will they play? The stadium is too big a venue."

"True, and we don't own it," Becca says. "The women will play their games at the practice facility. All I have to do is add more seating behind the nets on each end, and we'll have a capacity of twelve hundred people."

"Oh," I say slowly. "So the cost of hosting those games will ultimately be pretty low."

"Right!" Becca agrees. "All the big costs are for personnel. Creating jobs in Brooklyn is a good idea, anyway. You can help me figure out who to hire."

"You need a female GM," I say immediately. "Someone who understands both hockey and business. And a coach, but those are easier to find. There's a lot of under-appreciated coaching talent in women's college hockey."

"This is going to be so much fun," Georgia gushes.

"It is! The world needs women's hockey. And now I think I need a cookie."

"Go." Georgia shoos me toward the counter.

When I come back, Georgia and Becca have moved on. They're discussing the finer points of appetizers. "Mini quiche can be great or terrible." Georgia's voice is full of gravity. "Pigs in blankets are more reliable."

"Good point." Becca makes a note.

"Planning a party?" I ask, sitting down with my cup of coffee and my cookie.

"Yes we are," Becca says. "We're hosting a little shindig at the hotel after the Game that Shall Not Be Named."

"Don't call it a victory party," Georgia warns me. "We're superstitious."

"I wouldn't dream of it," I promise them.

"Are you flying to Texas to see it all go down?" Becca sketches a pig in a blanket into her planner.

"Maybe," I hedge. "I'm supposed to head out to a juniors tournament the following day. But I haven't bought any tickets yet."

"I think you should come with us," Georgia decides. "And Tank would agree with me. This game is going to be harder on him than anyone."

"It is," I agree. "I'm considering it."

I've been considering it all week. But there's a wrinkle I can't talk about. The Dallas game happens to fall in the midpoint of my cycle. And I'm honestly not sure whether that's a point in favor of making the trip, or not.

Am I really crazy enough to be *that* woman? The one who secretly tracks my fertility to try to give my boyfriend the baby he thought he could never have? Is that true love? Or just plain cuckoo?

Tank told me he can't go there again. And I told him he didn't have to. When I said that I'd love him no matter what, I meant it.

But a little voice in my head keeps asking: *What if it just happened? What if you could have it all?*

What if. What if. What if…

"Why don't you fly out with Nate and me on the Gulfstream?" Becca says suddenly. "We could brainstorm ideas for the women's team all the way to Texas. And you could leave for your tournament the day after the game."

"Okay," I say quickly. *Too* quickly. Becca just handed me the excuse I needed. A free trip on her private jet. And an opportunity to help women's hockey.

This girl is going to Dallas.

This girl feels a little funny about it.

THIRTY-ONE

Queso is Magic

TANK

"YOU NERVOUS?" Silas Kelly asks me as we get off the jet in Dallas.

"Nah." After almost a decade in the Show, a game is only a game, right? It's just Tuesday.

But maybe I spoke too soon. The minute the bus pulls up at the stadium, my confidence starts to veer a little sideways. Suiting up in the visitors' locker room feels wrong. And sitting on the other bench will just seem freaky.

Not that I'm letting it show. During the pregame rituals, I ignore all the strangeness and try to concentrate. I tape up my stick, and then tape it up again. Nothing to see here.

There's tension in the room. Castro sits across from me, chewing his lucky peanut butter sandwich like it's life or death. Silas is—as usual—stretching his body on the floor, getting limber to mind the goal. But he's also eyeing us, one by one, wondering if we're ready.

Coach walks by, grabbing my shoulder pad and giving it a hard squeeze. "Don't let him rile you up."

"I won't," I grunt. There's no need to ask who he means. All week Palacio has been talking smack on Twitter—making predictions, and making sure the whole world knows that my production is down this year. He's all about the bullshit mind games.

I *can't* let that fucker win.

"Listen up, guys!" Rebecca trots into the room, wearing a purple dress and matching heels. "Tonight, rain or shine, we're having a victory party in the hotel lobby."

"What?" Castro yelps. "Did you just *jinx* us? Have you *met* hockey players?"

"I thought you might say that," Rebecca says with a smile. "But victory means something special to me tonight. This is only one regular-season game. It doesn't matter all that much."

"It does to me," O'Doul grumbles.

"Be that as it may," Rebecca says, undaunted. "Nate is in Dallas with us tonight, and this is the city where he proposed to me. So that's a victory right there. Furthermore, the last time we had a victory party at this hotel, they served the most *amazing* queso dip, and I've been thinking about it for two years."

"That's what Tex-Mex will do to you," I mutter, and Rebecca grins.

But she's not done talking. "And, lastly, I love the whole bunch of you! So why wouldn't I feel like celebrating? I already feel victorious. Now go do your thing, and I'll see you afterward. For queso and champagne, no matter what."

Coach stands up and does a slow clap. "Hear, hear! Becca is full of wisdom tonight, boys. We have to do things a little differently tonight."

"Like, score and stuff," Castro grumbles.

"That would be nice," Coach agrees. "But tonight is really about *attitude*. Whoever keeps a cool head will win this game. They're gonna play dirty. They're gonna chirp like insulting you is the newest Olympic sport. Don't fall for it. Whoever stays out of the penalty box tonight gets first dibs on the queso dip at the party."

A bark of a laugh escapes me. Who are these nutters, anyway?

Castro looks back at me and just shakes his head. "Fucking Dallas," he says.

"FUCKING DALLAS!" the rest of the team yells back.

I crack up right here on the bench. And for a hot second, I feel like I'm in the right dressing room after all.

It gets weird again, though, when we skate out for the pregame ceremonies. I get chills as I'm hit with the familiar lighting and acoustics. Every stadium has its own vibe, and every team's home is a little different. I spent so many years of my life right here.

God, the sweat I left in this building. In this *city*. When I left, I had some regrets. But it's dawning on me that I don't anymore. I earned a championship ring here, for starters. Who could regret that? And I can truly say that I gave Dallas everything I had.

Just like I gave Jordanna everything I had. That's all a man can do. His best.

There's no more time for epiphanies, though. We stand in two long rows while the announcer calls out the starting lineup, and spotlights zigzag across the freshly surfaced ice.

The fans go wild for every Dallas player, as they should. Then they provide a smattering of polite applause for my new teammates as the Brooklyn team is announced.

Until we get to me.

"Number 27, and formerly of Dallas, MARK TANKIEWICZ!"

I expected a little cheer, just because there have to be kids in the stands still wearing my jersey. But the place roars for me. It's fucking *deafening*.

Whoa. I'd be a liar if I said it didn't matter to me. The roof is *shaking* as these Dallas hockey fans spend a long minute recognizing my contribution.

I'm not going to forget this any time soon.

When I glance across the ice at Bart Palacio, though, he is not a happy man. Like it might kill him to admit that we did some good work on this ice together. After tonight, I do not have to put up with that prick for a nice long time. Now, there's something to look forward to.

I put my hand on my heart for the national anthem. When I check Palacio's face again, he looks murderous. It calms me down an iota, because I finally feel like I'm on my way back up. Bart has more to lose tonight than I do.

If I can just remember that for the next two hours, things might just shake out right.

The crowd quiets down as we get into position for the first faceoff. I love that first silence—when everything stops except the pounding of our hearts. The moment is pregnant with possibility. Anything could happen, and no mistakes have been made.

Then the ref drops that six-ounce hunk of rubber, and we all leap into action at once. Castro wins the faceoff, flipping the puck back to me, and I flip it to O'Doul, who moves up.

The game is a tight, dirty scrum from the first minute. Dallas goes right for the kill, unsparing with their sharp elbows and slashing sticks. There's more cursing than on a naval submarine and more untempered testosterone than in an army battalion.

Keep your head down and skate fast, I coach myself.

Palacio isn't having it. His role, apparently, is to get up in my face. "Smug little bitch," he growls as I guard him. "Still got a limp dick? Didn't see any coverage of you with the puck bunnies in Brooklyn."

"Is that the best you've got?" Honestly, it's not that hard to tune out his patter.

Trevi and Campeau battle it out, trying to make some opportunities. But—Jesus—Palacio's snarling face is always in front of mine. And when I catch a pass from O'Doul, Palacio goes in hard. He slashes my ankle so egregiously that I shout in pain.

But I still get the pass off. And where is the fucking whistle? They don't call a penalty. Fuckers.

When my shift is up, the trainer slaps some tape on the bleeding gash. "You okay?"

"Yeah," I grunt.

But when I take the ice again, it's just the same. Palacio's ugly mug is everywhere I turn. That's when I start to get frustrated. I trip him, because I need to see how he looks spread-eagled on the ice.

Immediately, the whistle's shriek pierces the air, and the door to the penalty box opens. Of course I'm given a two-minute penalty. Shoot me already.

O'Doul sprays me with ice chips as he comes to a stop beside me, and I brace myself for a tongue-lashing. "Remember the queso dip," he says.

Wait, what?

"Settle down, okay? Just don't fight him. That's what he wants. We'll kill this penalty and move on. Just settle."

"Okay," I grunt. Even if he's not mad, I am. I glide toward the box, grumpy as a bear.

I don't *ever* look at the crowd, because who has the time? But maybe it's the red hair that catches my eye. Bess is basically tattooed on my subconscious at this point. And when I look up, we immediately lock eyes, as though my soul knew exactly where to find her.

I hadn't even known she was coming to Texas, but she's the only person I can pick out in a room full of eighteen thousand people. If that's not a sign from above, then I don't know what is.

And she gives me a big, happy smile, as if we've just run into each other at the cookie shop or in the park—someplace far away from here.

It calms me down immediately. *Okay. Breathe.* I give her a smile before sitting down on the bench. I watch the PK team give Dallas the runaround for a hundred and twenty long seconds. And I vault out of there the moment the door opens for me.

Then I'm back in the grind again, while Dallas takes cheap shots wherever they can get 'em. The game is sweaty and still scoreless.

I'm very careful not to draw another penalty, although Palacio does his evil best. When I skate into the corner to nab the puck, he's right there on my ass. I get the pass off to Castro, but Palacio flattens me against the plexi with unnecessary force, somehow managing to grind his fist into my ribs.

The crowd cheers.

No whistle.

"Aw, honey, good hands," I gasp, trying to get the oxygen back into my lungs. "But no nookie until after I win."

He lets out an angry roar, but I feel strangely calm. The game isn't over yet. Bess is here in Dallas, and Castro suddenly has a look on his face that tells a story. His chin lifts by a half an inch as the puck flies towards him.

Suddenly, I can just *see* how it's going to go down. I picture Castro's pass. And then I sense a low, perfect shot through the five-hole.

And I'm already in motion, feinting toward the blue line. Palacio's body follows, shifting my opponent out of the way for Castro's pass, which is coming right at me, just like I predicted.

I lower my stick toward the ice at the perfect angle, back-handing it toward the keeper's skates. The goalie tries to butterfly over it, but it's too late. The puck sails through his legs, and the lamp is lit before I even remember to blink.

It happened just like I planned. And for a moment, I'm too stunned to celebrate. Then the Dallas crowd roars its disappointment, and my teammates are grinning from ear to ear.

"FUCK YOU," screams Palacio.

Fuck you, too! I say via a smile. As I skate back to the circle, I can see now how the game will play out. Palacio will be pissed, and the rest of the Dallas bench will be rattled.

"They're gonna fall apart," I say to O'Doul as we get into faceoff position again. "Watch."

My team captain actually winks at me in response. A wink. Like we're in some kind of Broadway musical.

The puck drops again, and everything spools out like I pictured it. Fine—like I *visualized* it. Doc Mulvey might know a few things.

I must be open to the fucking universe now, because I can see Palacio's face getting redder on every play. And I can hear him dragging out every slur and taunt ever hurled across a span of ice.

"He just told me I'm like a tampon," Trevi says as the ice girls do a quick cleanup during the media break. "Only good for one period." He snorts. "Musta been saving that one up."

"Yeah? He told me he'd seen better hands on a digital clock," Baby Bayer says.

"Well, I got a Hispanic slur," Castro says, guzzling his water. "He called me a *beaner*, and told me to go back where I came from.

I told him—that's Minnesota. And we're playing there next month, so…" He shrugs.

"He's flipping his shit." Crikey chuckles.

"Nobody promised him any queso dip, obviously," O'Doul adds.

"QUESO DIP!" yell two or three guys at the same time.

"Quiet, morons," Coach says. He taps me between the shoulder blades to indicate that I'm up again. "Stay cool now."

"Will do," I promise. Because getting that goal past Palacio made staying cool a hell of a lot easier.

And now I have no trouble visualizing the scoreboard, because it keeps lighting up in our favor. We put four goals on it by the time we're through.

THIRTY-TWO

Another Epiphany

BESS

WHEN THE BUZZER goes off at the end of the Dallas game, Tank looks gloriously, transcendently happy. I hadn't known his face could smile that wide.

The final score is 4-1 in favor of Brooklyn. That asshole Palacio managed to flick one past Silas in the third period, but it was still a major victory, and everyone in the increasingly quiet stadium knew it.

"Let's hustle," Becca says, tugging on my arm after the buzzer. "We have a party to set up."

"You're not going to stay and give a statement?" I ask.

"Nah. Georgia is handling it. The press doesn't need to hear any posturing from the owner tonight. Let Tank have the last word. Besides, someone has to make sure the cheese is hot and the beer is cold."

"I like the way you think," her husband says. "This way, ladies. The car is waiting."

I'm whisked to the Ritz-Carlton bar by the Rowley-Kattenbergers. The hotel staff fall all over themselves to serve Rebecca, so it takes shockingly little effort on our part to set everything up.

230

"I can't believe you ordered these!" I say, holding up a napkin. It says: *Congratulations! We knew you could make Dallas cry.* "What were you going to do if we lost?"

"Put 'em back on the jet for the March matchup." Becca shrugs. "But I didn't have to, did I? Excuse me!" She waves down the hospitality manager. "Could you bring out about four times as much queso dip as I asked you for? I bragged about it to my hockey players, and we can't let them down."

"Yes, ma'am," he says sweetly.

I finish laying out the napkins, while Becca inspects the bar setup. "Well." She claps. "This will be fun. I might run up to my room and fix my lipstick. They could be another forty minutes."

"Go for it," I encourage. "I'm going to check my email. You never know who's having a weeknight calamity."

After she flits off, I sit down on one of the comfortable banquettes that line our roped-off portion of the bar. It's *supposed* to be comfortable, anyway. The sexy, red, lacy thong I bought myself is abrading my ass. Sexy undies are another thing—like heels and makeup—that make me feel like I lost my copy of the Girl Manual. When I'd waltzed into a Brooklyn lingerie shop yesterday and asked for something splashy, I'd simply gone with the salesgirl's suggestions.

Boy, am I sorry now. Holding a strip of lace between my ass cheeks had sounded like a bad idea at the time, but I'd hoped it was one of those things that would make more sense after I tried it. Like avocado toast or Uber.

But no. That perky little salesperson had steered me wrong. Not only am I uncomfortable, but every time the lace pokes me in the fanny, it reminds me of the other reason I'd come to Dallas. To seduce my man.

He'd looked so wonderful tonight—confident and radiant. Like he's finally found his footing. I can't wait to congratulate him. And I wouldn't want to do anything to dent that big smile.

I shouldn't have come. No—that's too harsh. I shouldn't follow through with my Day 14 seduction. It's not right to expect something that he may not be able to deliver. It's not fair. Even if he never suspects.

So I won't do it. We won't have sex. He may not like that but…

A tiny, invisible lightbulb goes off over my head. On the way in, I'd seen a store in the hotel lobby. I can buy some condoms, like any other girl who's planning for a little fun in a hotel bed.

God, why do I make simple things so complicated?

I spring up off the banquette — my panties abrading me again — and head for the lobby store. Five minutes later I have a three-pack of Trojans in my purse, and I'm feeling so much better about myself that it isn't even funny.

In the lobby, I plop down to check my messages. There's nothing much there, thanks to Eric, so I use some of my spare time for people-watching.

A couple walks in through the revolving doors, and I watch them pause to take in their surroundings. The man is carrying a sleepy, preschool-aged child, and when he spots the check-in desk, he turns to his wife. They execute a complicated handoff, because the little boy is floppy and tired.

His mama speaks softly to him as she carries him over to the sofa across from mine and sits down. "There we go," she says, stroking his hair as she settles against the cushions.

He rolls, curling up into a sleepy ball on her lap, adjusting his head as if her thigh were a pillow.

They're so cute that I'm smiling like a fool. He has copper-colored skin, and lush, dark eyelashes that brush his round cheeks as he dozes. And — this is the kicker — he's wearing a Dallas jersey over skinny black jeans.

And? The jersey says *Tankiewicz*.

My heart thumps a little faster, and I realize several things, one right after the other. First, there's no joy greater than buying shrimpy clothing for shrimpy people. And shrimpy hockey jerseys are the ultimate item in my opinion.

Second, Tank must see little kids wearing the Tankiewicz jersey all the time. He's probably been looking at them for years and wondering why he's the only one in Dallas who doesn't have a tiny Tankiewicz.

My heart starts to break for him all over again, but then I

notice one more thing about this family. Mom and dad are white. And their child isn't.

Another tiny, invisible lightbulb goes off over my head.

I must be staring, because the mom smiles at me. "He usually has a normal bedtime. We aren't terrible parents, I swear. Once a year we get hockey tickets, and a hotel room for after."

"Fun," I say quickly. But I can't take my eyes off her beautiful, sleeping child. "Could I…" I stop myself and try to figure out how to phrase the question. "Would it be terribly rude if I asked if he's adopted?"

Her eyes widen and then warm. "He *is*. We adopted him in China when he was almost two. Traveling there to bring him home was the most amazing experience I've ever had."

Now I have goosebumps all over my body. "Was it difficult to be placed with a child?"

"Yes and no," she says. "You need lots of patience, because adoption is slow. There's so much red tape, and it's wildly expensive. So you have to be ready for all that. But I really liked the agency we worked with. Would you like their name?"

"I would," I say slowly. Then I hand my notebook to the woman, along with my pen. She takes it and starts scribbling.

When he was almost two. My chills double down as it hits me. I became motherless at the same age, and then I'd grown up with people who hadn't really wanted me. Aside from my brother, I'd been nothing but a burden on everyone in my life.

Maybe there's a child out there somewhere who doesn't have even that much. A child who's in an even worse situation.

A child who needs me.

"Here you go." She hands back my notebook. "My name is Clara, by the way."

"Thank you, Clara. I'm Bess."

"I also wrote down my phone number. If you need to talk it through, you call me some night after eight, okay? I'm happy to tell you what I learned."

"Really?" My voice cracks. "I'd like to do that."

She smiles at me. "It's a difficult, wonderful experience. Think it over."

"There's no doubt that I will."

When her husband comes back with room keys a few minutes later, I watch him pick the sleeping boy up off his mother's lap and tuck him against his chest.

Something clicks into place inside me. Something big.

I pull out a notebook, flip to the first clean page, and start scribbling.

THIRTY-THREE

Room 412

TANK

"OH GOD," Georgia Trevi says, staring at her phone. "I can't believe he did that."

I'm shoving a chip covered in queso into my mouth, so it's Trevi who has to ask, "What's the matter, honey?" He looks over her shoulder. "Bart Palacio doesn't have anything better to do than yap on Twitter?"

"He says: *Actually, we won that game. With better referees, and no bad penalty calls, it was 1-0 in our favor.*" She groans. "He's the Donald Trump of hockey."

"Don't waste another minute on him," I say. "He's not worth it."

"Tank has a point, baby," Leo agrees. "Come play darts with me. Looks like Heidi just beat Castro."

Of course she did.

I shove another chip into my mouth and scan the party. There are throngs of jubilant hockey players and a few wives and girl-friends. But I don't spot any shockingly red hair anywhere, and I don't have any messages from Bess on my phone.

That's strange. I didn't *dream* her, did I?

"Hey!" Anton Bayer claps a hand onto my shoulder. "You're just the man I was looking for."

"How's that?"

"I got a song I need to sing for you."

"A song?" That's a frightening idea. The man is wearing a guitar, though, so I guess he's serious. "What did I do to deserve this honor?"

"You beat Dallas, man!" Castro says. "We live for this. You took Palacio down in front of the whole fucking world."

"Baby Bayer likes to write songs to show his appreciation," O'Doul explains. "Just roll with it."

"Okay?" I glance around one more time, hoping to spot Bess, but she's nowhere in view.

Anton starts strumming an intro. And since I lived in Dallas all those years, I know the song immediately. It's *Deep In the Heart of Texas*. But when he starts to sing, I realize he's changed all the lyrics. "The stars at night are not very bright!"

Right on cue, Castro, Trevi, O'Doul and some others let out the series of four fast claps that come with this iconic song.

"Deep in this parrrrrt of Texas," sings Anton.

I groan, and everyone else cracks up.

"The locker room has a strange perfume..." *Clap clap clap clap.* "Deep in this part of Texas."

"You really shouldn't have," I chuckle.

But he keeps on singing.

"They skate too slow and their slapshots blow..." *Clap clap clap clap.* "Deep in this part of Texas."

The rhyming gets—if possible—even more dubious. Anton rhymes "moron" with "score on" and "hockey with cocky."

He's a big goofball. I'm loving it. But then the last line knocks me for a loop.

"They're a bunch of twits who traded Tankiewicz..." *Clap clap clap clap.* "Deep in this parrrrrt of Texas!" He lets out a whoop. "Welcome to Brooklyn, man! Except for the excellent cheese dip, you're better off with us."

Everyone cheers. I feel my face getting red, because somewhere over the last couple of difficult years I forgot how to take a compliment. "Thank you, Anton," I manage to say, even though my throat is tight. "Who knew you were so multitalented? My only other gig is modeling underwear. Some night when we've had more tequila I'll demonstrate."

"YES!" Heidi Jo shrieks while every hockey player yells "Noooo" at the same time.

"That was awesome," Becca says, grinning from ear to ear. She puts a hand on my arm. "It's official, Tank. You're one of us now. How come you don't have a margarita?"

"I was just about to take care of that," I assure her. "But first I was wondering if you saw Bess tonight?"

"Oh yes! She flew down to Dallas on the jet with us. We had a two hour meeting about my secret project. Then, after the game, she helped me set up this room." Becca glances around. "Check the lobby? She said something about having to return a call."

"Good tip. Thanks."

First I stop by the bar and ask for two margaritas, which are served in heavy glasses. Then I carry both drinks toward the lobby, scanning the generous space for my favorite girl. I've almost given up when I step around a large potted plant and spot her on a sofa, hunched over, scribbling away in a notebook. I walk over to her, but she doesn't look up. Whatever she's doing, it's deeply engrossing.

"Bess? Honey? Is something wrong?"

Her chin snaps up, and her eyes widen. "Tank! Hi!" She closes the notebook so fast it makes a slapping sound. Then she leaps to her feet and promptly winces. "Surprise!"

I laugh. "Are you okay? Did you hurt yourself?"

"No! I'm just having a small wardrobe malfunction." She clears her throat. "Never mind that. Congratulations! I'm so excited about your win. You have no idea."

"This is for you." I hand her a margarita. When I get one of my hands back, I use it to pull her a little closer and kiss the top of her head. "Thank you, baby. I didn't know you were coming to Texas. But I sure am happy to see you."

"It was a sneak attack," she says with a small sigh. "But then I had an epiphany and a big idea, and I have some things to discuss with you."

"Everything okay?" I ask, suddenly worried.

"Everything is *great*." She beams at me. "Cheers!" She touches her margarita glass to mine. "To big wins and important victories."

We drink. "Now tell me your epiphany."

"What about the party?" She points toward the bar. "Did you see the napkins?"

"The napkins are first rate. But you're more fun than any party, honey. Any day of the week."

Bess blinks. "That's the nicest thing you've said to me all day."

"I haven't seen you all day." I put an arm around her shoulder. "Do you have a suitcase?"

"It's checked with the bellman."

"All right." I steer her toward the desk. "Honestly, you shouldn't miss this queso. We just won a game because of this dip. So let's see what I can do…" I stop in front of the concierge's desk. "Excuse me, could you send up the lady's suitcase to my room? And I'd love to order some room service as well."

"Certainly." The young man grabs a pad and a pen. "Do you know what you want?"

"The queso dip and an order of those fish tacos. And anything the lady wants. It's going to room four-twelve."

"Right away sir."

God bless the Ritz.

Bess hands over her claim ticket and finalizes our room service order. I tip the concierge and then steer Bess toward the elevators. "You hitched a ride with Nate and Becca? That's fun."

"It was," she agrees. "And hot damn, that game was *incredible*. You don't know how happy it made me to see you come out on top."

"Yeah?" I put my hand on her ass as the elevator doors open. "I'll give you another demonstration of coming out on top. How long do you think room service will take?"

I don't let her answer the question. I lean over—mindful of the drinks we're holding—and kiss her. *Finally*. This is already one of the best nights of my life, and it's about to get better. She smiles against my mouth and wraps me in a one-armed hug.

She's strangely quiet, though. I plan to get to the bottom of that in a moment.

Ding. The elevator announces its arrival on the fourth floor.

"Come with me," I say, taking her hand. "I got big plans for you." I lead her to my room and usher her inside.

She walks over to one of the chairs, kicks off her shoes, and sits cross-legged. Then she sips her drink and watches me remove my suit jacket.

"You look like a girl with a lot on her mind," I say, taking off my tie next.

"That's true," she says quietly. "In a good way, though. Do you ever feel like things are sliding into place for you?"

"Sliding into place? The first thing that comes to mind is a dirty joke," I admit.

She gives me a slow smile. "I love you. Do you know that?"

"Yes." I pause in the middle of unbuttoning my shirt. "I do know that. And I'm really fucking happy to see you."

"I'd hoped you would be."

I chuck my shirt onto my open suitcase. "So come over here and kiss me." I sit down on the bed and crook my finger.

Bess takes another sip of her margarita. Then she sets it down and walks over to stand in front of me. She puts both hands on my shoulders and leans down to softly kiss the corner of my eye. And then my cheekbone.

Goosebumps rise on my arms as she gently makes her way down to my lips. The kisses are the sweet kind you only get when someone loves you so much that they don't even know where to start.

And I feel electric—not with lust, exactly. Not yet. But with something even better: *certainty*. This woman is mine, and I'm hers. We found each other twice, I guess. This time I've got more miles on me, but hopefully I'm also wiser.

When you've got something great, you can't let it go. Bess and I are going to work out, or I'll die trying.

Her kisses get deeper, and I wrap my arms around her soft, warm body and pull her down on the bed. I roll, until we're side by side, our kisses becoming more urgent.

I suddenly remember that she'd said something about an epiphany, so I pull back and hug her. "Talk to me. What's sliding into place for you? In a non-dirty way, I mean. 'Cause we'll get to that a little later."

She runs a hand through my hair. "Mark, last time I told you all my big plans, it didn't go so well. But I think this time it could be different."

"Don't be afraid." I hug her more tightly. "I'm not going to freak out again. Promise. Even if you say you want to try to get pregnant. I'll man up and figure out how we can do that."

"No," she says quickly. "That's not what I'm here to say."

"But it's day fourteen."

She goes absolutely still in my arms. "You counted?"

"I can't shut it off, honey. I mean—I'll try. But it will always be in the back of my mind. That little *what if*."

"I thought about it, too. I'm not going to lie. But then I realized I didn't want to do that to us. We're more than that. I love us too much to be all about the babymaking."

My heart is in jeopardy of exploding. I roll on top of her and give her another kiss. "We can still have all the sex, though, right?"

"All of it," she whispers. "I bought condoms."

"What?"

"Condoms. For later. So we wouldn't even have to think those thoughts."

I laugh suddenly. "Okay. I'm down with it."

She strokes my cheekbone, looking up at me. "Now I need to ask you something. I had a conversation tonight that completely rearranged my thinking on the subject of kids. Mark, would you ever consider adoption?"

"Sure," I say easily. "With you? Anything. That's your epiphany?"

"Yes." She rolls out from under me and sits up. "And not as a backup plan. At first I really wanted my own baby. Because my childhood was so…" She frowns.

"Harrowing?" I supply. "Horrific? You don't tell me much, Bess. But I know you went through a lot."

She flinches. "I hate talking about it."

"You can if you ever want to." I kiss her palm. "I'll always listen."

She weaves her fingers through mine. "See, I thought I needed to have my own baby as a way of fixing my childhood. As if all the things I did for my own child would make my parents' neglect less real. *God* this sounds stupid when I say it out loud."

"No, honey." I pull her into a hug. "It doesn't sound stupid at all. Besides, I don't think anyone can give an articulate answer to why they want kids. They just do. You don't even need a reason."

"Here's the thing," she says to my bare chest. "Being an unwanted child shaped my whole life. But now I have the chance to turn some small person into a *wanted* child. It would mean a lot to me to adopt. I think I could be a great mother to someone who had a rough start."

"I think that's beautiful." I rock her gently, hoping she never wants me to let go. "I don't know anything about how adoption works. I think it takes a really long time, honestly. But if you're game, then I'm game. I'd be honored to take that journey with you."

Bess presses her fingertips against the corners of her wet eyes. "Thank you."

"I'm here for that." I kiss the top of her head. "Tell me what you've learned. Let's see that crazy notebook of yours. We'll eat room service and google the fuck out of adoption."

Bess's smile is a little watery. "It's a plan."

There's a knock at the door. I set Bess on her feet beside the bed. Then I get up to answer it, looking a little ridiculous in my trousers and nothing else.

A bellman rolls Bess's suitcase in, and he's followed by a room service delivery person. The scent of Tex-Mex makes me—if possible—even a little happier than I was before. "Where do I sign?" I take the bill from the server and add a generous tip.

"I'm so happy to see my suitcase," Bess says after they leave. "Can I change into something more comfortable?"

"Of course. Especially if that's a euphemism." I turn around and finish removing my suit, hanging up the trousers and the jacket so I can wear them again before our next game.

When I turn around, I almost swallow my tongue. Bess is

standing there in a flame-colored lace bra, and matching lace panties. "Holy fuck. Are you trying to kill me?"

"If I am, then it's a murder-suicide," she says. "Lace itches. Who knew?"

"Come here," I growl. "I need a closer inspection."

She gives me an uncharacteristically shy smile. "You don't think I look ridiculous? Like I borrowed a lingerie model's underwear?"

"*Never*," I assure her. "Bess, take it from an underwear model—you've got the *goods*."

"You charmer." She laughs and comes closer to me.

"If those need to be taken off, I want to be the one doing the taking."

"Do you, now?" She kisses my neck.

"You'd better believe it." I run my hands down her smooth skin, and then show her just how it's done.

THIRTY-FOUR

I Did Not Get Out of Bed

BESS

WHEN I WAKE up the next morning, I'm face down on the silky hotel sheets, my naked limbs tangled in the covers. I feel completely at peace, even before I'm conscious enough to remember why.

Oh, right. Tank is beside me. His presence comforts me on a deep level. When I'd finally fallen asleep in the wee hours of the morning, it was with the bedrock certainty that we were on the same page about the future.

Apparently he's awake, too. I hear typing.

I turn my sleepy face toward him and open my eyes. And, whoa, I will never get over that view. The hottie in bed with me has two days' worth of stubble and a broad, muscular chest that I want to lay my head upon. But doing that would require moving from this comfortable spot.

"Bess, honey," he says, putting a big hand on my head. "How much reading about international adoption did you do last night?"

Together, we'd gone over the various options. And—at first glance—it had seemed like an international adoption might be our best path.

"Not much." I yawn. "Why? Are you doing some research?"

"Yeah." He flashes a smile at me. "I woke up early and started thinking about it. Then I couldn't get back to sleep, because I love this idea so much."

My heart soars just hearing him say that.

"But did you know that all these countries require a couple to be married for two years before adopting?" He gives me a serious frown.

"I saw that. But it's okay." I yawn again. "We aren't racing the clock anymore. It's not about fertility. We have time."

He strokes my hair. "I love your attitude about this. And I love you. We're going to do this, aren't we?"

"We're doing this," I agree. "And maybe the delay turns out to be a blessing. We'll have time for us, and *then* time for a child who needs us."

Tank's hand goes still on my hair. Then he closes my laptop with a snap. "I have to run out for a few minutes."

"What for?"

"Egg sandwiches," he says. "And coffee."

"Mmm." I sigh. "That sounds so nice. Do you know I love you?"

His voice is low and super serious when he answers. "I do know that, honey. Don't go anywhere, okay? I'll be back as soon as I can."

"Isn't there a team brunch you're supposed to go to?"

"That's later. I'll be back, okay? Wait for me."

Wait for me. He has no idea how good it feels to be asked. "Always."

After he leaves, the room gets quiet again, and I drowse on the pillow. If we adopt a child, I'll have to learn to cook. What kind of mother can't make scrambled eggs for breakfast?

I'll have a few years to sort that out. Unless we don't try for an international adoption. If we go the foster-parent route, it could happen more quickly.

None of this will be easy. I'll need to work with at least one adoption agency—and maybe more than one, if we pursue different avenues of adoption. And then, when we get closer to success, I'll hire an office assistant to give Eric and I even more flexibility.

It will all go into the new five-year plan. Just as soon as I get out of this bed.

Spoiler: I do not get out of the bed. The sheets are soft and the pillow is fluffy and my man is roving the streets of Dallas, hunting down a deli that makes egg sandwiches.

He takes surprisingly long, and my stomach is growling by the time I hear the telltale beep and click of the room door opening.

"Do they not have delis in Dallas?" I ask, rolling over to look at him.

Tank is not carrying a bag. He's not even carrying two coffees. I'm having dire thoughts, but then I catch his expression. His eyes are smiling so hard that it changes his whole face. "Bess, honey."

"What is it?"

He walks over to the bed, where I am still lying lazily on my tummy. He kneels down beside me. "Let's start the clock."

"What?" I stretch my sleepy limbs. "What clock?" He leans a little closer and I find myself nose to nose with Tank. "What are you talking about?"

"The two-year clock, Bessie. Let's not waste time." He chuckles. "I hope you're not the sort of girl who wants a video of this to post on social media. 'Cause that's gonna be awkward. Bessie, will you be my wife?"

Wait, what?

Tank takes my hand and kisses my palm. "Will you marry me, ASAP? So we can have two years of fun and then adopt a baby or toddler who needs a home?"

Suddenly, this man has my full attention. My head springs off the pillow. "Seriously? We're doing this now?" My heart is in my mouth, because I hope to God I haven't misunderstood him.

"I never claimed to be a romantic. And maybe I'm doing this all wrong. But here goes." He fishes something out of his pants pocket. It's a little box. He opens it to reveal a diamond ring. "I didn't know your ring size. And I had to bang on the window to get the store to let me in early."

He's still talking, but I'm just staring at the beautiful thing in front of me. The generous emerald-cut diamond is set sideways on a dainty, narrow band. There's a row of tiny diamonds on either side of the center stone. I've never seen anything like it.

It's *stunning*. And my poor little brain is trying to grapple with the mystery of its sudden appearance.

"I want you, Bessie. All of you. I want your notebooks full of plans, and I want you to move into that apartment with me. Your commute will be longer, honey. You'll have to cross the street." He kisses my palm again. "Say yes."

"Yes!" My throat closes up, making it hard for me to speak. "Of course I'll marry you. Any day of the week."

"Careful," he says, his green eyes dancing. "I might pick tomorrow. Because I know this is right, and I'm not a patient man." He carefully plucks the ring from its velvet cushion. "Let's just try this on."

I gasp when it fits perfectly. I shouldn't be so surprised. Tank and I are a good fit. I know it in my heart. I know it the same way I know a rookie is going to grow into a hall-of-famer.

Tankiewicz is my hall-of-fame man. He always has been.

"Do you like it?" he whispers.

"I *love* it. So much. Almost as much as I love you." All I can do is stare down at my finger.

He laughs. "Maybe this isn't how you pictured your marriage proposal. So now I'll slow down and wait until you're ready to brainstorm a wedding plan. Or is there already a notebook for that? Have you ever thought about your dream wedding?"

"Never," I whisper. And that's the truth. Even when I'd told Zara I'd marry Tank in a heartbeat, I hadn't believed it was a possibility. Marrying Tank sounded as realistic as turning mice into coachmen.

"We'll think of something that works for two busy people," he says. "I just needed you to know that I'm serious about our future together. And if you want to start the clock on adoption, I'm here for that."

I wrap my arms around him and squeeze. "You really know how to make a girl happy."

"I'm working on it," he agrees. "Can I feed the girl some brunch now? About that buffet—what do you say we sneak you in?"

"Okay," I say, realizing this means I have to make myself presentable. "Give me six minutes."

"We're already running late," he says. "So it doesn't matter. Take your time and shower if you feel like it."

"That includes a shower," I say. "I'm speedy."

"You really are the perfect woman," he says, chuckling. "Off you go."

I wear the ring to brunch. Which means I'm practically floating as we ride down to the lobby together. The comfortable pressure of Tank's hand in mine as we step into the dining room is the only thing tethering me to Earth.

"There they are!" Georgia says, beckoning us toward one of two long tables where the team is assembled.

"Where'd you go last ni—" Becca's eyes grow round. "Is that a *ring*?" she shrieks.

Georgia lets out a happy little scream, too. "Get over here and let me see!"

Tank, chuckling, gives me a little nudge in their direction. "You sit. I'll find the food."

My friends wave me in like buzzing bees to the hive. "This is so pretty!" Georgia says.

"Did you know this was coming?" Becca wants to know.

"Heck no. It still doesn't seem real."

"That makes two of us who got engaged in this hotel!" Becca's smile is electric. "Isn't Dallas a great town?"

"*No*," O'Doul insists from a few seats over. "But we'll agree to disagree."

"I'm feeling some warm fuzzies about Dallas, too," I admit.

"What kind of wedding are you having?" Georgia asks. "Big? Small? Are you going to wait for the summer break? Hang on— you could get married on your birthday. Ten years to the date you met! That would be romantic."

"Well…" The question of starting the adoption clock is going to be a consideration. I love that Tank wanted to do that for us—that he'd leaped out of bed and bought a diamond ring to show me that he was onboard. "We might not wait," I hedge. But I won't go into detail until I get a chance to discuss it with my...

Fiancé. Wow. I can't believe I have one of those.

Becca makes me get out my phone and pose with the ring as she takes some pictures. "Hold this coffee cup," she says, framing another shot. "And now this flower." She grabs a rose out of the centerpiece on the table. "Your manicure needs a touchup," she clucks. "We'll do that after breakfast. A girl can't show off her new ring with chipped polish."

Georgia rolls her eyes. "It's really okay to ignore her. Becca, let the girl have breakfast."

I look over my shoulder, and my inner Cinderella practically strokes out at the sight of Tank approaching the table, carrying a tray that's loaded down with dishes, and wearing an expression that's both happy and relaxed.

Jewelry may sparkle. But nothing beats the sight of a strong man carrying coffee and breakfast. Nothing.

O'Doul puts down his coffee cup and starts a slow clap. After a second, he's joined by Silas and Leo Trevi. And then everyone joins in. Jimbo—the equipment handler—stands up and whistles.

"Thank you, thank you all," Tank says, setting the tray down. "It was a beautiful goal last night. I'm glad you appreciate that." He gives me a cheeky wink.

"Who knew?" Leo says.

"I did!" Becca chirps. "I knew it all along."

"I doubted him," Castro says, shaking his head. "But I'm happy to be a little bit wrong about this."

"A little bit?" Coach Worthington says from the end of the table. "Son, he's making you look bad. Your girlfriend is probably wondering where she went wrong, thinking you were a catch."

"Coach!" Castro gasps, looking over both shoulders. "Keep your voice down."

Everyone howls. And then they give Castro even more shit about having the balls to propose. Poor Castro.

"Did Dave hear the good news, yet?" Georgia asks as Tank sets an omelet in front of me.

"Nope," I admit, as Tank claims the seat next to mine.

"Dave is going to flip his lid," O'Doul says with a chuckle. "His little sister marrying a hockey player. Can I be there when you tell him?"

"Sure, man," Tank says. "You can ice my face after the punch."

Everyone laughs, but I make a mental note to call Dave from the airport later and tell him the good news. Although it's tempting to tell Zara instead, and let her cushion the blow.

I'm not that big a wimp. But it's tempting.

"What about Henry?" Tank says quietly, his hand finding my knee. "Let's take a picture for Henry."

"Oh," I whisper. "Let's. Becca, would you mind taking one more?"

Tank hands over his phone, and then he wraps an arm around me, holding my diamond-clad hand in sight of the camera.

And we smile together.

After brunch, we head back up to the room to get our things. I'm going to Ottawa for that tournament, and Tank is headed to San Jose for another game.

When it's time to meet the team bus, I go downstairs with him, even though I have another hour before I have to check out. I feel so happy, I don't want to let him out of my sight.

"Oh, jeez," he says under his breath after we enter the lobby.

I'm just about to ask what's wrong when I see a pretty brunette straighten up and walk toward Tank. She's wearing a stylish dress, heels, and delicate little pearls in her ears.

Jordanna.

On instinct, I put my left hand into the pocket of my jeans.

But she only has eyes for Tank. "Mark. Hi," she says a little breathlessly. "Do you have a second?" She finally glances at me, and the glance wonders if I wouldn't just get lost, please.

"I need to make a call," I say stupidly. Then I turn away.

"No, Bess," Tank says. "Hey—"

I disregard him and ferry myself over to a sofa that's a short distance away. It's not far enough. I can hear Jordanna loud and clear. "I'm sorry to interrupt your morning."

"Then why did you?" he asks tightly.

"Because I have two things to say to you, okay? And you don't answer my texts." I'm watching her out of the corner of my eye, and she looks shaky and uncertain.

And, damn it, now I actually feel sorry for her. I want to hate her for breaking Tank's heart. But if she hadn't, all my wishes wouldn't be coming true.

Also, I want to hate her for knowing how to walk in those spiky heels.

She takes a nervous breath. "Nice goal last night. You looked great out there. I watched on TV."

"Thank you," he says quietly.

"And I just wanted to say I'm sorry, okay? I'm sorry for everything. At the end, I told myself it was your fault that we couldn't work through it. But it was never just your fault. And I'm sorry I made you feel like it was."

I watch his back rise as he takes a deep breath. "Thank you. That's nice of you. I probably could have handled it better, too."

"We both could, maybe. But I said some things I regret. That's all. I'll let you get back to your teammates and your—" Her eyes dart over to where I sit."

"Fiancée," he says slowly.

Jordanna gasps so audibly they probably heard it in San Jose. "Oh. Wow." She looks at me again, and this time it's not me who looks away. It's her. "She's not—" She swallows hard. *Pregnant.* She doesn't say the word, but I hear it anyway.

"No, Danna," he says with a shake of his head. "No."

"Oh." She takes a deep breath, and some of the color returns to her face. "God, I'm sorry. It's none of my business."

I can hear Tank's chuckle. "No, it isn't. But, look, you need to get to a place where you can say that word without almost passing out, okay? Trust me, it's the only way to move forward with your life."

She brings both hands up to her mouth. "Okay. You're right. I know. I lost my mind there for a second."

"I understand why. I really do. But I hope you can find a way to make some peace with the way things turned out. You deserve that as much as I do." He reaches out and gives her a quick, hard hug.

It's so generous that I don't even feel a stab of jealousy. Not a big one, anyway.

"Be well, Jordanna. Now I have to get back."

"Goodbye, Mark. Congratulations."

"Thank you."

She walks away, as my poor little conflicted heart thumps inside my chest. I wonder how much it cost her to do that.

Tank comes over and sits wordlessly down beside me, his suitcase at his feet.

"Well," I say. "That was..." I don't even know what word to choose. Awkward? Sad?

"Ill-timed?" He laughs.

"Is this weird for you?"

"Getting emotionally mugged by my ex-wife? A little."

"No, I mean doing it all for a second time. Buying a ring. Kneeling down and asking me to marry you. Do you have déjà vu?"

He smiles, and tucks an arm around me. "No, honey. Not at all. It's like, if we'd lost to Dallas last night..."

"Which you *didn't*," I put in gleefully.

"But if we did. I'd be sweaty and tired and demoralized. And the next forty-eight hours would have sucked, right? But eventually I'd want a rematch. I'd be ready. I'd be hungry for it."

"So you're going to kick marriage's ass and make it cry? You're going to win?"

"I already have, honey. This is what winning looks like."

He cups my chin and kisses me.

THIRTY-FIVE

Glass Slippers and Everything

BESS

IT'S TOTALLY possible to plan a wedding in three weeks. And, honestly, I'd recommend a hasty wedding to anyone. You don't have to fret over all the decisions, because there simply isn't time.

"Take the first venue that's open on your date," my brother had suggested as soon as he got over his shock at my news. "Don't look at the price, I'll pay it."

It hadn't occurred to me to have my brother contribute to my wedding. But when I realized that the impulse was some kind of macho reaction, I let him get out his checkbook.

Besides, the man has a daughter, and he ought to know what he's getting into in case he decides to have more.

The rest of my wedding planning happened at top speed, too. I selected the first invitations the printer showed me. Then I gave the florist and the cake baker free rein to exercise their crafts.

"This wedding will be small," I told them. "It will be held in a Victorian-era mansion, and it's two weeks from today. You do your thing, and I'll love it, I promise."

When it came to dress-shopping, though, I needed guidance. Becca swooped in to help me choose the gown in a single afternoon of shopping.

"It doesn't have to be a bridal gown," I'd said. "My only rule is that it can't be strapless, or I'll spend the whole night worried that it will plummet to my ankles as I accidentally flash the guests."

"Noted," Becca had said. Then she'd promptly found a long, white, velvet burnout dress in my size on the rack at Bloomingdales that made her squeal with delight.

I might have squealed, too, just a little, over its boho vibe, empire waist, and un-fussy V-neck. The burnout pattern reminded me of antique wallpaper. In a good way.

Even as the dress was being wrapped, Becca had demanded that we go shoe shopping next. "They have to be fabulous."

"I can't learn to walk in heels in the next fourteen days, Bec," I'd told her. "They can't be *that* fabulous."

"Fine. Your dress is a maxi length, anyway. Let's see what they have in a ballet slipper style."

Agreeing, I'd tried on a couple options. But then I'd spotted something shiny and weird on a display in the corner. "What are those?" I'd asked the young saleswoman.

"Oh, we call those the glass slippers. They're made by an Italian designer, but they have a Cinderella look to them."

"I want to try them on!" I'd said, sounding exactly like someone's evil stepsister.

"Everybody does," the saleswoman had said, retreating to find a pair in my size.

"Are they too weird?" I'd asked Becca as I'd strode around the shoe department in the strange, shiny slippers. But I was a little in love with them already, the same way I'd fallen for Tank across a steak dinner. "Am I crazy?"

"It's your wedding, Bess," she'd said. "And you're going to look like a bohemian fairy sprite in this groovy dress. These shoes are killer. Although you'll have to let me paint your toenails, because they will show through."

I'd bought the shoes, and, of course, I'd let Becca work her pedicure magic.

And I am, just three weeks after Tank's proposal, listening to the muted strains of a string quartet playing as my guests take their seats in the rented mansion's ballroom. I'm sporting a pumpkin-colored pedicure and pale pink nails. My hair has been tamed into a loose, wavy knot at the back of my head.

"Isn't there supposed to be a rehearsal before the wedding?" My brother takes a sip of wine and leans against the carved mahogany mantelpiece of the library where we're waiting. "Will someone announce the starting lineup? Are we singing the national anthem? How will I know what to do?"

"David," Zara chides, powdering my nose to prepare me for my big entrance. "All you have to do is walk your sister down the aisle. Don't tease, or she'll think you're going to check the groom against the boards."

"Sorry," my brother says. "I'm just trying to make jokes so she won't be nervous."

"I'm not nervous," I say, and it's 85 percent true. So long as I make it down the short aisle without tripping over anything, I won't be nervous at all.

There's a knock on the door, and Heidi steps in. "Two minutes until faceoff," she says, her brand new engagement ring flashing in the light from the chandelier.

"Thank you Heidi," I say.

The week after Tank proposed, a sheepish Jason Castro came into my office and asked me how much he could afford to spend on an engagement ring. "Not because Tank shamed me into it," he'd said. "But because it's time."

Eric had snickered into his coffee while I helped Jason look at his accounts and decide on a budget.

"You look ridiculously beautiful," Heidi says. "You're setting the bar really high, here."

"She's right," Zara agrees, stepping back to admire her work. "We have to get you into dresses more often."

"What for?" I ask. "I think your work here is done." I take one more glance in the mirror. I look like an honest-to-God princess. It hardly seems real.

"Show time!" Dave says, putting his wine glass down on the mantel. "Let's do this. Zara, honey, you're first, right?"

"Here, baby." Zara hands me the bouquet of orange roses that the florist chose for me. "Ready?"

I nod and take a deep breath, and she slips into place in front of my brother.

The string quartet begins to play a minuet, and my heart rate doubles. *This is really it!* Although Dave is blocking my view of the ballroom, so I can't see Tank yet.

This mansion we're renting is owned by an Upper East Side museum. It's the perfect space for my little wedding—sixty guests, many of whom are hockey players.

The music changes, and Zara steps out to join Tank's mother for a short walk up the aisle.

We'd decided against a formal lineup of bridesmaids and groomsmen, so only our closest family members will take part in the ceremony. I rise on my tiptoes and peek over Dave's shoulder to get a glimpse at the other reason we're getting married in a hurry.

Henry Kassman is easing himself onto a tall director's chair at the front of the room. His nurse hovers in the first row, but Henry carefully seats himself without assistance and smiles. He's wearing a pinstripe suit and a red tie.

He doesn't show it, but he's in a lot of pain. That's why I wanted this wedding location—it's less than a mile from his apartment building. I was hoping it would be possible for him to come. And here he is. "You were wrong, kid," he'd told Tank. "You said you wouldn't get married again. And now I'm holding the invitation in my hand."

The music changes again. *Here comes the bride.* My pulse jumps and the world seems to slow down.

"That's us!" my brother says gleefully, offering his arm. "This is fun. I never gave anyone away before."

"You will," I remind him, taking his arm. "Someday Nicole is going to call you up to say that she met a nice hockey player—"

Dave grunts. "Hush. Everyone is standing up." He guides me forward. We step out of the library, and I get my first look at the crowd. Smiling faces are turned in our direction as Dave leads me slowly forward. I've never seen so many candles and flowers.

"Bessie—you know I love you, right?" Dave whispers.

"Yes," I whisper back.

"And that I'm really happy for you. Even if he is a hockey player."

"Yes," I repeat, squeezing his arm.

Dave stops walking as we reach the front, and I get my first up-close look at my groom in his gray tux. He's perfectly shaved, which is different. But the look on his face is even more unusual. It's completely disarmed. He tilts his head to the side and smiles at me, his green eyes glittering. Like he can't quite believe this is real.

"The man knows he's lucky," Dave whispers. "That makes this a little easier for me." He takes my hands and turns to look at me. "This is where I leave you, Bess. But I'll never really leave you."

"I know," I choke out. "Now shut up before you make me cry."

The people closest to us chuckle. There's Eric Bayer with Alex. And Rebecca and Nate. And Silas, Delilah, and Castro.

I'd come to New York to get a life, and make a five-year plan. Five months later, I have a life that looks nothing like I'd planned —it's more amazing by every measure.

Dave leans in and gives me a kiss on the cheek. "Go marry your boy."

Henry Kassman's face splits into a big grin. He gives me a slow nod.

So I do it. I step forward, where Tank is waiting to take my hand. He lifts it to his mouth and kisses my palm, gazing at me as his lips brush my skin. There's a look in his eyes I've never seen before. He's *humbled* by this.

And so am I.

Somehow my bouquet gets handed to Zara. Dave takes his place beside his wife, and the minister begins to speak. I miss most of what he says, because I'm too lost in the moment. I'm holding Tank's hands as he stares into my eyes. His thumb makes a gentle swish across my wrist, the same way it did when I got flustered and introduced myself to him in Nate and Becca's backyard.

We didn't bother with a rehearsal, so when it's time for the vows, it's the first time I've ever heard Tank say the words. "I, Mark, take you, Bess, to be my wedded wife, to have and to hold, from this day forward..."

Just wow.

"…To love and to cherish until death do us part."

Then it's my turn. I clear my throat and do my best. It's all so humbling that my voice shakes. I must do okay, though, because the minister pronounces us to be man and wife. And then Tank kisses me while the whole room cheers.

Cinderella has nothing on me.

THIRTY-SIX

Everybody Likes Sweet Potatoes

TANK

One Year Later

"IF HE FINISHED THE PEAS, try the sweet potatoes again," Bess calls from the bedroom. "Everyone likes sweet potatoes."

I look down into the soulful brown eyes of our foster child Roberto, who is six months old. "*¿Escuchas eso?*" I ask him. "*A todos les gustan las batatas.*" *Everybody likes sweet potatoes.*

Roberto kicks his fat little feet and bounces in his chair.

I dip the tiny spoon into the pureed sweet potato and lift it to his lips. Roberto takes the food into his cherubic mouth. And one second later he blows a raspberry, spraying sweet potatoes all over my Bruisers T-shirt.

"Aw, baby. Really?" I sputter, while Roberto giggles. "*Honey!*" I call. "Not everyone likes sweet potatoes."

"My bad!" Bess says in the distance.

"*Necesitamos un Zamboni,*" I tell the small person in the high-chair. I grab a paper towel and dampen it. Then I use it to wipe bits of pureed sweet potato off every surface of the room, starting with Roberto's round little face.

"Oh boy," Dave Beringer says, walking into my kitchen, his own seven-month-old son on his hip. "Looks like someone detonated a small anti-sweet-potato device in here."

"That happened," I say, pulling the baby out of the chair and detaching his bib.

"I can hold two at once," Dave says. "You need a fresh shirt."

"I'll take a baby!" Zara says, popping into the kitchen. She snatches Roberto from me and starts kissing his chubby cheeks.

Is Bess still in the bedroom? It's taking her a long time to get ready for the team Christmas Eve party. At *least* fifteen minutes. I guess I'm spoiled by her quick turnarounds. "Anyone need more coffee?" I ask our guests.

"I'll take one," Dave says. "Didn't get much sleep last night."

"Really? That hotel is pretty great. Did you try the croissants?"

"It's not the hotel's fault, and those croissants are killer," he says. "But this guy has forgotten how to sleep through the night." He pats his son on the butt.

"Ouch. Bess and I have been lucky, I guess." Roberto has only been with us for about ten days, but he's a good sleeper. "If only he liked sweet potatoes." I'm still wearing this wreck of a shirt.

"How do you do it?" Zara asks me as I pour her husband a cup of coffee. She gazes into Roberto's eyes.

"It takes a few days to learn their quirks," I say. Roberto is foster baby number three.

"No," Zara says, smoothing down Roberto's curls. "How will you hand him back?" She looks up at me. "Isn't it awful?"

Why yes, it is. But this is what we signed up for. "Roberto has a mom who loves him. That's why it's okay." We're doing a very special kind of foster care. We take in immigrant babies who are temporarily separated from their parents. In Roberto's case, his mother was injured on her journey from South America. She required surgery in a facility that can't accommodate infants.

So for a few weeks—we don't know how long—he needs a temporary home. That's us.

Our involvement was Bess's idea. I'd been skeptical, but she'd wanted to help. And it's so damn brave of her that I couldn't say no. She impresses me every single day.

It turns out that taking care of these babies is easily the most rewarding thing I've ever done—rocking a child who misses his mother. Feeding him. Holding him as he falls asleep. It's humbling.

Bess will cry a little on the day we have to hand him back to the social worker who will return him to his mother. But only because she wishes him the best. If they're lucky, his mom will win her asylum case and stay in the US. If they're less lucky, they'll be deported to Venezuela.

Either way, they'll be together. Roberto won't remember this time when Bess and I stepped in to care for him for a few short weeks. But we'll never forget it.

Dave takes the cup of coffee, and then holds it out of his redheaded son's reach. "This party starts soon, right?"

"Yup. Let me change my shirt and see if Bess is ready." I hold out my hands to Zara. "Shall I take him back?"

"Not a chance," she says. "Let me make sure Nicole hasn't spilled her milk all over your living room." She carries Roberto out of the room.

"It doesn't matter what Nicole spills," I say as she leaves.

"You say that now," Dave says. "But it's hard to get the smell of sour milk out of some things. Like, for example, a Honda Pilot. It's crazy the stunts these kids pull. But I hope..." He puts his hand on his baby son's hair as the sentence trails off. "Someday I hope you get that chance. To take care of a baby who calls you *daddy*. Because you guys deserve it. And the kid will be so lucky to have you."

"Thank you," I say gruffly. "Our chance will come."

And here's one surprising thing about my marriage—Dave Beringer has been solid gold. It was nice of him and Zara to haul their growing family down to New York for the brief holiday break in my game schedule. Bess loves having her family around her. As a bonus, Dave gets to see all his old friends.

"Go change," he says now. "So we can drink eggnog and play ping pong."

"On it." I leave the kitchen and head for the bedroom. "Bess? How goes it?" I ask when I find her in the bathroom.

Startled, she slams a drawer and then stands up, turning around quickly. "Fine! Great. Where's the baby?"

"Zara is making goo-goo eyes at him in the living room." I

study Bess for a second. She looks a little pale and also vaguely guilty.

"Ready to go?" she asks, tucking fidgety hands into her back pockets.

"Almost," I say slowly. "Give me a minute to wash the sweet potatoes off my face. A Roberto no le gustan."

"Sorry." Bess winks. "You look sexy like that, though."

"You liar."

She stops on her way out of the bathroom, her hand on my arm, her clear blue eyes smiling up at me. "It's the truth, though. It would take a hell of a lot more than some baby food to dull your shine."

After she leaves, I catch myself grinning at my reflection. She kills me. I'm so lucky to have had this second chance with her. I'm glad I wasn't too stupid to take it.

I shuck off my T-shirt and toss it into the hamper. Then I grab a clean button-down from our closet and wander back into the bathroom to comb my hair. Our commute to this party will be easy enough —an elevator ride up to the penthouse level of our building. And since we all chipped in to cater the party, we don't even have to bring a dish.

My team is having a hell of a season so far. But everyone's so busy. We need this three-day break.

One of Bess's bathroom drawers is slightly ajar. It's the one she'd slammed. I nudge it with my knee, but it won't close. Something is stuck. I open it, finding the culprit immediately. It's a vitamin bottle that's standing upright instead of lying down. Just as I'm tucking it back into place, I catch the label. *Folic acid.*

Goosebumps rise on my arms. As far as I know, there's only one use for folic acid. It's something pregnant women take. My ex took it for years, just in case.

I actually have chills right now.

But, hang on. When I freaked out at Bess last fall, she took some steps toward considering a solo pregnancy. Buying a bottle of folic acid would have been one of them. This bottle is probably just old.

And then there are the condoms that we use. Bess pulls them

out at certain times of the month, and I go along with it. She said we shouldn't waste time thinking about conception. And it works. I never think about it.

Until right this second.

Alone in the bathroom, I let out a strangled laugh. It's Christmas Eve, her family is here, and we're on the way to a party. I obviously have to keep on *not* thinking about this.

I carefully close the drawer and finish buttoning my shirt.

Three hours later, the party is winding down. The sky is darkening outside the big windows. The kids are starting to yawn, including the one I'm holding.

I've had a fine afternoon. I'm full of roast chicken and cheddar grits and wilted greens and cheesecake. And beer.

"Ante up," Leo Trevi says, shuffling the deck.

I put two chips on the table and rock the baby while I wait for him to deal.

Earlier, I lost gallantly at ping pong to Heidi Jo Castro. As one does. Now there's a warm, sleepy baby in a carrier on my chest. He's zonked from crawling around on the rug and watching my niece Nicole bounce around the party, stealing cookies off the dessert table. She's three and a half now, with cinnamon hair in two pigtails on either side of her round little face.

That's what Bess's daughter would look like.

Oh, boy. Most days my brain doesn't do that. And I really wish it would stop now.

Roberto presses his cheek against my chest and makes a sleepy little complaint. I pat him on the back. "Duerme ahora." *Sleep now.*

Castro shakes his head beside me. "Nunca me dijiste que podías hablar español." *You never told me you could speak Spanish.*

"No preguntaste." *You didn't ask.* And, in truth, my Spanish is pretty rusty. "When I was a little boy, my dad was a ranch hand in Washington state. There were some Spanish speakers who worked there, and I liked talking to them. Then I took Spanish in high school and college. I hadn't spoken a word for years until we needed to convince the social services agency that we should be eligible for the temporary foster care program."

"Ustedes dos son santos." *You two are saints.*

"We're not," I insist. "It's a small thing. Look at this place." I wave in the general direction of the sumptuous party room, the food and drink. "We live in paradise. I'm only sharing it for a few weeks."

"Until the little guy rips your heart out on the way out the door." Castro clicks his tongue. "How do people give them back?"

"Well, he has a mother—"

"I know you said that. But still."

"We'll get our chance. It's an adoption agency that manages this temporary foster program. When they finish our home study at the end of next year, they won't forget what we've done."

"Ah," Castro says. "Okay. So you could have a baby in a year?"

"A year and a half, minimum. Probably more like two. But that's all right with us. We got time."

A soft hand lands on the back of my neck. "Oh, you have a pair of aces!" Bess says.

Everyone else looks up in shock.

"Kidding!" Bess says with a laugh.

"But now they know I *don't* have a pair of aces," I complain.

"Who draws a pair of aces, anyway?" She kneels down to peek at Roberto. "Hi, sleepy. Can I take him?"

"He's pretty comfortable right now," I point out. "If you pick him up, he'll get the sleepy screamies." It's wild to realize that I already know this. Ten days is long enough to fall into a rhythm with a baby.

"All right." She puts her hand over mine. "But when he wakes up, it's my turn."

"You'll get yours, I promise." I'm leaving on a trip the day after tomorrow. Bess will be a single (foster) mom for a few days. But she has help from her new office assistant and a babysitter we hired for a few hours a day so that Bess can run across the street to make calls in her office.

"Don't bet too much against Heidi," Bess says, stroking my hair.

"Like I'd be so stupid."

"You're already a hundred bucks down to her," Castro points out.

"True, but I lost it very slowly and carefully."

Laughing, Bess kisses me on the top of the head and then wanders off to talk to Zara and Georgia, who seem to be mixing up a batch of frozen margaritas. The whirr of the blender startles Roberto in his sleep a minute later, and I have to pat his back until he settles again.

Then I lose twenty bucks to Heidi, who's a better bluffer than anyone on the hockey team. She takes me with a pair of fours, for God's sake.

"Yes!" she whisper-shrieks, mindful of the napping baby. "Ante up, people."

"Oh boy," Anton grumbles. "This better be my last hand."

Across the room, Bess is holding a frozen margarita in a pretty glass. And I decide I'd rather chat with the ladies than lose at poker. "I'm out, ladies and gents. It was a pleasure losing to you."

Slowly I stand, careful to support Roberto's head, so that it doesn't flop and wake him up. I cross the room, and all the women give me that smitten face that they reserve for men holding babies.

It's a perk, honestly. I'll take it. But where is Bess?

At first I think she's given me the slip, but then I see a flash of red in the corner behind a tall, potted plant.

Hmm. What's that all about?

THIRTY-SEVEN

Plant Killer

BESS

AS SOON AS I'm out of sight of my friends, I tip half my margarita into the soil at the base of the fern. I'll hold the glass until the rest of it melts, and nobody will notice.

I can't believe it's come to this. I hope tequila doesn't kill designer house plants.

My little secret is getting harder to hide. I'm mildly nauseous all the time, although I don't actually vomit. Except for one time at work. And Eric was on a call the whole time and didn't notice my quick departure from the room. He can't understand why I gave up coffee, though. And sushi.

"Wow, you guzzled that. Was it tasty?"

I practically leap three inches into the air and spin around.

Tank's gaze goes from my glass right down to the small puddle of frozen margarita melting into the potted plant's soil. Then his chin snaps upward and his gaze collides with mine. "Bess, what—"

"I just…" *Have no convenient way to finish this sentence.* And I can practically see it all clicking into place behind his eyes.

"*Jesus,*" he breathes. "No way. Are you—" He swallows hard. He doesn't want to say it out loud.

It's scary to say it out loud. And this is why I've become a nutter who poisons potted plants. "Yes," I choke out. "I'm sorry."

"Holy…" He takes a deep breath. "I thought I was crazy."

I give my head a violent shake. "You're not. And I'm sorry I didn't tell you sooner. I didn't know what to do."

"How far?" he asks, reaching out to take my hand in his.

My fingers close around his, and I immediately feel more centered. "Ten weeks."

He looks around for a second, as if trying to figure out if someone is pranking him. Like he just can't grab onto the reality. Still holding my hand, he sits down hard on the window seat. "*Ten*. Ten weeks? And you didn't tell me?"

"I'm so sorry," I echo just as Roberto wakes up from the sudden motion.

He picks up his little head and yowls.

With shaking hands, I reach down and unclip the sides of the carrier, lifting his warm body out, and cuddling him to my shoulder. "Tank, I didn't know what to say. Keeping it a secret felt wrong. But telling you seemed mean, too. Because I didn't want you to get excited for nothing."

"Wow, okay." He reaches an arm around my body and leans his head against my hip. "You feel okay?"

"Yes," I say quickly. "Mostly. Well, I feel like barfing pretty often, but it doesn't actually happen. I'm exhausted all the time. But—God—I'm just whining right now. I'm fine. We're fine."

"This is a shock." He takes a deep breath. "How did it happen?"

"Um, the usual way?" I pat Roberto's small back. "I did such a good job forgetting about the whole thing that I guess I forgot about the whole thing. And then I didn't pull out the condoms on the right days. Tank, I'm *sorry*."

He raises his finger and thumb to the bridge of his nose and squeezes.

"I hope you can forgive me. I didn't know what to do. I'm sorry to stress you out."

He shakes his head. When his hand falls away, I have the shock of a lifetime. His eyes are red-rimmed and wet. "Come here." He pats the bench next to him.

I sit. It's never a hardship to do what Tank asks of me.

He wraps both arms carefully around me and the baby. "I love you. I would rather have dealt with this together, Bessie. I'm not as fragile as that. *We're* not as fragile as that."

"But it would kill me to disappoint you," I say quietly.

"You can't, Bess." His voice is raw. "Not with this. So long as we're together, I have everything I need."

Anton Bayer's head peeps around the big potted plant. "Oh noes! Are you guys okay? How much did Tank lose at poker, anyway?"

Tank laughs, swiping at his eyes. "I'm not losing at anything."

"What's happening?" My brother comes to stand beside Anton. "Is something wrong?"

"Not a thing!" I say, sniffling. "I'm just…pregnant."

"Holy shit. But I thought…" My brother laughs. "Never mind what I thought. Here's to more redheads!" He raises his beer as a toast.

"*Maybe*," I hedge. "It's early."

"Does anyone else know about this?" Tank asks.

"No way. Just the doctor. If I couldn't tell you, I wasn't telling anyone."

"Tell us what?" Becca asks, moving Dave out of her way so she can see me. "Wait. Did you dump out the margarita I made you?"

"I'm sorry," I say because apparently I'm apologizing to everyone today. "I'm off alcohol until late July. Hopefully."

Becca gives a little shriek.

"Late July," Tank says slowly. "Oh my God. Wow. I'll be on vacation."

"Right after you win the cup!" Becca says with a smile. "A girl can dream. Would this be an awkward time to tell you that I'm due in June?"

"You're kidding!" Anton shouts. "It's gonna be baby city around here."

That's when the party turns into a back-slapping, congratulating outpouring of good cheer. Tank stands up and accepts all the congratulations and teasing that come his way. Including: "Nice job, *Sure Shot*."

I suppose that joke was inevitable.

It's a few long minutes until I get my husband alone again. We sneak out of the party and take the elevator back to our quiet apartment. Tank lays the sleeping baby in his port-a-crib and then joins me on the sofa, where we just hold each other for a few minutes in contemplative silence.

"Mark," I whisper eventually. "I love you so much. I'm sorry I didn't tell you."

He runs a hand down my hair. "It's okay, love. I know you were trying to spare my feelings. I was very clear that I didn't want to try for this. But since it's here, I have to tell you I'm so excited I can hardly breathe."

I let out a quick breath. "But no pressure."

He chuckles and then wraps his strong arms around me. "It's okay, Bess. We're okay."

"Can I just say that I still want to adopt? So badly. We might need a bigger apartment."

"Well, I still want to adopt, too." I kiss her on the temple. "That won't change. If we welcome another baby into the world first, then our adopted child will have a sibling."

She shivers suddenly. "Wow. This is starting to seem real."

"You and I are already real," I whisper. "No matter what happens with the baby, I'll be here for you."

She swivels to face me. "And I'll be here for *you*," she agrees. "I promise."

There's nothing more that needs to be said after that. So I kiss her instead.

The
End

Thank you for reading Sure Shot!

Don't miss the Brooklyn Bruisers bonus scenes!

Did you know there's a book for Eric Bayer, too? Grab your copy of Moonlighter. Or turn the page for more Sarina Bowen titles!

Also by Sarina Bowen

Acknowledgments

A special thank you to Claudia, Jo, Jenn and Natasha for reading early and catching the last few errors. Thank you to Edie for your tireless editing in the midst of a scary time.

Thank you to Hang Le for your beautiful work, and to Wander for this photo.

Thank you to Emma Wilder for producing the Sure Shot audio book as all the studios closed and production times lengthened. Our motto: we shall not stress over this.

CPSIA information can be obtained
at www.ICGtesting.com
Printed in the USA
LVHW021526010920
664769LV00018B/3492